"ARE YOU SURE YOU WANT to do this?" McNamara asked.

"Yes." Hannah punched the number for the floor she wanted.

"They won't let you leave, you know? The law is very clear and very specific. It's not like before, when you ran away before you committed yourself to training. You're making the deliberate choice to break the law after you'd been warned. They will put you in jail."

The elevator headed up one more floor. She didn't shake in fear for the entire ride. "They'll try. If you want to return to your office, I'll understand."

McNamara laughed. "Oh, no. I'm not missing this for the world. Watching you use your ability is a privilege Hannah. Too bad the rest of the Committee can't see it that way."

Copyright © 2018 by Debra Jess
All rights reserved.
Published by Debra Jess, Corp.
978-0-9966656-8-1

In accordance with the U.S. Copyright Act of 1976, the scanning, uploading, and electronic sharing of any part of this book without the permission of the publisher is unlawful piracy and theft of the author's intellectual property. If you would like to use material from the book (other than for review purposes), prior written permission must be obtained by contacting the publisher at P.O. Box 9241, Daytona Beach, FL 32120-9241. Thank you for your support of the author's rights.

This novel is a work of fiction. All characters, places, and incidents described in this publication are used fictitiously, or are entirely fictional.

Cover Design by Deranged Doctor Design
Formatting by The Killion Group, Inc.
First Edition: September 4, 2018.

If you would like to know more about the Thunder City Series or about any of Debra Jess's other stories, you can subscribe to her newsletter or her Bookbub page at:
http://debrajess.com
Risk. Reward. Romance.
You can also follow her on any of these social media sites:
Facebook, Twitter, Tumblr, Pinterest, Bookbub, Instagram
If you want to be notified when Debra Jess's next novel is released, please sign up for her mailing list by going to http://www.debrajess.com

Your email address will never be shared and you can unsubscribe at any time.

BLOOD HUNTER

A THUNDER CITY NOVEL

DEBRA JESS

PRAISE FOR
BLOOD SURFER
(A THUNDER CITY NOVEL, BOOK 1)

BLOOD SURFER delivers a fast-paced tale of danger and romance set in a world well-imagined world of vivid characters, superhuman and otherwise. Recommended. ~ Richard Lee Byers, author of The Reaver and Blind God's Bluff.

PRAISE FOR
BLOOD HUNTER
(A THUNDER CITY NOVEL, BOOK 2)

The latest novel by Debra Jess is full of fast-paced action and intrigue. BLOOD HUNTER is a roller-coaster of fantastic action and star-crossed romance in a world where...everyone believes that justice is on their side...The Thunder City series takes a hard look at the social and political issues in a universe straight out of the comic books. Blood Hunter reminds us that not everyone with super powers is a hero. ~ Sylvia Spruck Wrigley, author of Domnall and the Borrowed Child

To my mother, Bonny, my father, Michael, and brother, Eric. I love you all so much and I couldn't have written this book without you.

CHAPTER ONE

One week after the events in Blood Surfer.

"Scott, they have guns." Hannah Quinn curled into Scott Grey's embrace. They were standing on the deck of the *Elusive Lady* while the crew guided the yacht toward the dock at the north end of Thunder City's harbor, near the commuter ferry. His strong arms wrapped around her shoulders to pull her even tighter to his chest. What had they done to warrant what looked like an entire squad of police officers armed with rifles to meet them here? She hadn't been expecting a parade — just some peace while the harder-to-see emotional wounds scabbed over. She was desperate to hold back the flood of memories of the horror show she'd left behind, the body of her fake mother lying face down in the dirt.

"I don't know what this is all about." Scott let go of her and reached for the comm unit hooked to his jeans. "Let me call Thomas."

Hannah kept her eyes on the harbor's boardwalk as the yacht's engine slowed. She wasn't the only one who'd seen the guns. The crew must have noticed as well, and now the yacht floated just out of reach of the slip. Thomas must have seen the guns, too, and ordered his men to keep her and Scott out of reach of whoever waited for them.

They had dressed carefully that morning, Scott wearing Thomas's clothes and Hannah wearing Catherine's. Long pants, shirts with long sleeves, and ugly brown gloves Thomas had stashed in an emergency kit. All the better to keep them from touching each other, skin-on-skin.

Thunder City laws were clear about preventing alternative humans who hadn't proven they had control over their abilities from touching anyone and accidentally triggering their powers.

Even though they'd been trying so hard to obey the laws of Thunder City and not touch since they had rescued each other from the quarry prison, Hannah had made a point of healing Scott of his wounds. Miranda Dane's mercs had given her just enough time to heal Scott of the worst of his injuries before they kidnapped her. She had wanted to finish the job before she returned to Thunder City, where the opportunity would be taken out of her hands.

As the *Elusive Lady* drifted closer toward the harbor, Hannah saw still more police. Some stood out in the open, dressed in dark blue. Others shifted positions among the rooftops of the shops lining the boardwalk. She scanned the roof of the hotel at the far north end. Just because she didn't see anyone, didn't mean they weren't up there.

Scott released his comm and returned to holding her, the pressure around her shoulders comforting. "I'll bet you they aren't just any cops, either. Thunder City would have sent Division Six."

"What's Division Six?" Hannah's heart skipped a couple of beats. The last thing they needed was to get on Thunder City's bad side. Thunder City was the one city where alternative humans could live in safety, out in the open, just like their normal counterparts.

"They're a subdivision within SWAT, trained to handle Alts."

Why would Thunder City send Division Six to the harbor to meet the *Elusive Lady*? How did they even know she and Scott were on board the yacht? Had Thomas called ahead? Why would he tell Thunder City anything?

The *Elusive Lady's* crew slowed its engines even more, just feet now from pulling into the slip. Thomas had chosen the harbor because it was closer to Harbor Regional Hospital. Doctor Rao had stayed behind at the quarry to help take care of the wounded but insisted that Hannah get proper medical care at the hospital as soon as possible.

At least her ribs hurt less than they had immediately after the quarry raid, and Doctor Rao had determined she had no broken bones. Despite his medical talents, though, there was only so much Thunder City's Alternative Human Medical specialist could do on the yacht. Only time would heal her still swollen cheeks, by now only lightly blushed where Miranda Dane had hit her. If only she could heal herself the way she'd healed others, the way she'd healed Scott so he wouldn't have to go to the hospital too.

"At least they're not pointing their rifles at us." It was a stupid thing for her say, but she was determined to not panic. She was bruised, but not broken, not the way Miranda Dane had wanted her broken. "This is because of me."

"Maybe." Scott's hand left her shoulder to pull out his comm unit again.

"I'm right here." Behind them, Thomas Carraro surfaced from below deck. He'd changed out of his T-CASS uniform into beige khakis and a white polo, more or less what she and Scott had borrowed from the *Elusive Lady's* wardrobe, albeit in different color variations.

"Did you arrange for a security escort?" Scott asked his father.

"No, I didn't. I don't know what this is all about."

"Maybe we shouldn't dock here." Hannah swallowed back her fear as the yacht glided into the slip. "We should dock at your estate. It's private property, right? They can't follow us there."

Thomas stepped in front of Hannah and his son, blocking their view. "They could follow us, but no one gets onto the estate without triggering our defense systems, so why don't we stick to the plan and see what they want. It could all be just a misunderstanding. If trouble starts, we'll deal with it. I can't imagine they want anyone dead. That's not the way the Thunder City police work. You two might not want to stand so close together, though."

Scott unwrapped his arm from around her shoulders, but Hannah grabbed his hand in hers, the gloves making the gesture no less intimate. He squeezed, his long fingers strong and gentle. The message was clear: he hadn't left her side since the raid, he wouldn't leave her now.

"I'll go first." Thomas started down the plank his men lowered onto the dock. "Don't follow until I give the signal."

Hannah watched Thomas descend to the dock. From Scott's belt his comm unit crackled.

"Gentlemen, what seems to be the problem?"

Thomas had turned on his own comm so both she and Scott could hear what was happening below. A man in a dull brown suit, with thinning hair, approached from behind the police, his tie blowing in the breeze off the harbor.

"I'm Doctor Johnson. We've met before, at the Medical Society gala last year. I'm representing the Oversight Committee and I've reviewed the preliminary report submitted by Captain Spectacular about the quarry raid. I'm here to make sure that Hannah Quinn and Scott Grey are secured in the hospital."

"How convenient." Hannah could see Thomas place his hands behind his back. "I was about to bring both of them to the hospital myself. I don't believe we need an escort, however."

Scott leaned down to whisper in her ear. "Thomas wants us to stay put."

"I disagree," Doctor Johnson continued. "They're both dangerous. The Oversight Committee saw the security footage from the quarry, how easily Ms. Quinn crippled Miranda Dane's mercenaries. We also saw Mr. Grey translocate a bullet already fired and direct it into Mayor Dane's head. Both need extra protection for their own good."

"Protection or detainment?" Hannah could see Thomas turn his head giving Division 6, which had surrounded him, a long, slow gaze. "There's a difference between protecting someone and detaining them. What I see here is an attempt to detain Hannah and Scott."

"What does he mean?" Despite Thomas's warning, she stepped closer to Scott. "Are we going to be arrested?"

Scott's hand drifted up to stroke her hair, the glove

not smooth like Scott's skin, but clingy and tugging at the strands. "Not while I'm around."

"You can use whatever word you wish." Johnson pointed to the *Elusive Lady*. "Nevertheless, the Oversight Committee has ordered both Hannah Quinn and Scott Grey to be taken into custody."

Custody. The word balled up in the back of her throat. She stepped back into Scott's embrace, damn the laws. Miranda had had custody of her, had murdered her real mother for it.

Custody also triggered images of locked doors. Every night, while she'd tried to sleep in the bedroom of the *Elusive Lady,* she'd insisted on the door remaining open. The one time Scott had closed it, to give her privacy while she washed herself, she'd suffered a panic attack. Miranda had locked her in one of her prison's freezers to prevent her from escaping. She couldn't escape the cold even in the bright heat of late summer.

"No one is going to have custody of me." Her anger melted her frozen fear. She knew exactly what she had to do, only this time she'd have Scott with her. "Not now, not ever. We have to get away from here."

Custody. The word froze Scott to his very core as he pulled Hannah closer to his heart. The heat from her body added to the sweat pooling under his long-sleeved shirt. His mother had surrendered custody of him to Thomas when he was thirteen. He couldn't have guessed that she and Thomas would fall in love and get married.

Even though Thomas had become more than just a father to him — a true champion in Scott's mind — the sting if his own mother giving him up without an obvious fight had hurt more than he had realized.

"No one is going to have custody of me." Hannah raised her chin, even as she lay her head against his chest. The conviction in her voice matched his own. "Not now, not ever. We have to get away from here."

"No one is going to get their hands on either of us. Not like this, but let's wait and see what Thomas has to say."

Hannah relaxed against him once more. Scott wished he could give her assurances everything could be worked out, but he didn't know for sure. He hadn't lived in Thunder City for years; he'd never had Alt abilities until a few days ago. He'd never had to tangle with the Oversight Committee, a committee his own mother had created to work with the Norms of Thunder City to ensure the safety of all Thunder City citizens — Norms and Alts alike.

Voices rose from his comm unit, Thomas's voice soothing despite the harsh conviction. "Neither Scott nor Hannah have been convicted of any crimes. They're no different from the Star Haven Newcomers. None of the Newcomers were detained when they crossed Mystic Bay."

"They should have been," Johnson said. "If we had detained the Newcomers, Electrocyte wouldn't have taken a man hostage and nearly electrocuted him to death. Electrocyte would still be alive as well."

Scott winced. He'd shot Electrocyte to stop the Alt from killing the president of the ferry company. He'd also almost killed his own brother, Nik, in the process. If Hannah hadn't bloodsurfed through Nik, his brother wouldn't have survived. Scott wondered what else the Oversight Committee had planned for them. For him?

Johnson waved a piece of paper in Thomas's face.

Thomas snatched it and read it. "One moment," he said, then he turned his back on Johnson, forced his way between the Division Six team members who blocked him, to return to the boat.

"Scott, Hannah. I'm sorry, but the Committee has given Johnson the legal authority to take you both into custody. The situation with Electrocyte was never settled because of Miranda's interference. I can launch a legal challenge on Scott's behalf on that angle, but," an anguished looked crossed Thomas's face, "Thunder City's laws are clear. Until both of you can prove you can control your powers, you're subject to the Oversight Committee's supervision."

"They'll separate us." Scott looked at Hannah. He'd promised to stay by her side. They both needed each other's strength.

Thomas nodded. "It's going to be a long haul no matter what sort of spin I put on this. Hannah might be able to pass in a few days because she's been bloodsurfing since she was a child, but Scott, your power is brand new. We don't know what you're capable of yet. Since you can push objects in motion away from you as well as pull them toward you, that's far beyond anything we've ever seen before."

Thomas took the sting away from Scott's instinct to shove the piece of paper down Johnson's throat. "What about Electrocyte?" Scott asked. "Can they still arrest me for killing him?"

"I don't know. It's complicated. Your extradition to Star Haven was illegal because the order was forged, but Thunder City had agreed to it on principle." Thomas reached out to touch Scott's face, a show of affection Scott had grown accustomed to over the years, but this time Thomas pulled back at the last second, with a quick look over his shoulder.

Scott's anger burned away his shock. Thomas had been the bedrock through Scott's teenage life. No one should make him withhold his touch, but they both had Hannah to consider. Scott looked down at her. "What do you think? What do you want to do? If you want to run, we'll run."

Sadness, tiredness, disgust — it all crawled across her face. "Thunder City was supposed to be different. I was supposed to find shelter here."

"I'm so sorry, Hannah." Scott risked a light kiss on the top of her head, hidden by Thomas, who blocked Johnson's view of the two of them.

"If we run," she said, "we'll really be burning our bridges with Thunder City. There is nowhere else where we can live in the open as Alts. There will always be someone chasing me." Her heavy sigh shattered his heart all over again. "Let's do this and get it done. I can prove my control easily enough. I'll show them what a Blood Surfer can really do."

Scott couldn't hide a small grin of pride. He could always lean on Thomas, but Hannah's strength would see her through with or without Scott by her side.

"All right," he said. "We'll do this. Together."

CHAPTER TWO

They descended to the dock, Thomas in the lead, Scott by her side.

They won't hurt us, they won't hurt us, they won't hurt us, Hannah chanted to herself. It didn't calm her down because she wasn't afraid this time. Not like when she and Scott had first escaped Star Haven, when Miranda had chased her out of Star Haven Memorial Hospital. This time, she let her anger lead her.

She'd known Thunder City had its own laws about how alternative humans were to be treated, but she hadn't understood what those laws would mean to her. The reason Star Haven and Thunder City clashed so often was because of how differently they treated Alts. Star Haven wanted alternative humans deported or dead. Miranda had achieved that goal with the Alt ban. Thunder City, led by Catherine Blackwood, Captain Spectacular, was supposed to be a sanctuary city where Alts could live without fear. Alts didn't even have to wear masks if they wanted to use their abilities in public.

Division Six surrounded the three of them as soon as their feet hit the ground, rifles not quite raised, but at the ready. Thomas stayed within the tight circle, putting himself between Scott and Hannah and the police.

"Separate them."

Hannah couldn't see Johnson, but already the authoritarian voice grated on her nerves. Rough hands, gloved like her own, grabbed her and pulled her out of Scott's grip. Pain shot through her rib cage. Her face and neck muscles refused to flex with the increased pressure of keeping her balance. A half-scream escaped her lungs.

"Stop it! You're hurting her!"

Scott's voice. She could hear him through the roar of blood in her ears, but the spots swimming before her eyes made it impossible for her to see anything. More hands yanked at her clothes.

"Enough!" Thomas's voice. "What the hell kind of doctor are you? You're hurting her. You're hurting both of them."

"You know the laws, Carraro. I saw them on the deck of your yacht. You've allowed them to violate our laws long enough. Untrained Alts cannot touch or be touched. It's too dangerous."

Hannah staggered. The death grip on her upper arm cut off the blood flow to her forearm. Her fingers throbbed.

"They're wearing gloves and proper clothing. I saw to that," Thomas pleaded. "They haven't broken the law. This isn't necessary."

Where was Scott? Hannah ignored her stiff muscles and stood up straight. The bright sun made her already wet eyes tear up even more. She could see him on the other side of Thomas, who was still arguing with Doctor Johnson. Division Six had him surrounded, each officer with a gun pointed at him.

"I'm not blind, Carraro. Your wife's report clearly stated that Miranda Dane had your son beaten to coerce

Hannah Quinn into surrendering. Even from here I can see he has no bruises. Either Catherine lied or this one — " he jabbed a finger in Hannah's direction — "healed him. A direct violation of our laws."

"Let her go. You're hurting her." Scott's voice, sounding anguished.

Thomas appeared in front of her, ignoring the sputtering Johnson. "Officers, listen to me —"

"Step away," one of the officers ordered.

"She's hurt," Thomas continued, holding his arms out toward Hannah, to fold her into his embrace. How she wanted to run toward him, but the cop still had an iron grip on her arm. "She needs medical attention. We're going to the hospital anyway. Manhandling her isn't necessary —"

"Step away, or you'll be arrested as well."

If they arrested Thomas, what would Catherine do? She created the Committee but clearly she didn't control it. Not if this Johnson guy could show up with Division Six and take her away from everyone she'd come to care about. In her mind's eye she could see herself at the hospital, strapped down to a bed, the door locked behind her just like the freezer door.

Panic overtook reason. Division Six's clothes and armor kept them covered head to foot. No skin-on-skin contact was possible, so there was no way she could use her bloodsurfing skills to defend herself, unless…she looked up. The cop wore a ski-mask style face helmet to cover his skin, but he still had to breathe.

This is going to be gross. In a second, Hannah whipped off the glove on her left hand and jammed two fingers up the cop's nostrils.

Inside. She found herself in the lateral nasal artery, but quickly jumped into the corresponding vein. Traveling down, she swam into the facial vein and eventually the external jugular vein for her trip to the cop's shoulders.

Just like Miranda's mercs, she knocked out the shoulder, elbow, and knee joints in what felt like a minute inside, but more like a few seconds outside. The freedom to move without pain made her faster, giddy, almost joyful. A piece of her anger broke free and vanished. She swam up to his vocal chords and paused, looking at the undulating muscles. He was screaming. She could hear him over the wind of this breath rushing from his lungs. When she was a prisoner in the quarry, she'd slashed the mercs' vocal chords to keep them from calling for help.

It would serve the cop right if she denied him his voice, just like they were denying her. She had a temper. It had taken eighteen years and the promise of freedom the Blackwoods had given her to realize just how much of Miranda's abuse she'd internalized.

Yet, this Division Six officer didn't need to have his vocal chords destroyed because of her anger. Who knew what Johnson had told him about Catherine's report? Hell, she didn't even know what Catherine had reported. She'd never thought to ask because it hurt too much to think about and it was just a preliminary report anyway. She couldn't purge herself of her past. She could only move forward and she couldn't do that from inside someone else's body.

Part of her wanted to stay in here to avoid having to deal with the consequences of her actions, but no — she'd made this choice. No one was going to hurt her ever again without payback. Even if they were cops.

When she emerged, she found herself on the ground next to the cop's body. Above her stood the rest of Division Six, all of their guns pointed at her.

"Let me through."

Johnson spoke as he shoved his way toward her, his teeth bared, his ugly brown suit disheveled. She rolled off the cop with hands raised, ready to fight again.

"You've done enough damage as it is." Thomas yanked Johnson back. "You'll get her killed."

"She just attacked an officer. Look at her." Johnson pulled his collar out of Thomas's grip. "She's ready to attack again. I *will* have her arrested this time."

"You'll do nothing of the sort," Thomas insisted. "You've overstepped your boundaries. You were supposed to escort her to the hospital. This is a gross misuse of your position and I'll have you removed from the Committee."

One of the other officers lowered his gun. Hannah thought for a second that Thomas was getting through to them, so she lowered her arms. Instead, the cop grabbed her by the back of her neck. Her neck couldn't handle the violent movement and the sharp resistance pulsed through her muscles. She protested again, with a shriek of pain. She reached up again, looking for skin, anywhere she could make contact.

Before she could blink Scott appeared, out of the blue, right in front of her.

"Scott, where did you —"

Before she could finish, Scott punched the cop and ripped her out of the cop's hold. Scott had her back in his arms, but the whiplash movement was too much for her to handle, and blackness returned as the world swirled to darkness.

⁂

Scott held onto Hannah for dear life, his face buried in her neck, expecting to get shot or at the very least, tased. Nothing happened for a minute. He could hear his own staccato breaths, but nothing else. No shouting, no shooting, not even the smell of salt or the sound of waves crashing into the harbor.

He lifted his head a half-inch to look over Hannah's shoulder. Instead of the wooden boardwalk, soft light-blue carpet cushioned his knees. He knew that color. He lifted his head the rest of the way and saw he was in his childhood bedroom, the one at the Blackwood estate.

"Hannah?"

She pulled her head away from his shoulder, her face buried in his shirt, her eyes squeezed shut, wet with tears.

"Hannah it's okay. We're okay. You can open your eyes now."

She moaned and her head flopped to one side.

"Hannah, don't pass out on my now. Please." He tapped her cheek as gently as he could. "C'mon, Hannah, stay with me."

Her eyes opened, the bright green still stunning even with tears. He could tell the exact moment when she recognized where he'd brought her.

"Scott, we're — "

"Yeah, I know."

"How — oh, my God. Your Alt power. You translocated us from the harbor back here."

The wonder in her voice dried her tears and matched his own shock. "Yeah. Not just from the harbor to here, but away from the cops trying to 'cuff us."

Hannah turned to him. "You're amazing."

Scott would have debated the amazing part, except they didn't have time. Division Six would track them here first, even if it was just a guess. "We need to get out of Thunder City. If we stay here, they'll arrest us for attacking the cops."

He adjusted his arms around Hannah, to give give her more leverage to remain standing as she remained pressed against his whole body, not just his arm.

"I blew it," she said. "I let my temper get the better of me. Why couldn't I just go with them?"

"You shouldn't have had to." He guided her over to his bed. "This isn't the way Thunder City treats Alts. Catherine wouldn't have allowed this. If she hadn't stayed behind at the quarry, she would have defended you."

"How do you know?"

Scott shook his head, once again amazed that he would defend his mother. "The Star Haven Newcomers were given gloves and clothing, and were assigned to trainers to help them along. Johnson is twisting the law to make it cold, ugly. Something else is going on around here."

"How are we going to get out of town?" Hannah pulled away to sit on his bed. Scott remembered the last time she'd been in his bed. He tucked that wild memory away while he reached over to help her lie down, but she waved him off while she toed off her sneakers, groaning.

Scott shed his gloves and knelt next to Hannah, his hands massaging her arms. Why shouldn't he? They were already wanted. How much worse could it get? "Division Six has my guns, my comm, and my wallet. We can't take any of the cars in the garage because the cops will just put out an APB for all of the Blackwood vehicles."

Hannah closed her eyes. "And I don't have any guns, phones, or money. How long before you think they'll find us here?"

"Not long enough." Scott's mind raced. He had no friends in Thunder City, no one he could call on who would put their own freedom on the line for him. There was Juan back in Star Haven - no, those bridges were burned when the news media exposed him as an Alt. There were other ways out of town, but first he'd need money. "Stay here. I'll be right back."

He brushed his lips on her forehead before he headed down to the first floor. It only took a minute to get to Thomas's office. The office offered the comfort of the same warm colors found on the *Elusive Lady*. Books lined the bookshelves and a small bar stocked with Thomas's favorite liquors.

Scott gripped a set of books and pulled them off one of the bookshelves. Using his thumb, he forced the back panels to pull away from the shelving. Behind the panels, a safe appeared. He keyed in the combination along with his thumb print.

Thomas had never kept any secrets from Scott, including access to his private safe. Thomas had a history of playing fast and loose with the law, and always kept cash, phones, and fake IDs handy for the entire Blackwood handy. "Just in case," he'd told his newly adopted son with a coy wink, trusting him even as a young teen to make good decisions.

Scott scooped up two of everything, but as he did, his fingers brushed up against something in back of the safe. He pulled out a Ruger, a newer model than the one Division Six had taken away from him. Scott reached in again and pulled out a box of ammo. Thomas never used guns. He preferred to outthink his opponent. It also kept his father in compliance with the agreement Catherine had signed to not arm T-CASS in deference to police training. Scott wasn't a part of T-CASS and Thomas knew that. It was a clear signal that this gun was for Scott's use. He loaded it now and slipped it into his holster.

The weight of the gun against his chest comforted him. Next he headed toward the guest room given to Hannah when she first arrived at the estate. He grabbed a pair of black yoga pants and a blue athletic shirt from the closet. Then he headed for the master bedroom, grabbing one of his mother's oversized beach hats and a pair of sunglasses, before he raided Thomas's side of the bedroom for jeans and an oxford shirt before returning to his bedroom. He'd owe both of his parents a new wardrobe before this came to an end. If it ever came to an end.

Don't think like that. Hannah deserves peace. I'll find it for her. If I have to translocate us to the opposite side of the planet, I'll find it.

The old rock posters ruffled when he breezed past them back into his bedroom. "I have money, phone, and a fake ID for me. The problem is — Thomas doesn't have an ID that will fit you. You'll have to use the one he created for Catherine."

"As if anyone is going to mistake me for Captain Spec." Hannah sat up with a wince, giving the beach hat a side eye. Regardless of what she thought about his sense of fashion, she took the clothes, the phone, and her new ID.

"Don't worry about that part. We just need to get to the train station." He stripped off his shirt and slacks. He knew Hannah watched, but now wasn't the time for *that*. Still, he couldn't help but show off as he slipped on Thomas's jeans.

"The train station?" Hannah looked a lot less scared

and more interested while he zipped the fly.

"Yeah. It's still early enough for the morning rush hour. Hundreds of commuters milling about, noise from the trains, and lots of families leaving for a weekend getaway before school starts. If we're lucky, no one will notice us." The jeans fit fine, but the shirt was a little tight.

"How are we going to get there?" Hannah slid off the bed and reached for the yoga pants. Scott couldn't help himself — he watched Hannah get dressed, just as she had watched him. Instead of enjoying the view, the bruises on her body stoked his anger. He remembered pushing the bullet into Miranda's forehead. The satisfaction of that memory was the only reason he didn't put his fist through the nearest wall.

"I'm going to translocate us there."

Hannah paused before slipping on her shirt. "No. Scott, you can't."

"Obviously, I can. I got us here didn't I?"

Hannah pulled the shirt down and stood there, arms crossed, snap and color returning to her face. "Look, I get it. Your ability is amazing, but it's not a toy. All the dangers Thomas had warned you about — getting us stuck inside a wall or halfway sunk into the ground — "

" — and told you about," Scott interrupted.

"We had a brief conversation." Hannah admitted. "All those dangers aren't something you can ignore. You got lucky pulling me away from Miranda. You got lucky translocating yourself toward the cops, too, and then both of us here. At some point though, your luck will run out. You've only translocated us to places you could see or that you knew would be empty. A train station filled with people is something entirely different."

"I know that, but it's either the train station or we just wait here to be arrested. You can't run, not in your condition."

He could see the fear return to her eyes. Arrested meant locked doors and worse.

She sighed. "If only I had kept my temper."

"It's not your fault." He hugged her. He needed to feel her next to his heart, her head tucked right under his chin. They were a perfect fit.

She stayed there for a moment, but only for a moment. "All right. If we're going to do this, let's do it."

He watched while she piled her hair on top of her head, tucked it under the hat, and slipped on the sunglasses. His doubts returned when she stepped back into his arms. "You're familiar with the train station?"

"It's been a while." More like a decade. He'd never really had a reason to use the train to get anywhere.

"What do you remember about it?"

Scott had to close his eyes to think. "The clock tower. In the center of the lobby. It's huge so everyone can see it. It sits in the middle of a small garden. The garden is decorated for the change in seasons or for a holiday, but it's roped off so no one tramples over it."

"Aim for the garden, then, so we don't wind up inside the tower."

"Right."

Hannah tilted her head back, looking him in the eyes, while wrapping her arms around his waist. The faint sound of sirens wafted through the window.

"Close your eyes," Hannah instructed. "Think about the clock tower garden. You know you want to be there. We need to get there. Make it happen."

He closed his eyes and thought about the garden, calling up a vague memory of stanchion ropes messing his hair as his toddler-self made a beeline for the rocks lining the garden. He wanted to pick up the rocks so bad, to collect them for whatever childish reason he'd decided was important at the time. He'd almost made it too, until Catherine noticed he'd wandered away and pulled him back to the right side of the ropes.

Nothing happened. The sound of sirens grew louder.

"It's not working." Why? It worked just fine at the harbor. He hadn't even thought about what he wanted to do, it just happened.

Hannah placed a hand on his heart. "What were you thinking about when you translocated to me at the harbor?"

"You. I was thinking about you. They were hurting you and I wanted to make it stop. Next thing I know, I was right next to you."

"And after you punched the cop?"

"Safety. I wanted to get you somewhere safe."

"So, your bedroom was the first thing to pop into your mind?"

"Yeah. This room," he looked around, "It was my safety net until — " He stopped. Evan had apologized for almost killing him during a teenage prank. He didn't want to think about it now. He didn't need anger. He needed focus.

"So, if I'm in danger, it works?"

What could he say? "I'm sorry."

"Don't be sorry, just — " She looked over his shoulder. Her green eyes went wide. Her scream damn near shattered the windows.

Thinking about sharpshooters, Scott grabbed Hannah and closed his eyes.

The high pitch of brakes squealing and a loudspeaker announcement melded with Hannah's scream. He opened his eyes to see short clipped grass under his feet. Hannah was still cradled in his arms. Next to him was the faux brick of the clock tower.

"Hannah?" He unwrapped his arms from around her shoulders.

She looked around. "It worked. You did it."

"I guess I did. What did you see out of the window?"

Hannah gave him a confused look. "What?"

"What made you scream? Was it Division Six?"

"Oh, no. There was nothing outside your window. I just screamed so you'd think we were in danger and trigger your power."

Scott almost laughed, but settled for shaking his head. "Let's get out of here before we attract attention."

CHAPTER THREE

Hannah stared at the train rolling into the station from under the brim of her hat, willing it to move faster. She'd hidden in the restroom while Scott had bought their tickets at the window. News from the quarry raid played on the overhead televisions in a repeated cycle, but so far no one had recognized her.

Just a few more minutes and they'd be on the train. There were at least four major cities south of Thunder City. This train was a commuter and stopped at each of them before it reached the end of the line. It didn't matter where they got off the train, as long as they could remain anonymous.

As long as they could stay together.

"Don't move."

The words were quiet, whispered just loud enough for both her and Scott to hear. Scott had heard too because he stiffened beside her. Hannah closed her eyes. It was too much to have hoped that they'd make it onto the train. Scott didn't turn around either as the train glided to a stop.

"You're going to walk off this platform without giving me any fuss, or I will take you down hard."

Hannah risked looking over her shoulder, pulling her sunglasses down her nose. Hard brown eyes stared back under a large scar through the guy's left eyebrow. He was shorter than Scott, but wider in the shoulders, giving him the look of a brawler. Overconfidence rolled off him like steam. She didn't remember seeing him at the Arena before the quarry raid, so she guessed he was Neut, a neutral, working for the Oversight Committee instead of T-CASS. She could work around overconfidence, though. Whoever he was, he wore regular clothes — blue jeans and t-shirt — which made her think he really didn't care specifically about her or Scott. This was just a job.

She turned away from the train to face the Neut, to make her stand with Scott at her back. "I've had dozens of people try to take me down over the last six months, including Division Six. They all failed."

"I'm different."

"They all say that."

Stand-off. She wasn't moving off the platform. Scott turned with her now. He wasn't about to move either.

"You think T-CASS is going to rescue you? The Committee figured you'd cause trouble. My crew is stationed all over Thunder City, waiting for you to reappear. We got paid a lot of cash do this job, and when we get paid, the job gets done."

At least she had confirmation of his Neut status. She could see his own comm hooked to his jeans, just like Scott's.

The doors to the train opened. Passengers already on board exited, threading their way past the passengers waiting to board. It wouldn't take much for the Neut to shove Scott and Hannah into the flow of traffic and force them to move with it. From both sides, new passengers pressed against them, glaring at the obstruction the three of them created, wanting to get on board quickly. The mix of perfumes and aftershaves tickled her nose.

Scott tugged on her shoulder, pulling her closer to the train, putting distance between them and the Neut. "Hannah and I are leaving Thunder City. Don't follow or you might end up like Miranda Dane's mercs."

An invisible grip clamped around her, forcing her even closer to Scott, and yanked them closer to the Neut. Pain shot through her again. Scott's hand, trapped between the invisible force and her stomach, pressed into her guts, forcing the air she breathed up and out her body.

"Now what are you going to do?" the Neut taunted. "You can't move."

The Neut stepped back. Hannah could feel her feet lift off the platform, her toes pointed down reaching for the ground. Scott squirmed against her back trying to free himself. The passengers had finished boarding and the train's doors closed with a final thump. They had missed their chance.

Hannah experimented with inhaling, trying to figure out how the Neut was holding them. Air dragged into her aching lungs. Telekinesis. The damned Neut kept smirking while he dragged both of them toward the edge of the platform.

"Let me make this clear." There was her anger again, riding roughshod over her fear. "You might be able to stop me today, but then you'll be stuck in Thunder City with me."

"Yeah, so?"

Hannah nodded as much as she could toward one of the overhead screens still steaming news from the quarry. "I learned a lot from Miranda Dane about how to deal with people who get in my way. I know how to take down Alts when they least expect it. Do you really want to be at the top of my hit list?"

Her heart pounded. The Neut paused to look at the streaming video on one of the overhead screens. Her feet hit the platform because the Neut broke his focus. The Neut watched her on the screen taking down Miranda's armed mercs while a giant mutant Alt rampaged.

"Think about what you're doing. You're holding an Alt who was raised by a woman who spent her life not just murdering Alts, but torturing them. You're also holding Cory Blackwood, son of Captain Spectacular. What do you think she's going to do when she finds out you accepted a contract to attack her son?"

The Neut turned away from the screen to look at her and Scott. "Captain Spec won't do anything. She's the one who created the laws in the first place."

"Yeah," Scott said from behind her. "But she's married to Hack-Man. He doesn't play quite as nice as she does. You're a Neut. So is he. You play in his pool. Do you really think he's going to let you get away with this? If nothing else, you and your crew will never see another contract."

Money talked, always. Another lesson she'd learned from Miranda. The Neut's face slackened, unsure. Maybe he had worked for Hack-Man at one time. Maybe he admired Captain Spectacular even though he didn't work for T-CASS. Without the telekinetic grip, Hannah could step away from Scott, draw a deep breath.

"What are you doing?" Damn it. Johnson, his brown suit now sweat-soaked, pushed his way past the train crowd. "You're being paid to keep them from running. Keep them restrained." Johnson puffed his way onto the platform. "Division Six is surrounding the building."

The invisible grip tightened again.

"Let them go."

Hannah had expected to see Thomas, but this voice sounded deeper, with an accent Hannah couldn't quite place. A tall man, in a much nicer suit than Johnson's, with hair almost the same color as her own, approached, waving a piece of paper.

"I have a court order overriding the Oversight Committee."

The Neut looked back and forth between Johnson and the new guy, but didn't loosen his hold.

Johnson tried to reach for the paper the other guy blew past Johnson, keeping the paper away from his grasp. He approached the Neut.

"I'm Doctor McNamara. Chief Pathologist for Harbor Regional and Thunder City's Medical Examiner. Let go of Ms. Quinn and Mr. Grey now, or you will be the one arrested here."

The Neut didn't obey, but looked over McNamara's shoulder at Johnson, who stomped over to McNamara.

"I demand to see this order."

McNamara gave the paper to Johnson.

"How did you get this so fast?" Johnson demanded.

McNamara didn't even bother to look at Johnson while he answered. Instead he looked at Hannah, scrutinizing her. "I was at the courthouse reporting for jury duty. I managed to get myself excused, and good thing too. You're not the only one who has lawyers at their beck and call. The judge has the authority to override the Committee and call for a hearing."

Hannah's vision started to swim. If she couldn't take a deeper breath soon, she'd faint. She could still hear just fine, though. McNamara's argument sounded tenuous at best, but she was grateful for his interference.

"This situation demands we keep these two separated and incarcerated until they can be trained or until Thunder City arrests them. Do you have any idea of what you've done?" Johnson demanded.

"Stopped you from running roughshod over the values of this city? Yes, I'm quite well aware of what I've done. Hannah Quinn and Scott Grey will be protected."

"They've broken the law," Johnson insisted.

"That has yet to be determined. For now, they are free. A hearing will determine what is to be done with them." McNamara snatched the paper away from Johnson and handed it to the Neut.

The Neut took the paper. After a moment of indecision, the harsh bond crushing her and Scott together loosened. Hannah groaned as her lungs expanded to their full capacity. Scott slipped his hand under her arms, keeping her upright, keeping her steady, his touch soothing her outrage.

While the Neut read the order, Johnson pulled out his phone.

"Division Six is receiving their orders from the Police Chief," McNamara said. "They won't support your attempt to arrest Ms. Quinn or Mr. Grey."

Johnson swore and put his phone away. He tried to get closer to Hannah and Scott, but McNamara blocked him.

"Don't you two even think about running." Johnson wagged a finger at her and Scott. "You've turned the safety of this city into a joke. There will be consequences." Then he turned toward the Neut. "You're fired."

The Neut shrugged as he followed Johnson off the

platform. "You paid in advance. No refunds."

Johnson stomped toward the exit with the Neut shuffling behind him. Hannah didn't care.

"Thank you," she tried to say, but her ribs contracted on the "thank" making "you" sound more like a wheeze. She leaned on Scott. Without her anger, all she had was her relief. It wasn't enough to keep her standing. Scott held her as she sat down right on the platform. The train had left the station during the showdown. The platform was empty except for a handful of stragglers. One or two gawked at her, but the rest were too busy with their phones. They probably had streamed the entire confrontation.

"I need to get her home." Scott knelt next to her. McNamara did the same, close enough to talk to her, but not to touch her.

"I can't touch you to take your pulse, so I'll have to ask you a few questions." McNamara paused to turn his head to cough into the crook of his arm. She could hear the clink of what she assumed was a cough drop scraping his teeth. "Is your heart racing? Are you in severe pain? You don't have a history of seizures or asthma, do you? Are you taking any medications?"

Hannah answered the questions as best she could. Her voice grew stronger as her heart rate decreased.

"Unfortunately, I can't tell without a direct examination if you're more damaged now than you were before Telekis attacked. You still need to go to the clinic."

Hannah swallowed, her throat still contracting around her voice. "Can you tell us what's going on? Why is this Johnson guy so determined to lock us up?"

McNamara started to answer, but an announcement over the PA system drowned him out. Hannah noticed a new crowd of passengers waiting for the next train had given her and Scott a wide berth.

McNamara tried again. "How about I give you two a ride to the clinic? There are others better versed in the law than I am."

Hannah looked up at Scott.

He shrugged. "Can you promise Johnson won't try to lock us up again? We were supposed to go to the clinic in the first place."

"I'll stake my reputation on it." McNamara stood while Scott helped her to stand. Her legs still quivered like jelly, but she could breathe as deeply as she needed. "Johnson will have to wait for the hearing to be scheduled before he can challenge the court. It will take a couple of days at least."

Hannah could only nod at this point, her energy gone, and her voice along with it. She accepted McNamara's promise, but her thoughts already raced ahead about how to escape Thunder City once again. McNamara couldn't promise that Johnson wouldn't return to court and prevail, and she hadn't survived the quarry raid to be locked up by an egomaniacal doctor. Next time she ran, if she had to run, she would have Scott with her, and that would require extra planning.

The three of them weaved their way around the crowded platform and headed toward the exit. She'd already been to the clinic once, but she hadn't looked at it with the eyes of someone who would have to escape. She wouldn't make that mistake a second time.

"How is Hannah?" Thomas asked over the phone.

Scott paced along the clinic's hallway, his hands back in gloves provided for him and Hannah by Doctor

McNamara. He pressed the phone closer to his ear and let Thomas's calm voice soothe his nerves.

"The clinic rushed her into X-Ray. She's in an exam room now, waiting for the results."

"Where are you?" his father asked.

Scott could hear muted voices in the background. Where was Thomas? "Outside the exam room. They brought us to the second floor to keep us away from the press. There's a crowd gathering outside the hospital next door. If the reporters manage to bypass hospital security, they won't find her right away. Where are you?"

"Downtown at the courthouse. Joanna's with me. We're waiting to schedule the hearing for you and Hannah. We want both of you at the same hearing, no splitting you up. We also need to counter any roadblocks Johnson builds."

Scott remembered Joanna Culp, Thomas's personal lawyer. She was a shark born in the twin fires of cybersecurity and human rights law. She hadn't handled Scott's adoption by Thomas directly, but she was always in the background, reviewing every piece of paper before Thomas signed.

"Tell her I said hi." Scott doubted Joanna would care if he said hi or not, but Thomas had raised him to be polite when it mattered. Staying on Joanna's good side mattered. "What about me and Hannah? Where should we go after this? I don't think Hannah will have to stay overnight in the clinic or in the hospital."

He could hear Joanna's voice in the background. Thomas paused before he said, "I think it would be best if you stayed in the penthouse for now, with Hannah staying at the estate. Even if we get the hearing scheduled soon, we can't change the law, and Johnson is looking for any excuse to separate you two. I'm sorry, Scott. I know this is overkill, but let's try not to exacerbate the problem. You two can still communicate, but being seen together, even completely covered and wearing gloves, is going to be provocative for the next couple of weeks."

Scott nodded, but realized Thomas couldn't see him. "Okay. I'll call Garrett and arrange for him to move my stuff to the penthouse." Not that he had much. Some clothing and a few personal items. Everything else he owned was still back in Star Haven. Another thought occurred to him. "What do you know about Thunder City's Medical Examiner? A guy named McNamara?"

Another pause. "Not much. I've met him at a few charity events. He's been here quite a while, though he got his degree elsewhere. Good man. Does his job. Stays out of the politics as best he can. I trust him."

Thomas trusted him. That should have been all Scott needed to hear, but it didn't settle his uneasy feeling about why McNamara had gone to such lengths to help them. The pathologist had brought them to the clinic, used his status to get Hannah seen right away, then apologized before he returned to the hospital. Before he left he'd handed Hannah two cards.

Call me before you leave the clinic. I have a few questions I need to ask you. Here is my business card and a security key. I'll give you directions on how to use the security key to get to my office when you call.

He'd wanted to speak to Hannah, not to Scott. That much had been clear. "He seems to be on Hannah's side. Can't figure out his angle, though."

"I think I have an idea of what he wants — "

Scott could hear Joanna's voice again, cutting off whatever Thomas was going to say.

"The judge wants to see us," Thomas said, talking faster. "I'll call you later. Go to the penthouse and wait for me. Catherine and the twins are on their way back to Thunder City. Don't worry too much about McNamara."

Scott slipped the phone back into his pocket. Catherine, Evan, and Alek were flying back to Thunder City. Catherine wouldn't have left the quarry unless she was convinced that T-CASS had it secured from any meddling from Star Haven. Before the quarry raid, Scott wouldn't have been so relieved at knowing he would see his mother again.

The exam room door opened. Hannah stepped out looking better than she had at the train station, her eyes more clear and sharp and her dark red hair pulled back into a knot at her neck. Scott fought the urge to pull her into a kiss, an urge he noticed she fought too as she walked into his personal space, but then glanced over her shoulder at the doctor who had followed her out of the room.

"She'll be fine," the woman in the white coat said. "Doctor Rao's examination was on the spot. A few bruised ribs, but those will heal along with the contusions on her face. Nothing requires a hospital stay. Do you have any questions?"

Hannah shook her head. "No, I don't have any questions."

The doctor nodded. "Call if you notice swelling or have difficulty breathing. No exercise or lifting heavy objects. Do make another appointment, though, for next week. There will be a prescription for a painkiller at the front desk you can pick up before you leave." The doctor hesitated. "You won't want to leave through the front door, though. In fact, you might want to call security to escort you to your ride."

"Why?" Hannah asked.

Before Scott could tell her about the crowd out front, the doctor pulled her phone out of her pocket and turned on the streaming news app. "We've been expecting something like this ever since the news about the quarry broke."

On the phone's screen both Scott and Hannah could see a crowd gathered there. Hospital security stood at the entrance. Neither side engaged the other, and the volume was turned off, but even without the sound, Scott could see the crowd was agitated.

"Why were you expecting this?" Scott asked.

"A new Alt in town is always exciting." The doctor slipped the phone back into her pocket. "We always take extra precautions when they're brought here for their first exam. But an Alt that can heal almost instantaneously — "

The nightmare he'd been fearing since he'd met Hannah had started. Decisions had to be made. Who would have access to Hannah's ability and when? What would the citizens of Thunder City think about Johnson restricting their access to Hannah? Scott filed away a few ideas for later examination.

"We'll take the skyway on the fourth floor to the garage first, then over to the hospital."

The doctor nodded, satisfied. "If you'll excuse me, I have another patient I have to see."

She rushed off.

Hannah sighed and started walking toward the far end of the hallway, toward the elevators, while placing Catherine's beach hat back on her head. Scott followed, his hands behind his back. Thomas's security firm handled the hospital and clinic. Scott knew there were eyes everywhere.

"What did Thomas say while I was in X-Ray?" she asked.

"Nothing we couldn't predict. He's at the courthouse, scheduling our hearing. I'm going to stay at the penthouse, while you stay at the estate."

Hannah nodded, her head down, her sadness obvious, but not surprised. "What about your clothes and stuff? How will you get there?"

"Garrett can pack everything I have in an overnight bag. He'll pick me up here." It dawned on Scott that Garrett would have to deal with the crowds forming outside. "I'll have him come to the fourth floor of the garage and pick me up there."

"Lucky for you it's on our way."

"I think I should bring you to McNamara's office, then double back."

Hannah was already shaking her head. "No one in the hospital is going to hurt me, even if they recognize me under this." She flicked a finger under the hat's brim. "Security is going to be extra vigilant and Johnson's probably at the courthouse trying to stop Thomas. I'll go straight to McNamara's office. He'll take me back to the estate later today or I'll have someone else pick me up."

"What about the crowd outside?"

"Security can handle it. If they can't, T-CASS will."

"Most of T-CASS is still at the quarry," Scott reminded her.

Hannah shrugged. "I have power now. Everyone in Thunder City has seen me take down Miranda's mercenaries. By the end of today, they'll know about us fighting off Division Six. If Thunder City keeps threatening me, I *will* leave. I'd rather live in another city and not use my power at all, than be locked up again."

Scott put his faith in Thomas's security team's discretion and hugged her. "I'll go with you," he whispered in her ear. "If you decide to leave or if we have to run. Don't go anywhere without me."

"Never," she whispered back.

He released her from his hug. Side-by-side they made it down to the first floor and to the front desk without creating any further havoc. The guy sitting behind the desk didn't look up as he made Hannah another appointment for next week, then handed her a piece of paper for her prescription.

Hannah tucked the prescription into her back pocket, while Scott walked her back to the elevators and up to the fourth floor skyway.

"Are you sure you don't want me to go with you?" They'd reached the garage without saying much to each other. If Hannah felt as wiped out as he did, he couldn't blame her for keeping her thoughts to herself. He still looked around for potential threats, but the garage at this level was only half full, even in the middle of the work week.

"I'm sure." Hannah stepped away from him. "I need to make this trip on my own. If I can't get from here to the Pathologist's office on my own without causing a ruckus, how am I ever going to live a normal life in Thunder City? How can I convince a jackass like Johnson that I'm trustworthy? That I don't need to be locked up to keep everyone else safe?"

Her voice sped up and climbed an octave as she talked. He could see her pain, her eagerness to get away from him. Oddly enough, he understood. They'd stood by each other's side for so many days, maybe a short break was in order. Hannah had something to prove to herself, not to him or anyone else.

"Shhhhh, it's okay, Hannah. I understand." He backed away from her instead of moving toward her. "Go see what McNamara wants. I'll wait for Garrett here. If you need a ride, you can call him directly and he'll come back and pick you up here on the fourth floor."

Relief sagged Hannah's shoulders. "Thanks, Scott. I knew you would understand. I *will* call you later. After you're settled in the penthouse. I promise."

There's was nothing else left to say, so he kissed the tips of his gloved fingers and held them out toward Hannah. She did the same before turning her back on him and walking away.

CHAPTER FOUR

Guilt walked with Hannah all the way through the skyway. She knew Scott would watch her until he could no longer see her. Any other day, she wouldn't have minded his overprotectiveness. Today, she couldn't fight off the feeling of relief at being alone. She hadn't really had time to herself since the quarry raid. Either Scott, Thomas, or Doctor Rao had hovered over her. Thomas had a crew that milled about, doing their jobs. As much as she loved Scott and cared about Thomas, she really needed just a few minutes to herself, time to think without someone nearby to interrupt her thoughts. She had an escape to plan if it became necessary.

The skyway ended and she entered the hospital. She glanced over her shoulder and couldn't see Scott anymore. She stood up straighter, held her head high. All she was doing was going to see a doctor. People did that every day without fuss and bother. Her journey, short as it was, shouldn't be any different.

She followed the signs to the nearest suite of elevators. A few nurses passed by, wearing blue scrubs. Closer to the elevators, she started to see patients, some walking with IVs, others in wheelchairs. Her fingers itched to touch their skin, to bloodsurf and cure what ailed them, whatever it was. She fought back that urge, and changed her stance, keeping her head low. All the better to not see the security cameras discreetly placed at regular intervals along the ceiling.

Once she reached the elevators, she pulled out the phone Scott had given her and dialed the number on McNamara's business card.

"Ms. Quinn?"

The voice sounded smooth, soothing, until a cough ruined the effect. "How did you know?"

He tried to chuckle, but coughed again instead, this time punctuated with a sneeze. "My patients tend to be a quiet bunch. I rarely get calls not on my contact list."

Of course. He was a pathologist and medical examiner. He autopsied the dead. "You said you needed to give me further instructions to get to your location. I didn't know Pathology would be so difficult to get to."

"I can't imagine the morgue is on anyone's top ten list of places to visit."

It was Hannah's turn to laugh. Even she hadn't gone near the morgue when she was haunting the hallways of Star Haven Memorial. "No, I can't imagine it is."

"Well, then, here's what you need to do." She waited again as another sneeze interrupted his instructions. Whatever illness he had, it was getting worse. "Wait until you can catch the elevator when it's empty. Once you're inside and the doors have closed, run the short edge of the white keycard along the left edge of the floor selection keypad. There's a point where the card will slip behind the keypad itself. It will disappear for a moment, then reappear. Pull it out immediately. That will send the elevator down to the VIP floor of the hospital. Do you want me to stay on the phone with you?"

It sounded simple enough. "No. That's okay. It might take me some time to find an empty elevator."

"You may have to ride it up a few floors, then come down again." He coughed again. "A tiresome complication, but the VIP floor is sort of a half-secret. Not many people know about it. You understand, Hannah. It would be best if you kept the information about this floor and the key to yourself. For security reasons."

A half-secret. The Blackwoods are damn big VIPs in Thunder City. They must know about it. Maybe use the floor themselves? Scott might not know about it, though. He hasn't lived here for years. What do I tell him?

Nothing. Miranda's voice in her head. *You have to start protecting yourself. Scott knows you're going to the Pathology department. He doesn't need to know which Pathology department.*

No! I'll ask McNamara if it's okay to tell Scott first. Scott might already know. Thomas would have told him, and Thomas would have to know about the VIP level. His company handles security around here.

"I understand," she replied to McNamara. He shouldn't have to wait for her to finish her internal argument with her dead ex-mother. "I'll be there as soon as I can."

"Good. Turn right off the elevator. My office is the last one at the end of the corridor. Hopefully the cold meds will kick in before you get here, otherwise you'll hear me long before you see me."

Hannah hung up. The first elevator arrived with a crowd inside. They all got out. She walked inside and luck followed. No one entered behind her. She knew she was in trouble the second the elevator doors closed, though. Her body grew cold, remembering the temperature of the freezer in which Miranda had locked her. She white-knuckled the key card as she slid it down past the floor numbers as instructed. About halfway down it slid in, disappeared, then slid back out again. She snatched it and backed up against the wall, her eyelids closed so tight her eyeballs hurt.

You can do this. Won't take long. Can't take long. You were just on an elevator with Scott. Imagine Scott standing beside you, holding your hand. Don't be scared. Catherine wouldn't be scared. Miranda would want *you to be scared. Miranda wants you to cry. Don't give her the satisfaction.*

The lower the elevator dropped, the harder her body shook until the elevator doors opened to silence. As much as she wanted to jump out, her tremors forced her to exit with small steps.

You made it. The doors shut behind her, but she still stood there, hugging herself. *Nothing wrong with me that a good dose of courage won't cure.*

She turned right per McNamara's instructions and stopped dead in her tracks.

Tall, dark, and darth stood in front of an office door. The only office door at the end of a short corridor. He had a gun strapped to his hip.

He, of course, could see her standing there, like a lost kid in a horror movie. She couldn't see behind his mirrored sunglasses (and who wore sunglasses in the basement of a hospital anyway?), but she imagined he laughed at her. Not that he showed any amusement. He didn't show anything. Not a twitch.

Oh, hell. After the day you've already had, what could this guy do to you? She asked herself.

Make you a resident in the morgue? Catherine's bluntness spoke this time, not Miranda's disdain. Hannah slipped her hand into her pocket to get the key card out of her hand. The guy might work as hospital security, but if so, why was he armed so heavily and not in uniform?

Thoughts of blowing up Joe's brain flitted through her memories. She remembered her power during the quarry raid. She could heal, but she could also fight. She'd forgotten that in the elevator where there was nothing to fight but her own fear.

With more confidence than she felt, she approached the guard.

"Hi. I'm Hannah Quinn. I need to speak with Doctor McNamara and he said he would be in his office."

This close up, she could see a hint of heaviness in the guard's pale cheeks, along with some silver across his near-black hairline. The puckered tip of a scar poked his suprasternal notch from under his black t-shirt. He wasn't a young punk, but a man with experience and he had the battle scars to prove it.

A long moment passed, then with the tiniest of smirks he stepped to the side, opened the door behind him, and motioned her to enter. She passed by him with the cheeriest "thank you" she could manage. Once she had crossed the threshold, the guard slammed the door shut.

Click, click. The door locked and she was stuck inside. Trapped. She whirled around to face the closed door, her hand reaching for the door knob, trying to yank it open.

I will not panic, I will not panic. I will not panic.

"Ms. Quinn?"

A hand gripped her wrist.

"Ms. Quinn. Relax. You're safe here. You're safe with me."

That voice. She recognized it. From under the beach

hat, she saw a white jacket, a blue oxford shirt, and a maroon tie.

McNamara. Of course, he was here. It was his office. Why did she think she was back in Miranda's freezer?

She let go of the door knob.

"I'm sorry." She inhaled in an attempt to slow her heart. "I don't react well to closed doors. Reminds me too much of the quarry."

The door opened. Darth stood there, hand on gun.

"No!" McNamara gave her a gentle push backward so he could stand between her and the guard. "It's fine. You triggered a panic attack when you locked the door. She'll be okay, but let's keep the door open for a little while, shall we?"

Hannah peeked around McNamara. With his sunglasses covering his eyes, she couldn't tell if the guard was concerned, disgusted, or angry.

McNamara sighed. "Ms. Quinn is not a threat. The crowd outside, however, might find their way inside. Why don't you do something about that?"

The guard still didn't say anything, nor did he back off.

"We'll be fine," McNamara repeated, his voice louder, more forceful despite the rashness of what had to be a sore throat. "No one will find her down here without me knowing about it. Go check on the crowd."

As quickly as the door had opened, the guard closed it again, but this time he kept the latch resting on the strike plate.

McNamara maneuvered her over to a comfortable, executive-style chair. With light pressure on her shoulders, he encouraged her sit. Her legs collapsed with little resistance.

"I'm sorry." She had no energy to say anything else.

"I'm sorry, too." McNamara sat behind his desk, pushing several bottles of cold medicine to the side. "Today has been stressful for you. The Shield shouldn't have locked the door behind you. Would you like some water? We'll talk whenever you're ready."

The Shield? So, the guard was an Alt. Probably another Neut. She couldn't imagine someone like that working for T-CASS.

She must have nodded because a moment later, McNamara reached over his desk to hand her a bottle with the cap already unscrewed. She took the hat off, though. She didn't need to hide who she was down here.

"I don't know what happened." The words tripped over her dry tongue, so she sipped the water. "I don't understand why I keep reacting like that."

"Having a bodyguard is an unfortunate necessity, at least for the next month or two. The Shield came highly recommended, but he is quite intimidating. I understand why, but I do wish he would dial back the attitude when there's no obvious threat."

The panic attack subsided the more McNamara talked. For a moment, her eyes drifted shut as she listened to her heart rate slow and her breath fall back into its normal rhythm. In the background the white noise of rain drowned out the last of her panic. Quiet, soothing rain —

"Hannah?" McNamara rapped his knuckles on his desk, disrupting her peace. "Don't fall asleep on me."

Her eyes blinked open, her shock raising her heart rate again. "Sorry. For a moment there, I thought I heard rain. I was using the sound to help slow my breathing, but then it stopped when you called my name."

McNamara cleared his throat, a loud, raspy sound. "This far underneath the hospital, we get many a strange sound. It's more than likely water in the pipes from the bathrooms upstairs."

"At least I know what it is." She took one last deep breath to get herself back under control. "This has never happened to me before. The sound of the locks — they reminded me of the freezer Miranda shoved me into when she captured me."

McNamara waited, the picture of patience. What the newscasters had reported about the quarry raid and the events preceding it might have given him a clue as to what she was babbling about.

It took a few minutes, but she managed to regain some semblance of control. "You said you had a few questions you needed to ask me?"

McNamara cleared his throat as he folded his hands on top of the desk. "Yes, I do. You see, Ms. Quinn, the quarry raid has forced Thunder City and Star Haven to work together to uncover Miranda Dane's operation."

"We already know what she was up to." Hannah could feel her blood pressure rising. She couldn't help but interrupt McNamara. Even though her brain told her to slow down, to not let her anger get the better of her again, she couldn't control herself. She had to let the anger out or she would explode. "She was experimenting on Alts, trying to find the secret to their Alt power. She wanted to use me to control the Alt population in the quarry. Eventually, she would have used me to control the entire population of Star Haven."

McNamara sat back in his chair. "Is this fact or speculation?"

Hannah shrugged. "Speculation, but I've had more

experience with Miranda Dane than anyone else. If Miranda could figure out the secret to Alt power, she could create Alts that she needed and destroy the ones she couldn't control. Once Star Haven became dependent on me for health care, she could threaten to restrict access and do whatever she wanted."

"Has T-CASS found evidence of any of this?" McNamara leaned back in his executive chair, his hands folded on his stomach.

Hannah shrugged again, for lack of anything else to do to express her disgust. "Not yet. Thomas said something about the quarry computer systems set to a low level format, which I gather erased everything. But, like I said, I know Miranda."

McNamara nodded, taking his eyes off her to glance at his computer screen. "Well, Miranda Dane may have erased her computer systems, but she can't erase all of her evidence. I have sixteen guards and twelve Alts, including the mutant she created, that I have to autopsy within the next week. All killed during the quarry raid."

Hannah's spirits crashed and burned. She'd healed three Alts in the prison's infirmary before Miranda had shot them. The mutant would have to be Joe Austin, the one whose brain she'd blown up. The one who could be considered two dozen bodies all by himself because of his size. Yet there had been more Alt prisoners? More than one freezer? More than one infirmary? None of the Blackwoods had told her about there being more Alts in Miranda's prison.

The acid she had swallowed back earlier returned, but she held it back by gulping the rest of the water from the half empty bottle.

"Star Haven can't handle the case load." McNamara

pulled up more information on his computer screen. He sniffed again; his cold was worsening. "Their city Medical Examiner is currently missing in action along with half their city government. I have some contacts in Star Haven and a decent enough relationship with a number of prominent hospital administrators over there. Thunder City has asked me to negotiate an offer to perform the autopsies here and make the reports available on both sides of Mystic Bay. I could make the argument that with your inside knowledge of what happened during the raid, you could provide me with some insight for my final report."

McNamara wanted her to advise him on the job? Twelve Alts. Twelve dead Alts and sixteen guards. Flashes of Joe's brain blowing up under her command returned with a vengeance. Her stomach swirled around the water.

"You don't have to help me if you don't want to." McNamara leaned toward her, his concern obvious in the softening of his brows. "But, you belong in a hospital more than you belong anywhere else. If you can't work with live patients just yet, you may as well work with the dead."

Work with the dead. Show the Committee she could be useful without bloodsurfing. Maybe even get paid for her work so she wasn't so dependent on the Blackwoods. That had been her goal ever since she had first arrived in Thunder City. Get a job, support herself. Fit in so she could have a normal life. McNamara had no idea what a gift he was offering her.

"How will you perform an autopsy on Joe Austin? I...I didn't leave much of his brain after I..."

She couldn't finish, memories of what she'd done overpowering her voice. McNamara sat back up but, didn't expect her give a detailed description, thank heavens. She would have to tell McNamara, though, if not before the autopsy, then during the examination if he asked.

"We've rented the warehouse at the south end of the boardwalk along the harbor. We'll perform the autopsies there so that the Star Haven delegation can observe the process if they choose to without having to come downtown."

Without having to enter the heart of a city that loves its Alts. Another, more horrible thought occurred to Hannah.

"Is Miranda Dane one of the bodies you're going to examine?"

McNamara looked away from her gaze.

"Don't lie to me. Don't try to make this easier. Are you going to autopsy Miranda Dane?"

McNamara returned to lock eyes with her once again. "Yes, but you don't have to be there for that particular examination. I wouldn't expect you to be there. We'll save her for last and you can — "

"I want to be there." Hannah surprised herself with the strength of her voice. "I want to watch Miranda Dane's autopsy. I need to see for myself that she's dead. She holds — held — so many secrets. I need to see her body for myself."

I need to stop imagining she's still alive. I need to stop believing she can still hurt me. I need to get her out of my head.

"Are you sure?" McNamara's voice hardened, deepened.

Hannah took a deep breath and held it until the shaking stopped.

"I'm sure." Hannah tossed the bottle into the waste

basket. "How soon can I start?"

"As soon as you pass the test, which brings me to the second question. You need to prove you're able to control your power before Thunder City will let you work here. I can't possibly undertake so many autopsies while I'm sick. If I can arrange it with the judge and with the Committee, would you be willing to heal me of this cold as your proof of control?"

"Yes." The word was out of her mouth before McNamara had even finished talking. Her fingers twitched with the desire to heal him right now. Rip off her gloves, reach across the desk and touch him, skin-on-skin, and do what she did best. She wanted to work. She wanted to feel useful, but first, she had to prove that she had control.

McNamara leaned back again. "Wonderful. I'll make the phone calls right now. With luck, we can finalize the arrangements today."

For the first time in a long time, Hannah could feel herself smile.

Scott watched Hannah until she made it to the end of the skyway and rounded a corner. Maybe she was right and they both needed a break from one another. Even as he watched her disappear, and the urge to run after her was strong, a small piece of his heart sighed with relief at being alone for the first time since he had fallen out of that helicopter. He had never realized how much you could care for someone and still crave your own space.

After all, Catherine and Thomas had as solid a marriage as anyone else, but they didn't spend every second of every day hanging off each other. How could they when they both had two jobs: acting as CEOs of their respective companies, Blackwood Enterprises and Carraro Security, and managing T-CASS operations? No matter how busy they got, they made time for each other, but they also made time for themselves alone. Someday he'd talk to Thomas about how he managed a marriage like he and Catherine had.

Confident that Hannah wouldn't get into trouble between the garage and McNamara's office, Scott walked toward the concrete half-wall. The western view of Thunder City pointed at the Arena in the distance, with the airport farther along. Peering down at the street below, he could see crowds of hopefuls packed into the hospital courtyard, the overspill of people lined up along the boulevard. They wanted access to the Blood Surfer. The media had adopted Hannah's description of her ability and used it as her moniker, even though she hadn't joined T-CASS. They didn't give a shit about Hannah, the person. If the crowd demanded unrestricted access to her, things would get real ugly real fast.

He watched while what looked like hospital security set up a perimeter along the front entrance. At the same time other hospital employees moved a podium, microphone, and speaker to the center of the top step. The crowd grew restless, with some folks shouting at security, but no one tried to rush the steps to force their way through the front doors. At least, not yet.

Scott pulled out his phone and checked the streaming news service. The feed split between images from the quarry and the crowd at the hospital, all the while speculating about Hannah's healing ability and where was she now. If they only knew she was actually in the hospital, but McNamara had been discreet when parking his Cadillac. The journalist reporting for one channel said they had contacted City Hall and T-CASS demanding answers to her immediate whereabouts, but no officials had responded.

Scott wondered if Catherine or his twin brothers had returned from Star Haven yet. All three could fly across Mystic Bay in record time, but Catherine at least preferred not to make a show of her powers unless she had to. She would avoid flying directly over Star Haven, given that the Alt-ban was still in place. The twins, on the other hand, liked to show off for their fans and would fly over Star Haven just to antagonize the haters below.

Speaking of brothers…Scott shot off a text message to Nik, his eldest brother who'd returned from the quarry as soon as the raid ended, along with a snapshot of the crowd. If most of T-CASS was still at the quarry and didn't join his mother for the journey back to Thunder City, then the T-CASS ranks would be stretched thin. If Nik was busy working for his father, then he might not know about the crowd at the hospital. He definitely wouldn't know about Hannah being inside the hospital. Without giving too much detail, Scott told him about Hannah's whereabouts in case the crowd surged and made it inside. If that happened, Scott could get to Hannah before they did, but it wouldn't hurt to have back-up.

The message sent, Scott disconnected the line, turned around, and damn near smacked into a guy who hadn't been standing there thirty seconds ago. Before Scott could even get out a "hey, watch it," the guy shoved Scott aside. He dressed in black, wore sunglasses, and carried a Colt rifle like he knew how to use it.

Scott backed away while reaching for his Ruger.

"You'll be dead before you get off a shot."

Scott froze. The guy hadn't even turned around to see what Scott was doing, yet he knew anyway. "Want to tell me why you're on the roof of a hospital with a rifle?"

The guy didn't bother to look at Scott. His sole focus was the crowd below. "The Norms want a piece of your girlfriend. Riots are a bitch."

Scott risked pulling his weapon, but not yet taking aim. "If you fire into a crowd of unarmed Norms, you'll be the one who causes a riot."

"It's still a mess. I've been ordered to clean it up."

"Whose orders?"

"Doctor Russel McNamara."

Scott choked on the name. "He ordered you to shoot into a crowd?"

"No, he ordered me to protect your girlfriend from a threat. Those Norms down there are a threat."

"I can't let you do that." Scott raised his gun, took aim. "I won't."

"So, stop me."

Except the rifle was still pointed up, not at Scott, not at the crowd. He couldn't justify his shot unless this...whoever the hell he was targeted the innocent bystanders below, or targeted Scott.

Before Scott could shake off his quandary, the guy tossed the rifle and dive-rolled, landing in front of Scott. Scott dodged the fist flying at his face, saving himself from yet another black eye. He backed up, unable to fire at close range. He dropped the Ruger and raised his arms to deflect the blows.

They dodged and weaved around the cars. This guy was no amateur. Scott connected a few times, but he couldn't so much as knock off the guy's sunglasses.

"Stop it!" With a shove worthy of a third-grade brawler, Scott pushed the guy off of him. "What the hell are you doing?"

The guy wasn't even breathing heavy. "You've got some moves, but not enough. You lack motivation. Why didn't you translocate the rifle?"

Confusion froze Scott again. "I'm not allowed." It was a dick answer and he knew it. He had never thought to translocate the gun when he had the chance. Instead, he'd reached for his own gun.

"Since when do you care about the laws of Thunder City?" The guy backed up, but not far enough. "You almost left because your girlfriend told you to."

News of his and Hannah's escape from Division Six and the showdown at the train station must have hit the news cycle. "So what? Thunder City wanted to separate me from Hannah. We chose each other instead of Thunder City."

Scott couldn't see the guy roll his eyes under the sunglasses, but his imagination worked just as well. "So the red-headed hottie gives an order and you jump to? You don't even have the stones to make your own decisions. No wonder you failed."

"I didn't fail. I obeyed the law. Not to mention I need to practice. My translocation doesn't always work." Why did he confess his failure to a complete stranger?

"I just gave you a chance to practice. You blew it." The guy walked away to pick up the rifle.

Scott couldn't see where he'd dropped his own gun, so he ran past the guy to stand between him and the half-wall. He'd be damned if he was going to let some crazy-assed thug attack him, insult him, then shoot into a crowd. "I'm not letting you shoot."

The guy reached into his pocket and pulled out a

hospital ID. "I work here. The admins know about the gun. I won't shoot if the crowd doesn't cause trouble."

Scott stood his ground. Hospital ID or not, McNamara's approval or not, Scott was not going to take the chance. This guy wanted him to go away. Scott was going to stay if it meant protecting those below. Even if they did rush the hospital, he had to believe he could find Hannah before they did. This guy knew his way around the hospital better than Scott. He'd make this son-of-a-bitch take him to her one way or another.

From down below, he could hear the sound system squeak.

Putting his faith in Thunder City like he never had before, Scott turned his back and prayed that his instincts were correct. Below, a man in a suit stood on the steps leading into the main entrance of the hospital. The crowd surged forward, straining to hear every word.

As if out of nowhere, a bright orange T-CASS style uniform appeared on the steps. The color stood there for a second before replicating itself between the crowd and the podium, preventing the crowd from mounting the steps. Overhead, a bright white streak rocketed over the crowd. Another splash of color bounced into the air and arced into a gap between the crowd and the oncoming traffic from the boulevard. He knew the moniker of this particular Alt: Hopper. She must be part of a reserve team, one that didn't take part in the quarry raid.

The sound system boomed as the administrator talked. Scott couldn't hear the exact words. The low roar of disappointment rippled through the crowd. Some started to disperse right away. Others stayed put, hugging each other in grief, but not trying to enter the hospital.

"You see," Scott said. "No riot. T-CASS wasn't even needed to hold them back, but they're here now. You and your gun aren't needed after all."

The guy had lowered the rifle and stepped to the edge of the roof, to stand right next to Scott. "And you hate it, don't you? Not being down there with your badge. Not being able to show your girlfriend you're worthy of her."

His words hit hard. How could this random stranger understand Scott's frustration and anger so well, splatter it on a canvas right in Scott's path so he couldn't avoid it, couldn't pretend it wasn't there?

"It doesn't matter how I feel. I can't go back to Star Haven. I'm an Alt, whether I like it or not."

"Today. Maybe tomorrow. But, what of next week? There's a war brewing and T-CASS can't stop it."

"You mean Alts versus Norms? Maybe in Star Haven." Scott rolled his eyes. "Not in Thunder City. T-CASS is designed to make Norms feel more comfortable with Alts. It's what Captain Spec has worked for her entire adult life."

"If you think it's that simple, then you're an even bigger fool than your mother."

Sticks and stones. This time Scott let the insult to both himself and his mother pass.

"You say there's a war coming? That's hardly news. The Left Fists threaten war with Star Haven every other week. This isn't my first war."

"No?" The guy yanked Scott's shoulder, forcing him to stand nose-to-nose. They were the same height, but the guy still kept his sunglasses close to his face. "You think you're prepared? You think you know what this is all about? Your girlfriend has made you soft. She's distracting you from what's really happening in this city."

The roll of elevator doors interrupted him. The guy backed off, but only by an inch.

"Watch your back. We're not done, yet."

The guy marched away, back toward the hospital. The thick metal doors leading to the stairwell slammed closed behind him.

A conspiracy theorist, nothing more. Well, nothing more with a high-powered rifle and access to the hospital. Scott wasn't sure he wanted that guy anywhere near Hannah, but he'd promised Hannah she'd have her time alone with McNamara. He had to trust her instincts, and his instincts said following this guy down to McNamara's office wouldn't help her.

Scott looked at his empty hands. A real cop would have reported the encounter. A decent citizen would have called T-CASS. This thug wanted Scott's attention and he got it, but why did Scott give it to him?

What he had said about Scott wanting to be in the thick of the crowd with his badge...the thug had been right. If Scott trained with T-CASS, but chose not to work for them, he'd have no future in Thunder City outside of Hannah. He loved her, but he'd have to find a job if he didn't want to depend on his father for the rest of his life. Thunder City police sure as hell wouldn't hire him even if the city prosecutor decided to let his shooting of Electrocyte slide.

The thug, whoever he was, had managed to rip into all of Scott's fears, forcing him to examine them. What if he couldn't control his power? Where would he go?

Thoughts of leaving Thunder City without Hannah weighed heavy on his shoulders. She belonged here, he didn't. He never had. He loved Hannah, he loved Thomas, but was that enough to build a life? If he left, could he still build a life without them?

He looked at the disbursing crowd below, T-CASS in their bright uniforms milling around the Norms. Scott still couldn't find any answers.

CHAPTER FIVE

Hannah tried not to show her impatience as McNamara lay down on the hospital bed. Around her, all of the members of the Oversight Committee crowded into the operating theater, the only room big enough to accommodate everyone and still allow them to watch her, well, "operate." Even Catherine was there, standing behind Hannah, giving her support through her presence if not through physical contact.

Catherine had returned from Star Haven late yesterday afternoon to a flurry of activity involving her company and T-CASS and Thunder City. Yet, she had still taken time to talk to McNamara, after he'd brought Hannah home from the hospital, about his plan to use himself as a subject for Hannah's test this morning.

After a thorough grilling about safety, which McNamara handled with mixture of aplomb and gentle humor, Catherine had agreed to bring Hannah back to the hospital this morning, though she'd had Garrett drive them. No flying with Catherine unless it was an emergency. Hannah's test to see if she had control over her powers didn't qualify as an emergency.

"I'm ready." McNamara nodded at her.

Johnson was there of course, like a shark waiting for

chum. "You may proceed."

Hannah kept her growl of aggravation to herself. She'd like to see Johnson try to use that tone with Catherine, but for now, she pulled off a glove and touched McNamara's cheek.

Inside. She headed to his sinuses because all of his external symptoms indicated this was a head cold. She was right. A colony of rhinovirus skittered around, wreaking havoc. McNamara's immune system couldn't keep up with the trouble.

"So, you wanna play rough, huh?"

Hannah glared at the army of rat bastards floating in front of her. Those spiky blobs of overstuffed proteins thought they could run her over, push her around, mess her up real good? Well, they were nothing compared to Miranda Dane, so those slimy good-for-nothing cankers had another think coming.

"Time to separate the pros from the goobs," she shouted to no one but herself. "On the count of three!"

With a mere thought, she summoned an army of reinforcements - white blood cells she could command.

"One...two..."

Leave it to white blood cells to have no respect for a countdown or her authority. They charged past her already knowing how to kill a colony of wimpy rhinoviruses. Hannah assisted the assault by weakening each virus with a well-placed kick to where it hurt the most — the outer membranes.

If only she could kick Johnson where it hurt the most.

The weak viruses died faster with every pass Hannah made through their cluster. Hannah wanted to end this operation so she could take off both of her damn gloves in the outside world. She'd obeyed the letter of the law last night and kept the bulky gloves on even when she was alone, talking to Scott on the televideo in the video room.

They'd talked for hours, mostly venting their frustration about the Committee. They might have talked all night, but Nik had stuck his head into the room looking for Thomas sometime after midnight. Nik's interruption forced her to notice the time, which in turn made her yawn. Scott laughed and told her to go to sleep. She didn't even take the gloves off when she finally crawled into bed.

With the rhinoviruses defeated, Hannah pushed herself into the nearest vein and zipped through the rest of McNamara's body, checking to see if he suffered from anything other than the head cold. She found little to no plaque in the arteries, a healthy liver, strong bones, and just a touch of arthritis in the left hip. She eliminated the arthritis since it wouldn't take too long.

If only she could have Scott by her side. She didn't regret insisting on time to herself yesterday, but even after their phone call, she still woke up missing him. Maybe this was what love was supposed to be: wanting to be with a man who touched her so deeply she could feel his emotions even from across the city.

McNamara shifted on the hospital bed, backwashing her into his stomach. There was nothing else to fix and she didn't want to linger.

She reemerged into her own body still holding McNamara's hand. A small rebellion on her part. The Oversight Committee knew she needed skin-on-kin contact to heal people, but the assembled Committee collectively glared at her anyway.

Tough. The skin-on-skin contact sent shivers of warmth straight to her heart. How could she miss human touch so much when she'd had so little of it in her life? She didn't want to let go, but holding McNamara's hand longer than she had to would creep him out. It wasn't really his hand she wanted to hold.

"Congratulations, Doctor McNamara." She tugged her hand out of his, and forced herself to sound chipper. "You have the body of a healthy forensic pathologist."

He laughed as he sat up on the hospital bed, straightened his collar, and took a deep, deliberate breath.

"I have to say, I haven't had this much verve in three days. It's amazing what a lungful of oxygen can do for you. Thank you, Ms. Quinn. I do believe we have the proof we need to allow you keep the gloves off."

"I object." Johnson looked around at his colleagues. "All she's proven is that she has alternative abilities. She hasn't proven her control."

Hannah mashed her lips closed to keep from spewing a long stream of foul language at Johnson. McNamara swung his legs around to climb off the table. "On the contrary, her performance today coupled with what we've already seen from the video evidence proves she can control herself."

"All she's proven is that she can use her ability for evil. She's hurt more people than she's helped. She needs to be detained for further testing."

"Self-defense is not evil." McNamara made it to his feet, fists balled up ready for a fight.

A hand on Hannah's shoulder backed her away from McNamara. Catherine Blackwood stood there. The look on Catherine's face made it clear that Hannah wasn't to get into the middle of this argument. The angry flame in Hannah's gut flared. Miranda would have done the same thing to keep her quiet, but even as the memory of her ex-mother fed her rebellious thoughts, Hannah knew Catherine was right. No one wanted her opinion here.

"You'll still need a thorough examination." Doctor Rao nudged his way to the front of the Committee so he could take McNamara's pulse. "We've scheduled more blood work and a CT scan to compare against the baseline reports we have on record. We'll need to repeat the lab work we performed yesterday."

"Yes, yes. My body will be at your disposal *after* I finish my report on the quarry victims with Ms. Quinn's assistance."

McNamara glared at Johnson who glared right back, neither willing to concede the fight. Catherine Blackwood stepped up from behind to hand Hannah an opened bottle of water. Hannah took the water, but only sipped the contents. With a final glare at Hannah, Johnson stormed past her and out the door.

The icy contempt in the air rose a few degrees. The other doctors who'd watched her test said nothing.

"I'll take you home," Catherine said, her hand dropping from Hannah's shoulder to her back, guiding her back toward the hallway.

That was it? Hannah scanned the faces of the Oversight Committee members who passed by her: neurology, ophthalmology, general surgery, orthopedics, pulmonary medicine, and a few others. They chattered to each other in hushed voices, their glances at her fleeting.

Still no official pronouncement. She was free to go. The thick, dark-brown, unfashionable gloves she'd worn for the last week sat on a nearby counter. She decided to leave them there instead of throwing them in the garbage, afraid if she drew attention to them, the

Oversight Committee would change their minds and make her put them on again, or worse, try to lock her up again.

With Catherine at her back, Hannah opened the door leading into the hallway of the surgical suite.

Scott stood there, leaning against the opposite wall. Hannah stopped in her tracks, forcing Catherine to stop too. Her hormones spiked her pulse. It didn't take much, just slicked back black hair and gray eyes, squinting with mischief. His own gloved hands held a spray of flowers.

The rest of the world faded away to nothingness. If she were any other girl, she would have run to him, thrown her arms around his wide shoulders and wrapped her legs around his blue-jeaned hips. But she wasn't any other girl and her life wasn't her own. So she stood in the door and waited for him to make the first move.

"Catch!"

Hannah raised her hands as the burst of color flew at her, the flowers dropping into her ungloved hands.

The surprise on Hannah's face filled Scott's heart with affection. She'd caught the bouquet he'd tossed at her without gloves on her hands. She'd passed. The fact that the Committee allowed her to leave the exam room without gloves was all the proof he needed.

Scott curled his own gloved hands into fists, pressing his knuckles into flesh. It would take him longer to get to the point where he could prove his control, but as long as Hannah was staying in Thunder City, he had incentive to stay as well.

Hannah walked up to him, close, but not too close.

"They're beautiful."

Her face, more relaxed than he'd seen it since the day he'd met her, gave him hope. Joy glowed from her, a happiness she deserved more than anyone else in this room. How tempting to pick her up, press her against his chest, maybe even give her a quick spin.

He resisted the temptation. The Oversight Committee filed out of the exam room. They spotted him standing so close to her. Johnson tried to approach but Catherine held him back with a sharp word Scott didn't catch. He didn't want to see Johnson or his mother right now.

"No. You're beautiful," he said. "The flowers just enhance what's already there."

Her smile sent shockwaves of desire through his veins. The bruises on her face had faded even more since yesterday. Despite her conservative beige skirt and light blue blouse, she looked as if she could tumble into bed at a moment's notice. He wanted her there, in his bed, more than anything.—

He put his hands behind his back and leaned against the wall, hooking his thumbs into his back pockets. *See? I'm being good.*

Catherine wasn't having any of it. She pushed her way between them. "Cory."

He sighed. His mother's tone of voice, and her insistence on calling him by his birth name, spoke volumes. *You're here to cause trouble. You're here to make a point. Congratulations. Now, go home.*

Well, maybe he was here to make a point. The Committee had said he and Hannah couldn't have physical contact, but they couldn't legally stop him from speaking to her — yet. The Star Haven Newcomers could still live with their families. Preventing him from seeing Hannah in person was just some sick joke cooked up by Johnson. Some other day he'd have to ask Catherine about it, but he wouldn't do it here with so many people watching them.

He ducked his head, blood pounding in his ears.

If he were smart, he'd leave the hospital. When it came to Hannah, though, the smart thing to do clashed with his heartache. He needed to rebuild, but starting from scratch for the second time in his life — just moving into his father's place downtown reminded him of how much Thunder City didn't want him. Hannah could heal his physical wounds, but she couldn't help him with his loneliness. He needed more than just a loving girlfriend in his life. His resolve to use Hannah as his incentive to stay slipped further away.

"Fine. I'll wait here." He tilted his head toward the doors at the end of the corridor. "You two go on ahead. I have a training session at the Arena later."

Disappointment drooped Hannah's shoulders, as she too lowered her eyes. "I'll call you tonight. We need to talk. McNamara is taking me to the harbor with him."

McNamara again.

Instead of fighting the inevitable, he touched two of his gloved fingers to his lips and blew her a kiss. She did the same, before she followed Catherine, the doctors right behind her, not trusting Scott in slightest.

"Hannah Quinn."

The shout pushed Scott away from the wall. He watched a small woman overburdened by a shirtless toddler in her arms, push her way through the sparse corridor. She stepped in front of Hannah and Catherine, forcing them to stop. "I demand the Blood Surfer examine my child."

Taller than most of the doctors, Scott could see

the commotion over their heads. He shoved his way through the knot of white coats as Catherine pushed Hannah behind her. Good. If anyone had a larger stake than Scott in keeping Hannah safe, it was Catherine. No one could threaten his mother and not expect to get knocked on their asses. She created a barrier between Hannah and the woman.

"Hannah is not a doctor," Catherine said. "She cannot use her ability to determine what is wrong with your son. Perhaps some time in the future — "

The woman shoved the child into Catherine's arms, leaving Catherine no choice but to grab hold of the boy. The kid's head lolled to the side, his eyes closed, either asleep or drugged. Hannah stepped back, but not fast enough. Even as Catherine juggled the limp child, the woman reached around Catherine and grabbed Hannah by the arm. With a jerk, she forced Hannah forward, then smacked Hannah's ungloved hand onto the boy's upper body.

"Wait." Scott could see Hannah try to pull away. "I can't — "

This wasn't a random assault by a distraught parent, but a well-planned attack. The woman wore blue surgical gloves so she wouldn't touch Hannah's skin. Scott surged forward. Before he could reach the woman and pull her away from Hannah, the woman swung out and slapped Hannah across the face.

Hannah's shriek of pain was cut short as she disappeared, bloodsurfing inside the boy's body.

CHAPTER SIX

"No! Oh, no, no, no, no, no! How could you do this to me?"

What had she done? The shock of the slap had triggered her ability. The sharp sting reminded Hannah of her helplessness when Miranda had hit her.

Her proof of control shattered into millions of red blood cells. She wanted to scream, but who could hear her from inside the boy's lungs?

You're just pissed because the Committee was right. You don't have control. If you go out there with a temper tantrum, you'll only prove you're not mature enough to handle your own power. Don't give them yet another excuse to cage you.

Her rage burned too hot for her own words to cool down. She needed to swim off her anger, so she headed for the anterior spinal artery and surfed upward. Was the kid sick? Dying? Was he an Alt? She'd have to check his brain to find out.

She plowed through layers of gray matter until she reached the area where the interthalamic adhesion was supposed to be. It wasn't there, which wasn't unusual in a normal human. Not everyone had one, but if this child had been an alternative human, a thin black thread would have crossed the midline of the adhesion. Somehow the black thread tied alternative humans to their Alt power. Scott had one. Scott's brother Nik had one, as had Joe Austin.

Her heart skipped a beat. Pressure. She remembered so much pressure as she sucked air and liquid into Joe's skull. The visceral pain had blinded her as Joe's brain exploded under her touch and rocked her for the second time. She didn't want to think about Joe or how she had killed him. Not here. Not while she operated inside a child.

You killed him.

She surfed faster, as if she could outrun her own thoughts. What she wouldn't give to take it all back.

This is life and death. You can't take it back.

Her attack on Joe wasn't like disabling Miranda's mercenaries. She would heal the mercs if they'd let her, but she couldn't resurrect the dead.

She shoved Joe to the back of her mind and focused on bloodsurfing around the boy's brain. Something didn't look right. There were scars along the meninges. The brain itself didn't appear to fit inside the skull, a hair to too close to the bone in some places. The brain wasn't swollen, though.

She traveled back along the spine. *What the hell is that?*

The spine bulged just at the point where the medulla oblongata ended and the spinal cord began. She surfed closer to examine the damage. It appeared as if someone had sliced through the spine and all its interconnecting tissues, then spliced them back together again. Despite the detail of the splice, the job itself looked sloppy, as if the surgeon couldn't quite get a clean stitch. The swollen nerve tissues pressed against bone. The signals along the spinal cord operated at a rate slower than normal, bumping over the uneven growth along the newly healed wounds.

Why, though? What was wrong with the boy that had required such an operation? Who could perform such an operation? She'd read as much as she could about medicine and surgery while she had been on the run from Miranda. None of the medical textbooks discussed a condition that would require a surgeon to cut through the spine to heal someone.

On the other hand, she knew nothing of this boy. If she'd been given a chance to examine him from the outside before his mother slapped her, she would have known what she was supposed to look for.

Oh, there was her anger again, distracting her, damn it. She surfed faster. Scars aside, all of the boy's systems functioned within normal parameters, if a bit erratic here and there. The drugs in his system appeared to keep his immune system at bay. Fixing the damage wouldn't take long.

I demand you examine my child.

Hannah stopped dead in the middle of the boy's aortic arch. What was she doing? The mother of this boy didn't want her to fix what was wrong. She had asked for Hannah to look at the damage and report back. Like the Oversight Committee, the mother wanted a witness, not a healer.

Hannah floated closer to the aortic wall, confused. What was she supposed to do now? Why didn't she know? She knew every part of the human body, better than any doctor, but she couldn't identify the purpose behind the scars.

She needed to know.

When Miranda forced you to heal her prisoners, you ignored the causes of their injuries in order to protect yourself. When you healed Scott, you used brute force to heal his body before he died, and ignored the consequences of what you were doing. He hadn't wanted to you to regrow his missing ear. He never wanted you to fix his broken Alt powers. You thought you were so smart. You thought because you'd memorized human anatomy you knew everything, but you're not as smart as you think you are. You heal without considering what your patient really wants.

Frustration further stymied her instinct to heal. The temptation to smooth the scarring, to re-image the boy's immune system nagged at her. Except it wasn't just frustration, it was fear. Fear of what she didn't understand paralyzed her.

She'd never *not* healed anyone before, so she floated further down the descending aorta until she could skip along the upper true ribs and insert herself next to the boy's heart — which beat with a strong, steady rhythm despite the signal lag.

What should she do next? She couldn't answer her own questions, so she floated back out of the boy and into her own body, leaving him exactly as he was.

For the first time in her life, Hannah had failed to heal her patient.

Scott shoved himself to the front of the crowd. How dare anyone force Hannah to use her power without her consent? He knew better than anyone how much Hannah needed her freedom. After spending her life being manipulated and abused by a heartless killer, Hannah deserved to have a say over when and where she used her Alt ability.

His white-hot rage made him reach out to tackle the woman, but a strong pair of arms clamped around his shoulders and yanked him back.

"Let her finish," a sharp, deep voice admonished him. Scott shook off the arms. McNamara backed off, but repeated his warning. "Let her finish."

Scott glanced back at Hannah, still a barely-there outline of her body visible. Of course. No one knew what would happen to Hannah if they touched her shadow while she surfed. McNamara had prevented Scott from making a bad situation worse by blundering into the commotion blind with rage. Scott had been a cop. He should have known better. He should have assessed the scene, then acted. Scott nodded his thanks to McNamara, who retreated.

A minute passed, then another. No one moved. Catherine remained frozen in place. She looked at Scott, then the child — a boy, to all outward appearances — then back to Scott. Pulling one hand from the boy's back, she gestured. *Don't interfere.*

Scott obeyed, but he did pull his phone out of his pocket. Without even looking at the screen he tapped the code to alert Thomas. His company had built the security system for the hospital, and his team would have already alerted him, but he didn't know Scott was here.

Hannah reemerged after a third minute. She yanked her hand from under the other woman's gloves before she stepped away from Catherine and the child.

"Did you see?" The woman ignored her son as she shouted. "You saw what those butchers did?"

Scott watched Hannah, looking for signs of distress, a signal or a blink, anything to indicate she needed him. Hannah didn't respond to the woman's question. She just stood there with an odd expression.

Catherine leaned forward to hand the boy back. "What you did here today was dangerous — "

The woman shoved the boy back into Catherine's arms. "I don't want him. He's not my son. He's someone else's child. I demand the return of my child." She whirled on the doctors standing behind Scott. "You! You allowed this to happen. You said the transplant would save his life, but you stole him away from me instead. I want him back. I demand you give my son back to me!"

Scott wouldn't risk turning around to see who the woman was pointing at. Behind him, he could hear some murmurs and shuffling, but nothing that identified the culprit. The woman's hysteria built and the boy started to wake in Catherine's arms. Hannah appeared too fixed upon the boy to pay attention to the danger. Scott took another step forward. Someone needed to get the situation under control.

"Ma'am. I want to help you, but you have to calm down first."

The woman's breath hitched as he approached, slower this time.

"What is your name?"

"Betty Chung," she said after a moment.

"My name is Scott. Can you tell me what happened? Can you explain why you forced Hannah to bloodsurf through your son?"

"I know who you are." Ms. Chung took a half step away from Hannah. Good. The farther he drew the woman away from Hannah, the better.

"Everyone knows who you are. You love the Blood Surfer. Tell her to prove it. Make her tell them," she pointed at the doctors, "this isn't my son. Make them bring my child back to me."

This time Scott glanced around to see if she pointed to anyone in particular. He noticed McNamara had slipped away in the confusion, but no one responded to the accusation. The doctors looked as confused as Scott.

"This is not the boy I gave birth to." Ms. Chung moved closer to Scott, putting more distance between herself and Hannah. "This isn't my Jimmy."

Scott forced a small smile. "Well, it's nice to know the reporters got one thing right. I do love Hannah — but, Ms. Chung, I can't order her to do what you want. I can't force her to break the law."

"I've already broken the law. The law *she* created." Ms. Chung spat at Catherine's feet.

Catherine didn't react beyond tightening her hold on the boy, who'd started to squirm.

"Jimmy was an Alt," Ms. Chung continued. "He could create auditory hallucinations."

Catherine shrugged in the corner of his vision. He guessed that the boy's power hadn't been proven yet. Maybe he could throw sound or maybe it was just a fanciful tale created by a wishful parent. Sometimes proving a child had Alt powers wasn't as straightforward as normal people, especially parents, wished.

"Jimmy was full of life." Ms. Chung's voice broke. "He smiled and laughed and loved to run and jump. This one is a lifeless lump. He doesn't do anything. Doesn't like the same foods, doesn't laugh, doesn't recognize our dogs, doesn't even play with his toys. He's not my son. I want my Jimmy back."

Oh hell, Chung's eyes filled with ugly tears. His sympathy broke his anger. He reached out to comfort her, aware that his gloves didn't offer much. Hannah, at least, remained still and close to Catherine. "Ms. Chung, Hannah can't help you. She's not a doctor. She can heal people, but there's still a lot she needs to learn."

The doors at the far end of the corridor opened with a squeak of hinges. Hospital security slipped through followed by several police officers, called in by either Thomas's team or McNamara. Ms. Chung saw them at the same time Scott did. He'd managed another step forward. The young mother was within easy reach if she tried to attack Hannah again.

Instead of fighting, though, Ms. Chung's shoulder's slumped, resigned, knowing she was about to be arrested. It didn't matter what Ms. Chung thought. Her pain touched a sensitive core of Scott's own need to connect with his mother. He and Catherine had made tentative steps toward repairing their relationship. Seeing a woman who would sacrifice everything for her child, no matter how screwed up her beliefs were, rattled the cage where Scott had buried most of his pain.

He reached out to touch Ms. Chung's shoulder, but instead she grabbed his gloved hand. "Promise me you'll find him. Find my Jimmy. Don't let him remain lost forever."

Scott squeezed the poor woman's hand back. He had once told Hannah that he never made promises he couldn't keep, so he scrambled to find a way to not hurt Ms. Chung any further, knowing Hannah could hear everything. "I promise to look for him."

Ms. Chung sniffed and released Scott so the police could pull her arms behind her back. He winced at the sound of the 'cuffs clicking tight around her wrists, his fingers flexing with the ghost of the 'cuffs that had once hobbled him.

The police officers not burdened with escorting their prisoner dispersed to start gathering witness information. More people entered the corridor; some wore civilian clothes with hospital IDs around their necks. Catherine shifted the boy from one arm to another as she talked to them.

Hannah stayed by Catherine's side, but she watched Jimmy. She was looking for something, her eyes roaming the boy's upper body.

Scott's focus on Hannah distracted him from the police officer who approached him.

"Cory Blackwood?" It wasn't a question, just the necessary confirmation before she took his statement.

"Scott Grey." That's what it said on his driver's license. He didn't recognize the officer as one of the cops who handled him when he'd been called in for interrogation, but he could see the wary look in the woman's eyes. She knew who he was, no matter what name he used.

"Can you tell me what you saw?" The office pulled out a small tablet to take notes.

Scott kept his answer simple, sticking to just what he had seen. He didn't tell her about the promise he had made, or about Hannah's odd behavior.

"I guess we already know how to contact you if we have any further questions." The officer slipped her tablet into her pocket and moved on to the next witness.

Scott said nothing. If they didn't have his direct phone number, they knew they could get a message to him through his parents or T-CASS. He prayed they didn't call him downtown to give a formal statement. The thought of returning to the station where he'd been turned over to Miranda Dane made him sick to his stomach.

He swallowed back the bile in his throat and walked over to Hannah, but she didn't seem to notice. So long as Catherine was nearby, whoever lingered around from the Oversight Committee couldn't do anything about their proximity to one another, since they weren't touching.

"Are you okay?" he asked.

"I'm fine." Her expression grew darker, her frown more pronounced. "But Ms. Chung might not be wrong."

"About what?"

Hannah bit her lip in that adorable way she had when she was deep in thought. Scott shoved his hands back into his back pockets, tempted to rub her shoulders and release her tension.

"I don't know. I saw something inside. I can't explain it. I need to — "

Without warning, Hannah stepped around Scott, searching for someone in the thinning crowd of doctors.

"Where's Doctor McNamara?"

Scott looked around himself, but McNamara hadn't reappeared. "I don't know. He disappeared during the altercation. I think he's the one who called security."

Hannah growled, another cute habit he'd come to love even though it meant she was frustrated. She reached into her front pocket. Scott realized she was looking for her phone, but it would have dropped on the floor when she surfed, along with the flowers he'd given her. The flowers lay next to his mother's foot.

She picked the flowers up and found the phone underneath, looking none the worse for wear. Snippets of Catherine's conversation drifted toward him. It sounded as if she were waiting on Social Services to pick up Jimmy.

Hannah clutched the flowers close with one hand

while she started texting. While she worked, Johnson approached and handed Hannah her hated gloves. "You'll be scheduled for training shortly."

Hannah didn't even look at the man. She flipped screens, sending a text message instead.

"I'll take those." Scott reached for the gloves.

"You'll do nothing of the sort." Johnson pulled the gloves away from Scott's open hand. "*She* will take them and *she* will put them on and not take them off again until we tell her she may do so. *You* will leave the hospital, or I will have security escort you out."

With her hands full of flowers and phone, Hannah would have to put both down in order to put on the gloves. The easiest thing to do would be to hand both to Scott, but it would only exacerbate the tension if there was a chance that she and Scott would touch.

"Can I be of assistance?"

McNamara appeared. Whatever Hannah had planned to do about the gloves became moot when McNamara reached around her to take the gloves from Johnson with a motion so smooth, Johnson didn't have a chance to fight.

"I require a consultation with Ms. Quinn. I'll see that she puts her gloves on when we are finished."

"We can't permit you to have contact with her. She had no control." At least the other doctor turned his ire on McNamara, and not on Hannah.

"She has sufficient control around me." McNamara held out a hand to Hannah. Hannah gave him the flowers and took the gloves from his hands, her phone going back into her pocket. "I've already had contact with her. What happened this morning was an anomaly — "

"An anomaly we can't ignore." The doctor argued

back, taking a step closer to McNamara, his shorter stature not interfering with his outrage. "You're not on the Committee. You can't override our decisions without a court order. This whole demonstration would never had happened if you hadn't insisted your caseload should take priority over safety."

Scott wanted to punch both of them, for acting as if neither he nor Hannah were standing right there. He could tell Hannah felt the same, as she jammed on her gloves, her cheeks red.

"See. All done." She wiggled her fingers, to prove her point.

Her compliance meant little to the two doctors, who stood toe-to-toe now, their pissing match catching the attention of everyone else — including Catherine, who shushed hospital security with a simple wave of her hand.

"If you tried giving Ms. Quinn a little respect for what she has accomplished instead of tearing her down, you might find her more willing to comply with your ridiculous standards."

Whatever McNamara would have said next became moot once Catherine joined them.

"Gentleman, whatever the problem is, bring it to a close. You're creating a disruption." Ms. Chung's son, still snug in Catherine's arms, blinked but otherwise didn't react.

"With all due respect, Captain —"

"I understand your objections, Doctor Johnson, but Hannah has her gloves on. Cory has his gloves on. He's moved out of my home. There's only so much you can do in the name of safety. We took a chance and it worked. Dr. McNamara is cured and Ms. Chung has been arrested. I will make arrangements for Hannah's training as soon as I'm able." She juggled Jimmy from one arm to the other as the boy yawned and stretched. This time she addressed only Dr. Johnson. "The Committee will have to be satisfied with our efforts. Anything else and you risk losing them forever. *We* don't want that."

His mother had thrown down the gauntlet. There wouldn't be a Committee if not for her, and she had just challenged her own creation. No one wanted to lose Hannah to another city. No one wanted to let her go. They wanted to control her. They'd tried to cage her, but they had failed.

They'd have to get through him first if they tried again.

"I'll be calling another meeting about this." Johnson didn't try to couch his words as anything other than a threat.

"I understand." Catherine sounded more tired than anything else.

Stymied, Johnson stomped away. No sooner had the doctor gone out of earshot than Catherine rounded on Scott.

"It's time for you to leave."

Scott hated it when his mother was right, but even he knew his presence in the hospital would only make things worse for Hannah.

"I'll call you tonight." It was the best he could offer.

"I'll find a nice vase for the flowers." Hannah reached over to take them back from McNamara.

Scott smiled, but turned away before he could say anything else. Catherine watched them both. She wouldn't leave until he did.

"Scott."

He turned back to look at Hannah.

"You'll keep your promise to Ms. Chung, won't you?"

He'd made a promise to look for the "real" Jimmy. Whatever Hannah had seen inside the boy had her spooked. "Of course."

He would keep his promise to Ms. Chung, but first he needed a plan. He wasn't a detective, but he knew someone who was.

CHAPTER SEVEN

Scott walked away, leaving a cold spot on Hannah's heart. The urge to follow him, to hold him, to have him hold her and tell her everything would be okay, paralyzed her, because she understood all too well the consequences of disobeying the law.

Even though Johnson had also left in a fit of pique, she couldn't help but notice that one other member of the Committee had remained behind — an older female doctor, with a hint of pepper still showing in her hair, who watched Hannah unobtrusively from the other end of the corridor. Hannah refused to meet the woman's eyes, unwilling to give the woman the satisfaction of seeing Hannah struggle to obey. This woman was nothing, a mere shadow of Miranda. Once Scott had slipped through the door, the woman left too, but Hannah's rebellious anger stayed put.

Damn them anyway. You would think with all of the Newcomers around the Oversight Committee would have enough to keep them busy. If only she could find a way to keep the Committee too distracted to bother her.

The light tap on her shoulder made her jump. *Now who's the distracted one?* McNamara stood there, looking none the worse for wear after all the excitement. -

"My office phone forwarded your text message." He kept his voice low. Maybe he understood by instinct that she didn't want anyone else to know she'd contacted him. He slipped his hands into the pockets of his slacks. "Are you okay?"

A loaded question she chose to ignore. Instead, her voice quavered as she rambled. "Yes. Sorry. I didn't know where you had disappeared too. I'm fine. Thank you for jumping in like you did. Can I talk to you a minute? Privately?"

"Of course." McNamara motioned her into the nearest exam room, which was the same one where she'd healed him. "We gingers need to stick together."

Catherine had drifted back toward the doors. It looked as if she was giving the administrators quite an earful. Hannah gave Catherine a subtle wave, then motioned toward McNamara, then the room.

Catherine saw her signal and nodded, though she kept talking to the officials. It would seem everyone trusted her with McNamara, but not with Scott. Was it because McNamara was a well-respected physician and Scott was an Alt-killer turned Alt?

Stupid question. Of course it mattered.

She waited until McNamara closed the door. "I saw something I can't explain."

"In the boy?" McNamara hitched a hip onto the same exam table he had recently occupied. It was the same hip Hannah had cleared of arthritis.

"Yes. In Jimmy. That's his name. James Chung, I'm assuming."

McNamara looked curious, listening instead of rushing to the next item on his agenda. "If I recall correctly, you can see things on the microscopic level: bacteria, viruses, and the like?"

"All true." The details of her ability hadn't been made public. Only the Committee knew. How did McNamara know? He must have friends on the Committee. How else could he have been able to outmaneuver a guy like Johnson so that she could heal him instead of demonstrating her Alt power on lab rats?

"Well, I'm not sure I can help." His soft smile held light humor, even as he admitted to his confusion. "My patients are a pretty silent bunch. If they have anything to say, I usually don't find out until I get reports back from a lab."

"True, but you have a more unique perspective on anatomy than most of the other doctors in the hospital."

McNamara laughed, a low, gentle sound. "Fair enough."

"Also, I'd like to keep my questions just between the two of us. I don't want the Oversight Committee getting involved."

His smile faltered, and the worry lines on his face deepened. He knew she was up to something. He had to be calculating the risk to his career against his curiosity. Even though he'd hired her to work with him, the job could just be temporary, until the quarry raid victims had been examined. Maybe she'd overestimated his pull with the Committee?

The flash of neediness overcame her again. She needed Scott and the comfort he offered, even if he couldn't solve her problems. None of the Blackwoods could.

"The Committee controls so much of my life. The gloves, Scott — " Her throat tightened around her words, like a wad of gum stuck in her throat, but she pushed through. "If this is just a useless rabbit hole I've fallen into, I don't want everyone in the hospital talking about it. About me. There are so many rumors already. Ms. Chung wouldn't have attacked me if she hadn't seen me on TV. There are too many exaggerations out there."

McNamara's brow smoothed out, his confusion relaxing the more she explained. "I understand."

"Good, because I need to see Jimmy's medical records." She paused, waiting for a shake of his head or a refusal because of some hospital rule or other blockade.

Instead, McNamara tilted his head, with a look that said *please continue*. He listened to her, really listened. He wanted to hear what she had to say.

"I need to know what was done to him. His brain looks too big for his skull, but it's not swollen. The tissues around the spinal cord had been cut and stitched back together again, right above the atlas. The stitches looked sloppy — "

A flash of anger crossed McNamara's face, so Hannah stopped. Had she crossed a line? Had she offended him? Maybe he didn't like her criticizing his colleagues. Who was she, after all, but a teenaged Alt, and an untrained one at that?

The angry look passed almost as soon as it had appeared. "My apologies; I didn't mean to make you stop, but I don't recognize what you're describing. I can't imagine why anyone would cut the spinal cord. The certainty of paralysis alone makes me wonder what that poor boy was suffering from, that would compel a surgeon to perform such an operation."

Hannah's worry eased its grip on her stomach. So, what she saw didn't have an easy explanation. Her inner rebel wasn't grasping at trouble. She had a purpose. She had an anchor. If she couldn't have Scott by her side, she could at least have McNamara. He believed her. "Which is why I need to see his records."

McNamara's phone vibrated from his pocket. He gave her an apologetic look as he checked. "I'm sorry. I have to take this."

Hannah waited while he called his office, hearing his words while trying not to appear as if she was eavesdropping.

Four uh-huhs and a yes later, McNamara disconnected his phone. "I'm sorry for the interruption, but I have some important calls to make. My caseload timetable has moved up and I need to reschedule a few appointments. I'll have to work tomorrow instead of going down to the harbor to inspect the set-up at the warehouse. Have you ever watched an autopsy before?"

"No. I haven't, but it's not like I've never seen the inside of someone's body."

McNamara slipped his phone into his back pocket. "Perhaps you should. Just to prepare yourself. You really don't know how you'll react to an operation like this until you're seeing it."

Hannah hugged her arms to herself, her gloves making the comforting move less so. She struggled to think of what Scott had told her last night.

In a month or two, it'll be snowing. Everyone will be wearing gloves. It won't be quite as obvious.

"You're probably right. What time should I be here?" She would have to arrange a ride to the hospital with either Catherine or Thomas.

"Before eight o'clock. We'll make sure your hospital credentials are all in order before we begin." McNamara looked at the door to the exam room as if he expected to be interrupted. "Once you work for the hospital, you'll have access to Jimmy's medical records. The police might also access his records as part of their investigation of his mother. It will be noted in the system that you *are* accessing his records. This could raise a few red flags for the Oversight Committee. If they question you, send them to me. Don't talk to them unless I'm with you."

"What about Catherine?"

He hesitated. "The Captain can protect you too, but remember, she's invested in making the Committee work. She has interests outside of protecting just you. Also, her commitment is to Thunder City. If there's a crisis that T-CASS must handle, they look to the Captain to lead them. Despite her extraordinary power, she can't be in two places at the same time and the Committee knows this. Johnson will exploit it."

"How did a guy like that ever get on the Committee in the first place?"

McNamara shrugged. "Men like him will always find a way to disrupt the order and use safety as an excuse to sow the seeds of chaos. It makes them feel in control when they truly have no control."

Hannah didn't quite understand, but she knew what it felt like to be out of control. Her temper, her gloves, her power.

McNamara placed a hand on her shoulder. "You'll find your control. Just start with the small things."

It was as if he could read her mind. "Small things?"

"If you go to the Captain now and tell her you need rest, she will stop talking with the administrators and take you home. When you get there, you decide what you would like to eat for dinner and say so. Call Scott first, don't wait for him. You decide when you go to bed tonight. Don't let the Captain decide for you.

Small things."

She *could* control the small things if she wanted to. "Okay. Small things. I can make that happen."

"Good girl. I'll see you tomorrow in pathology. It'll be fine."

He slid off the table and motioned her out of the room. Hannah followed, but her thoughts were far from the city. If she could find some control for tonight, maybe receiving the bodies at the harbor wouldn't seem so daunting.

"Pull."

Like one of Pavlov's dogs, Scott stared at the red beanbag at the end of the ping-pong table. Need versus want. In order to pull the beanbag, he had to need it, feel it in his hand. Hannah had taught him that. She'd also mussed up his hair, giving him a reason to want something and not his comb. Thinking about that moment made him want more, but not the beanbag. He didn't need the beanbag. What would happen if he didn't need it?

Nothing, and he'd fail the test. Again.

Serena Jakes, Highlight, stood off to the side in a forest green skirt and pale blouse instead of her usual bright-yellow Alt uniform. "I said, pull."

He'd heard her just fine, the tone careful to convey the command without letting annoyance slip through.

Scott focused on the beanbag. He imagined the rough fabric against his palm. He could use the bag to stuff down the throat of the Alt who'd challenged him on the roof of the hospital. Another distraction he didn't want or need, but the potent curiosity clicked in his brain.

The beanbag disappeared and reappeared in his left hand.

"Shinzo, did you get that?" Highlight called.

Shinzo poked his head out from behind a screen where he operated a fancy, high-tech video camera. He wore the blue polo shirt and black slacks of Thomas's elite team. "I filmed it, but I won't know what we recorded until we analyze the video."

"I'll leave the analysis to you." Jakes sounded much less frosty talking to Shinzo then she did to Scott.

Scott tossed the beanbag back and forth between his hands, waiting for Jakes to turn back toward him.

Instead, an alarm honked from her comm. The same happened from Shinzo's. Scott waited while both checked their messages.

"We're done for the day." Jakes picked up her purse from the floor and headed for the door.

"Wait!" Scott said.

She turned, her brown eyes as cool as her voice. "Did you need something?"

"How about some feedback?" He dangled the beanbag from his fingers.

Highlight shrugged. "You're a smart man, Mr. Grey. Do the math. Ten successful pulls, twenty bags. You have a fifty percent failure rate and no pattern in regards to the size or weight of the bag. We'll do this again tomorrow and the day after until you can pull all twenty bags on command."

She left without another word.

Scott would have tossed the bag against the closed door, but Shinzo blocked him. "Sorry, Grey. I need to take the beanbag from you."

Scott looked at the beanbag, then back at the door.

Shinzo laughed. "Yeah, all the Goobs want to take a

swing at her at least once during training. It's not just you."

Scott doubted that, but then Shinzo had no reason to lie to him either. Instead, he tossed the beanbag at Shinzo so the tech could catch it. "What was the alarm about?"

Shinzo caught the beanbag and dumped it into a container. "Ghost called in a red alert and requested backup."

Nik. What the hell was his brother up to that would require backup? "Doesn't Thomas have better things for you to do than to clean up after a Goob during a red alert?"

"Not this time." He must have seen the worry on Scott's face, because he put down the container to talk to Scott without the distraction. "I wouldn't worry about it. It happens all the time. If Thomas needed me, I'd have left with Highlight. If you want details, though, you should call Thomas."

Scott considered it, but forced himself to dismiss it. Thomas would take the call, but Scott couldn't bring himself to interrupt his father in the middle of an operation. Scott wasn't T-CASS, but if he was he would know what was happening to his brother. Was this what it would be like for him if he stayed in Thunder City with Hannah but didn't join the family business of rescuing people? Always on the outside looking in and wondering if they were safe? Was this why Thomas had joined even though he had no Alt ability? So that he could keep an eye on his wife and stepsons, if not his actual son?

Another wrinkle in his path to deciding where he fit into the fabric of Thunder City. In Star Haven, he and his partner Juan had always worked extra shifts during a disaster. He'd met Hannah after the Left Fist gang had captured him, beat him up, and shoved him out of a helicopter. Juan had been helpless to stop it. It was the last time he'd seen his partner, his friend.

"So, you're just going to stay here and play with my beanbags?" he asked Shinzo, burying any thoughts about contacting Thomas, or Juan.

Shinzo picked up the container and wrote on it with a thick black marker. "All of the beanbags have to be sent to the University lab for analysis. See if you somehow altered them on the microscopic level. I get to read their reports and sum it all up for the boss."

Scott could feel his shoulders relax. Shinzo had no Alt abilities. Maybe that made the difference in attitude. Thomas's number two-in-command had nothing to prove. "Have you learned anything new about the Court of Blood?"

Shinzo paused, marker in his hand. "You know I'm not supposed to talk about it."

"To anyone who doesn't already know. Whatever you tell Thomas is going to get back to me anyway."

Shinzo paused, beanbag in hand. After a second, he continued to pack the beanbags, but must have decided Scott was right about Thomas never withholding information from his son. "I've found a half-dozen vague online references, all dated within the last few years. Most of it was buried so deep, no one who wasn't already digging would know to look for it. The few references I found were written by people who died soon after. Accidents. Sometimes only hours after the notes were written."

"Too coincidental to be accidents, you mean."

"Yeah."

Scott watched Shinzo organize the containers. "Are

you worried they'll come after you? I mean, is there a way they can track your investigation back to you?"

"No. I'm too careful." Shinzo set the last container into a tub on the floor. "If I did anything to put you or the Captain at risk, Carraro would kill me before the Court of Blood could."

"No, he wouldn't." Judging by Shinzo's grin, he already knew that too.

Shinzo picked up the tub of beanbags. "See you tomorrow."

"Yeah, see you tomorrow." And the day after that, and the day after that.

Scott headed back to the locker room. Shinzo seemed friendly enough, but Scott wasn't ready to ask the guy if he'd be interested in grabbing a beer after work. He checked his watch. It was too early to go home and call Hannah. He wanted to talk to her about Jimmy Chung.

He wasn't a trained detective. His ambitions had him working toward joining Star Haven's SWAT team, not toward obtaining a detective's badge. He had planned to ask Nik for advice, but if his brother was in danger —

His thoughts were interrupted by the buzz of his phone. A text message flashed on screen from a more than familiar number. Juan Costenaro, his partner — his former partner.

Are you going to be at the harbor for the evidence transfer?

Scott stared at the question. Juan had once told him that he lived in Star Haven so he wouldn't have to live and breathe the Alt *problem* every day. He supported

Mayor Dane's Alt ban. Scott hadn't disagreed with his partner and Scott himself had supported Dane's ban, too.

Yes. I'll be there.

Scott paused outside the locker room, waiting for his — friend's, partner's? — reply.

*I'm working security for the transfer of evidence.
I have a box of stuff from your apartment.
Your real apartment.
Where do you want me to leave it?*

The hope that Juan didn't despise him for what he'd become squeezed itself back into his heart where it couldn't hurt as much. Hannah held his heart now, but this was one ache she couldn't fix.

*Not sure. McNamara knows who I am.
If you can give it to him,
he'll hold it for me. Unless —*

Scott stopped typing wondering if he should even bother with his own question. What the hell, he had nothing to lose by asking.

*— Unless you want to meet somewhere
after the transfer? There's a
souvenir shop next to the hotel
where the tourist section begins.*

An eternity of loneliness passed as Scott waited for a reply.

Fine. After the transfer. I'll text you when I'm there.

Scott didn't respond, out of fear of pushing his luck. Juan's message made it clear this wasn't going to be a friendly meet-up, but he also didn't back down at the arrangement. Between this and the worry over his brother, Scott needed a mindless workout. Maybe burning off all of this excess emotion would also give him focus. He couldn't do anything about Nik or Juan, but he could work through the mystery of the guy on the roof.

Scott replayed their fight one step at a time while he changed into his workout clothes, then headed for the gym. The two of them were well-matched in height, weight, and strength, but the other guy had him outclassed in experience. Nothing Scott threw at him had any effect. He couldn't even knock off the guy's sunglasses.

Scott shoved open the gym door with a *bang*. The room was empty, giving Scott his choice of equipment. He stepped onto the nearest treadmill and set it for a punishing speed.

Why couldn't he hurt this guy? Why didn't any of his punches connect?

Scott almost tripped just as the treadmill picked up speed. A barrier. The guy must have used an invisible barrier to protect himself. That was his Alt ability. He'd known Scott couldn't hurt him when he'd picked the fight.

Scott pushed the treadmill even faster, trying to outrace his thoughts. This guy knew Scott couldn't hurt him, but did he know that he had the same ability as Scott's biological father? No, he couldn't. Cole had died before Scott was even born. No one talked about him, not even Catherine. Not even to her own son. Everything Scott knew about Cole had come from newspaper articles. Thunder City called him Shelter because he had an invisible barrier he could use to shelter himself and others around him, to protect them from bullets or flying debris.

The one thing Catherine did tell Scott was that his father had died a hero. It wasn't enough, but no amount of begging could get Catherine to tell him more. Nik, Alek, and Evan had shared a few memories of Cole, but it still wasn't enough. When Thomas came into Scott's life, Scott found a father figure of his own. His need to cling to the imaginary figure of Cole lessened as the years passed. He almost never thought about Cole anymore. In fact, he hadn't thought about his father for years — until now.

Did this guy, this Alt, know about Cole? If he did, how?

Having more than one Alt with the same or a similar power wasn't unusual. There had been a number of speedsters in Thunder City before and after Mach Ten had joined T-CASS. Casters like Spritz, Flame, and Cobalt could pull different elements from within themselves or from the environment around them. Alek and Evan — Rumble and Roar — showed off their identical ability to manipulate air molecules every time they flew to and from emergencies. There had even been a translocation specialist before Scott had arrived in Thunder City. Only Hannah had a unique power no one had ever witnessed before. That's part of what made her so valuable.

The treadmill slowed as the program wound to a

close, so Scott played with the thread his thoughts had gathered. His shoulder twinged. At least Hannah wouldn't see the bruise so long as he kept his shirt on. He doubted the other guy had any bruises, despite Scott's best efforts. If Cole could deflect bullets with his barrier, then no amount of punching could hurt this other guy. Scott would have to find another way to win a fight against him.

An hour later, Scott still had no answers, but he couldn't stay at the Arena all night either. He had nothing to go home to except Thomas's empty penthouse with a freezer filled with frozen meals. At least he could call Hannah.

Halfway back to the locker room, he glanced through the windows of a smaller gym used only by the Alts, not by any of the sport teams above ground. All the lights were off except for one spotlight. It lit a mat in the center of the room. No one stood there, just empty space.

Someone must have forgotten to turn off the light. Scott opened the door and felt around for a switch. As he watched, the light flicked off, then back on.

A signal, as clear as a flare in the midnight sky. He couldn't see much in the black, so he reached out and touched the back of the nearest bench. Behind him, the door slammed shut.

An ambush. It had to be. T-CASS must have planned a beat-down because they didn't want an Alt-killer soiling their sandbox. Where else but in the middle of the Arena could they get away with it? Thomas had designed the security for the entire Arena, not just T-CASS HQ below. No one could get in or out without his security team knowing about it, but once the Alts had passed the security scan, they could move around with no one monitoring them.

Scott stepped slowly into the light. He needed his weapons, but they were back in the locker.

"You won't need them."

The familiar voice growled from behind. Scott whirled around, facing darkness.

"You give yourself away."

He whirled again, toward the circle of light, but there was nothing.

"Whenever you think about using your guns, you clench your right fist."

Still nothing. Maybe he could try to use his Alt power, but how could he pull anything if he couldn't see his target?

"Whenever you think about using your Alt ability, you clench your left fist."

Son-of-a-bitch. Still hulked out in black with mirrored sunglasses, the guard from the hospital stepped in front of Scott. "Giving yourself away like that only makes it easier for your enemies to defeat you."

Scott unclenched his left hand, but kept his eyes locked on the guard.

"How did you get in here?"

The guard stood with arms akimbo. "What makes you think I don't belong here?"

Scott had guessed right. This guy was an Alt and T-CASS knew about him. They had to, or he'd never have gotten into the Arena. "Now what?"

"That's up to you, Grey. Do you want to waste your time playing with beanbags? Or do you want to really learn to use your ability?"

More spotlights lit up around Scott in a semi-circle.

At the center of each light was one of his weapons: two guns, two knives, one taser. The guard had broken into his locker, set up this display, and waited for Scott to walk by. All without getting caught.

"To what end?" Scott asked.

"I told you. There's a war coming. Your mother can't see it. Carraro can't see it either. You need to learn to fight. Fight the way a real soldier fights, to the bitter end with every weapon available to you. You need to learn the things T-CASS will never teach you."

"But you'll teach me?"

"Yes," the guard said.

"And what are you getting out of this? Whose side are you on?"

"I'm on your side."

"How do you know I'm on the right side?"

"I know you'll make the right choice when the time comes," the guard said.

Except the sides weren't defined.

The guard stood still, even as power radiated off him like hurricane-force winds across an open field. He wanted an answer from Scott. Did Scott want to train with T-CASS? With beanbags? Or, did he want to train as a soldier trained? Did he want to become a part of this theoretical war? Did he want to learn what this guy had to teach?

He thought about the beanbags. He remembered Highlight's disdain. His heart spoke before his brain could catch up.

"Okay," he said. "Let's do this."

The guard stepped out of the light, into the pitch black.

"Wait," Scott called. "At least give me your name."

The guard's voice answered as if he stood directly behind Scott. "The Shield."

His voice was the only warning Scott had before the first blow landed.

CHAPTER EIGHT

Hannah washed the last of the blood and skin from the table, her hands shaky. Garrett had driven her to the hospital earlier that morning. Catherine, Thomas, Alek, and Evan had to respond to a red alert called in by Nik. She'd asked what was wrong, but Catherine only said she shouldn't worry about it before leaping into the air with Thomas tucked against her.

Hannah could only sigh. More secrets. She had tried calling Scott, but he wasn't answering his phone either. She had given Eight-ball a thorough brushing to relieve her frustration. If she were with T-CASS, she would know, but if Johnson had his way, she'd be locked in a hospital room with no information at all.

McNamara trusted her, at least. He didn't talk down to her during the whole autopsy process. It took three times longer than it should have because he grilled her with a constant stream of questions, mostly about identifying various bones and organs. Though she believed in her heart she answered correctly each time, McNamara neither confirmed nor denied the accuracy of her answers.

When she bloodsurfed, she fixed whatever was broken and didn't worry about whether it was an appendix or a liver. The only time she had control of her life was when she was inside someone else's body. Last night she had dreamed of bloodsurfing through a body and just staying there.

The trauma inflicted on the corpse during the process didn't ease her anxiety. From the inside, a live human body had a beauty to it, a rhythm fueled by a beating heart, the flow of blood, the spin of cells as they split. Watching McNamara insert a needle into a half-opened eye, part some skin with a scalpel, and worst of all, cut through the skull with the bone saw, reminded her of how much she didn't know about how the body worked.

She also considered the secret she kept from him, the secret to what created Alt power. McNamara had said the body belonged to a Norm, but Hannah wished she could have bloodsurfed through the corpse to confirm his assumption. Instead she removed her plastic smock and tossed it into the red-lined trash can along with the latex gloves.

The second the gloves hit the bin, a bang louder than she expected echoed through the room.

"What was — "The sound of dogs barking followed the noise. " — that?"

McNamara paused the recorder he was dictating notes into and waited. "Security above us. It's tighter these days because of the transfer of bodies. Administration must have requested police dogs just in case the Star Haven anti-Alts issue another one of their empty threats. Sounds like they have it well in hand. I wouldn't worry about it too much."

The barking stopped almost as soon as it had started. McNamara started dictating his notes again, so Hannah figured whatever had happened upstairs had been handled. She checked the bio-hazard bin to make sure the lid was secured. If the Oversight Committee found out she'd exchanged her brown gloves for the latex ones during the autopsy, they could deal with McNamara. She was done talking to them.

McNamara ceased talking into the recorder he used for his notes and turned his attention to Hannah. "What did you think?"

"I don't think I have a future in pathology. It's so much different when the body — I mean, when the person is alive."

"I'm sure it is. I have one more scheduled for this afternoon, but you don't have to join me. If you want, I'll arrange for you to go home. You'll want to be rested for tomorrow."

Hannah looked down at what was left of the cadaver, then checked her watch. What did she have waiting for her at the Blackwood estate? Eight-ball. The rest of the Blackwoods would still be dealing with Nik's red alert.

"No. If I'm going to watch you do this to Miranda Dane, then I want to get used it. I *need* to get used to it."

"Very well." McNamara led her out of the room and into the next one. The other staff had already set up the cadaver.

"Hannah. I have to admit, I haven't paid much attention to the news reports. Not that I wasn't interested," he said, his tone indicating he thought she would care if he had not been. "So I don't know the details of your ability. When you bloodsurf, do you absolutely need the flow of blood to move around the body?"

Hannah put on a new apron and latex gloves, grateful for the change in subject. The less she thought about Miranda, the better. "No. I mean, at first, yes, I thought

I did, but while I was healing Scott I had to move outside of the bloodstream to finish healing him."

McNamara picked up a scalpel, but didn't start cutting. "Interesting. Did it make the process more difficult?"

Hannah thought about it as McNamara waited for her reply. "Not the healing part. I remember having difficulty figuring out which way to travel. I was surfing up his carotid artery, trying to get to his skull, but his brain had swollen so much, I couldn't push my way inside. So, I squeezed out of the artery. Without the flow of blood I had to climb using his bones as leverage to pull myself along.

"When I bloodsurf through the veins, arteries, and capillaries, it's so much easier because there's no thought as to where I'm going or where I am. I don't have to 'swim' under my own power. As long as I know where I want to go, I don't need as much energy to get there."

"I see."

McNamara still didn't start to cut. He was leading up to something. On the previous body, he'd had no difficulty asking her questions while doing his job. Now, he ignored the body, as if he found her more interesting than why this youngish-looking woman had died. It was an interest far more flattering than the Committee's, though. They acted as if she were the one with an agenda to bring harm to Thunder City. McNamara sought knowledge for knowledge's sake. It was refreshing to talk about her ability with someone who understood the human body, who understood her ability. Scott loved her, but her power was as much a mystery to him as it was to the Committee, or to T-CASS.

"Hannah — " McNamara hesitated one more time.

"It's okay. Whatever you're going to ask couldn't be half as intrusive as the Committee."

He smiled. "Can you bloodsurf through a cadaver?"

"No." She didn't even have to think about it.

"Are you sure?"

"No blood, no bloodsurfing."

"But, you just said you didn't necessarily need blood to travel through the body. You did it for Scott."

She had said that, hadn't she?

"I mean," McNamara continued, "have you ever tried? It doesn't sound like with your ability that you've ever lost a patient. So, forgive my morbid curiosity, but it also doesn't sound like you've ever had contact with a cadaver before."

Her tongue scraped dry across the roof of her mouth. "You're right. I've never tried. All of my patients survive. I've never had contact with a dead body before today."

"Would you like to give it a try?" He indicated the cadaver. "I would be curious to see if you could. Wouldn't you?"

This was getting too surrealistic. "I guess, but what about the Committee? I mean, they don't want me bloodsurfing at all."

McNamara frowned. "They're not here, and I'm supervising you. The recording device is off and the hospital's security system doesn't extend into the exam rooms for ethical reasons."

No one would know what he asked of her. Another secret. She should have been horrified, but instead excitement at the illicit idea electrified her. "Why do you want to know? What would it mean if I could? I can't resurrect the dead."

He leaned toward her, over the body. "You're so sure,

but have you ever tried? Can you imagine what it would mean to humanity if you could bring someone back to life again?"

Just thinking about that sort of power scared her. "I've read *Frankenstein*. Resurrecting the dead didn't work out so well for the monster or the doctor."

This time McNamara chuckled. "No, I guess it didn't, but you shouldn't confuse science fiction with reality. Remember, we live in a world where a woman can crush concrete with her bare hands and race a rocket into the sky."

Hannah still couldn't bring herself to take off her gloves and touch the cadaver.

"It's fine." McNamara leaned over the body to make his first incision. "I don't want you to do anything that makes you uncomfortable. Just be aware, I'm not going to be the first person to ask. Others will want to know. We'll work together to formulate an answer for when that day comes."

"Wait."

McNamara froze, the scalpel poised a half inch above the skin.

"You're right. You won't be the first to ask. Ms. Chung broke the law to force me to bloodsurf through her kid. It won't take long for others to demand answers. Best for me to find out now, for sure, so I can fight them later. I don't want to do this, but at least if I know for sure it can't be done, I can answer with a clear conscience."

McNamara straightened, giving her full access to the entire cadaver. She rolled the woman's arm toward her, so she could see where the median cubital vein should be.

Hannah removed the latex glove from her hand, and

surfed. An electrical *zorch* slammed her body back into herself.

"Ow!"

"What happened?" McNamara rounded the table to stand next to her. "Are you okay?"

Hannah shook her head. Her brain buzzed in time with her pulse. She took deep breath, waiting three or four beats before the sensation faded. "Yeah, fine. I hit a wall."

"Well, that's rude."

He made it sound like a joke, but Hannah could feel her rebel rising. She didn't like to fail. Not healing Jimmy stuck like glue to her pride.

"Let me try again."

"If you like." McNamara backed away giving her space.

Hannah put her hand on the arm again and pushed harder this time. Same thing, but the affect wasn't immediate. She made it past the skin before bouncing back.

"I almost made it." Her near-miss only fueled her determination. "Let me try one more time."

"Hannah. It's okay to stop whenever you need to."

"Yeah," she said, but this wasn't about McNamara's curiosity anymore. It was about *her* and what she could do, and the excitement of finding a new skill. She could do this.

She touched the arm again, and pushed.

Inside. She'd done it, but now what? Darkness surrounded her, the silence, the stillness. She tried to surf, but she couldn't move. She kicked as hard as she could and moved a few centimeters, but it was like surfing through wet cement. The cadaver gave her no support. The longer she stayed, the more energy she lost. Her strength faded as fast as she could think.

She hated it inside, she despised what she'd done. She had to get out. She used the last of her strength to push her way back to her starting point, using the walls of the vein to propel her backward.

Outside. She made it and inhaled as if she'd held her breath for hours.

"Hannah. Hannah. What happened?"

She blinked her eyes as if the wet heavy gum from the body forced them closed.

"I did it," she gasped. "I made it inside, but it was horrible. I couldn't move. There was nothing. Just dark, cold, and heavy. Don't make me do that again."

"Okay, okay." He gave her a light rub on her back. "Why don't you take five minutes while I get started. At least, now you know."

Hannah hobbled over to a stool sitting in the corner. Yes, now she knew she could break the barrier of the dead.

But, what will you use this skill for? What would Miranda do?

No. She refused to let Miranda into her head. Not now, not during the rush of success.

Hannah leaned against a cold counter while McNamara returned to work, his deep voice recording information as he examined the woman. Pathology might not be her calling, but she was glad she had McNamara on her side. For the first time, Hannah felt as if she had a pathway to her future. Scott would be proud of her.

Scott sat next to the picture window of the Chung residence. The morning sun lit the tidy Fargrounds neighborhood. He could see several cars back out of gravel driveways in tandem, while a dog walker maneuvered a pack of rambunctious mutts barking and straining against their leashes down the sidewalk. Typical families going about their typical day, unlike his own.

He wasn't far from where Thomas had kept a decoy home, the one he'd used to deflect people investigating "Scott Grey." People like Miranda Dane. Of course, this was before Scott's identity as Cory Blackwood became known.

On a small-screen television sitting against the pale yellow wall, a video of Jimmy Chung played. Scott watched with a keen eye and an open heart.

"Watch what he does next. You will see."

Betty Chung's sister, Rita, had bailed her out of jail, but it had been a close call as to whether or not the judge would set bail in the first place. He had also ordered Rita to take custody of Jimmy until a trial date was set.

On the TV screen, a video of Jimmy played. The boy crawled across their small yard and dove into a pile of grass, two yappy dogs bounding after him. Not finished, he plowed out the other side of the pile and whirled around, the cut grass that had clung to his clothes flying off him in a tornado.

"He sure looks like a happy kid," Scott said, for lack of anything else to say. His comment brought a sad smile to Betty's face.

"He was happy, and active. I wish I could show you his Alt ability, but you can't capture it unless you know it's going to happen. I meant to try, but then he got sick."

Betty halted the video, the image of her son's drooly smile huge on the screen.

"No one would believe me when I told them he had an Alt ability, but he does. I would hear sounds in the house when no one else was around. Voices, when I was alone with him in the room. Doors slamming shut when all of the doors in the house were already closed. The wind in the middle of a calm, sunny day." Her eyes filled with tears.

"I don't believe in ghosts." She paused with an apologetic glance at him.

Scott gave her a smile. He could appreciate the small play on his brother's moniker, glad he could provide her this small bit of humor. He also knew that Nik was safe now, after T-CASS had pulled him and one other out of a hairy situation over at the ship graveyard. He hadn't asked for the details about the rescue. He'd get those later.

"For the record," he said, "I don't believe in them either. Nik Blackwood is the only Ghost I'll ever believe in. Why didn't you alert the Committee when you first suspected?"

"My husband had left me, I had the divorce to think about, a new job to find, bills to pay, the typical childhood illnesses to deal with. By the time I put it all together, he was already losing his ability to balance, to walk. His vision became blurry. All of my friends said I couldn't know for sure if he was an Alt, that he was too young, but I knew he would need surgery. My mother had the same symptoms.

"I knew surgery on Alts required specialized doctors, different medicines. I hadn't wanted him to not have the surgery because of my suspicions. I regret that now. If they had known he was an Alt, the doctors would also have seen the changes I've seen. They would have spent more time with him. They would know the child they gave back to me was not my Jimmy. I wish I'd never taken him to that hospital."

Scott winced. He'd have to talk to his mother about improving communications with the public about Alt medicine. Yes, the doctors had to be careful about operating on someone who could potentially shift in the middle of an operation, like Blockhead, or shoot fire from their hands, like Flame, but on a child like Jimmy who had no shift potential? He'd have to double check with Doctor Rao, but he didn't see any reason why Jimmy's transplant would have been delayed if he had proven to be an Alt.

"So you haven't heard any suspicious sounds since the surgery?"

"No. Nothing. But, it's not just the lack of auditory hallucinations. It's his whole personality. Look at him." She pointed at the screen.

Scott looked again. The boy on the screen had a smile. He ran around like a race car driver, sometimes walking, sometimes crawling. Scott watched the way the boy moved with a critical eye.

"Ms. Chung. I'm going to have to do some more investigating. May I have a copy of that video?"

"Yes. Absolutely."

Ms. Chung made a copy of the video and pulled it from her laptop.

"Please, let me know what you find. I'm not allowed to go far."

Scott nodded and showed himself to the door. He stepped outside, heading for his Harley. He straddled it, thinking through his plans for the rest of the day. He had another lesson scheduled at the Arena. He wanted to meet with Nik and get the scoop on what had happened yesterday. He'd received a couple of quick texts from Thomas, and even one from Catherine, which surprised him. Nik was fine and so was the person he was...well, Thomas was non-specific about who it was Nik was trying to rescue.

Scott hadn't pressed for more information then, but he would today. He needed Nik's advice on how to proceed with Chung's case. Should he visit the sister next? Could he get access to Jimmy's hospital records? How would he handle talking to Jimmy's doctors when most of Thunder City thought he should be locked up?

He turned the ignition to his Harley and revved the engine. From behind him, another engine revved. Scott looked over his shoulder. Sitting on the roadway, not twenty yards from the Chung's driveway was the Shield on his own motorcycle. He wore no helmet, though Scott could have identified him by the leather jacket even at this distance.

Scott's curiosity about the bike almost had him turning off his own engine to approach the Shield, but the Shield had other ideas. He revved his engine again. The challenge was clear: *chase me.*

Before Scott could put on his own helmet, the Shield's bike screeched as rubber burned against asphalt and he was gone. Scott shoved on his helmet and careened out of the driveway. At this speed, he still had to gain lost ground.

The Fargrounds neighborhood didn't have that complicated a layout. Most streets lay in a grid fashion with small houses or townhouses lining each rectangular section. Each intersection had a stop sign. The Shield ignored most of them, barely slowing down to check for oncoming traffic before blasting through. The cop in Scott knew better than to not stop, so he lost ground as the Shield barreled toward the industrial section of town.

Traffic picked up around the warehouses, with trucks of all sizes pulling into and out of the loading docks. The Shield dodged them all, still without stopping, but also without trying any movie-style dramatics. Scott figured he'd be less careful too if he had a shield covering his body. Must be nice not to have to worry about broken bones or concussions.

They dodged and weaved their way through the Fargrounds in record time. Scott managed to keep pace, even with the Shield trying to lose him at every turn. The Shield even pulled the old "turn into an alley and turn off his headlight" trick when he thought he'd lost Scott one block back. Scott was hip to that trick and pulled into the alley right after the Shield did. The Shield then damn near knocked Scott off his Harley when he engaged in a game of chicken while getting back onto the main road. Scott dodged first. He had enough bruises from their sparring the night before. He didn't want to have to ask Hannah to secretly heal him again. This was his fight, not hers.

They broke through the last main intersection, leaving the Fargrounds behind. Scott wasn't familiar with this section of Thunder City. The railroad line lay ahead, though the station where he and Hannah had been ambushed was farther west. There wasn't much out here except larger warehouses, and beyond that, farmland. It was sort of like what the quarry was to Star Haven: unincorporated territory, not really attached to Thunder City, but still reliant on the City for basic services. It was no-man's land otherwise.

No-man's land. Unincorporated territory. Geographically a part of Thunder City, but not subject to its laws. Or at least, not subject to Thunder City laws without a fight. The Shield hadn't led him out here just to test Scott's high speed chase abilities, though the mysterious Alt was certainly doing that, too. He knew how cautious T-CASS was with training new Alts. He'd led Scott out here as a dare. He wanted Scott to use his translocation ability, but he knew Scott wouldn't break Thunder City's laws. Out here, the Shield could toss Scott into the deep end of the pool to see if he would swim or drown, without landing his ass in jail or getting expelled by the Oversight Committee.

Railroad tracks ahead. The morning rush hour was over, but the trains ran throughout the day. Scott could hear the blast of the horn as the train approached a long abandoned intersection. The train driver still followed the laws, even out here in the middle of nowhere.

The Shield sped up, heading toward the intersection at high speed. The guard arms rang out a warning even as they dropped to block access across the tracks. If the Shield didn't stop, he'd smash through the guard arms and hit the tracks at the same time as the train. Scott couldn't speed up fast enough to cut in front of the Shield and run him off the road.

The train couldn't stop. The Shield wouldn't stop. Did the Shield know for sure that his Alt ability would protect him? Had he done this before?

No time. Scott had no time to think this through, or wonder if he could save the Shield. He knew he'd fallen for the Shield's trap even as he telekinetically grabbed hold of the Shield and brought his own bike to a screeching halt.

The Shield and his bike disappeared a hair's breadth from the train as the engine careened past the intersection, horn still blasting loud and clear.

The Shield reappeared to Scott's left, the bike still in motion. The bike shot forward past Scott, but the Shield brought it to a controlled stop.

Scott couldn't stop shaking. He not only had translocated a live person, just as he had done with Hannah when Miranda Dane had tried to shoot her, but he'd transported a Harley moving at high speed. The adrenaline rush washed over his fear. He could see stars at the edge of his vision. Scott ripped off his helmet to gulp air.

The Shield twisted around on his bike to look back at Scott. Now that he was sitting only a dozen or so feet from the Shield, he could see the Shield's lips twist into a smirk. Then the Alt revved his cycle's engine and executed a perfect hairpin turn before he sped past Scott, back the way they came.

Scott didn't try to follow. He sat there and waited until the rush died. When his muscles melted into mush and the stars in his eyes disappeared, only then did he perform his own, less precise turn, and head back to Thunder City.

He'd done it. He'd saved the Shield, but the Shield hadn't needed saving. They'd both used their powers at full tilt, but at what cost?

Scott still didn't have any answers as he raced across the border and back into the city.

CHAPTER NINE

Hannah almost crawled her way to the video room, her dinner balanced on one of her gloved hands and a drink in the other. The plate was piled high with brisket, roasted green beans, and a small square of caramel-covered shortbread on the side. Garret hadn't seemed to mind when she'd asked if she could eat in the video room. Alek had called from the Arena and left her a message while she was with McNamara. Nik's emergency had left him bruised, but he would be fine. Alek hadn't left any details, and the news hadn't picked up the story yet. Hannah almost wished the media would hurry up. If Nik's investigation had led to something big, maybe the reporters would stop talking about her and the quarry raid. Really, just five minutes without being reminded about how different she was would be nice.

She wanted to call Scott right away, but her stomach couldn't wait. She needed to decompress after discovering she could bloodsurf through the dead - sort of. The sensory experience of dark, claustrophobic silence haunted her. When she'd said she never wanted to do that again, she'd meant it. McNamara had clasped her shoulder as he led her back to his office. His previous concern for her had disappeared behind his excitement at her "accomplishment."

Hannah slipped off her brown gloves, taking a moment to let the sweat between her fingers cool. Bloodsurfing into a cadaver had felt more like a trip into a Halloween horror house than an accomplishment, but she hadn't wanted to dull McNamara's enthusiasm. He'd supported her against the Oversight Committee and she couldn't afford to lose that support. Not when she couldn't have Scott by her side.

She activated the app for the televideo. Scott's face appeared after a second ring, his face pinched, his brows lowered. He looked just like she felt. —

"What's wrong?" she asked before anything else.

His face jerked away from the camera as if he were trying to hide his face. "Nothing. Just have a lot to think about. How are you holding up?"

Oh, I'm just fine. I bloodsurfed into a corpse. It was dark and creepy and just awful. Scott already looked troubled. How could she add to his burden by telling him she did something she would never, ever do again?

"I'm fine." She speared a green bean with her fork. "Just really hungry. McNamara autopsied someone while I watched. He said I should see at least one to make sure I could handle it. Hope you don't mind if I eat while we talk. Did you go for training today?"

"I'm glad you can eat after watching an autopsy. Not sure I could."

They both laughed a little at his comment. It was a good sign, and his troubled look eased.

"I just got back from training," he said. "I still have a fifty percent failure rate with beanbags, even after — ."

Hannah nibbled on her food. "After what?"

"Nothing. Just everything that's happened."

He either was referring to the raid, or to their escape

from Division 6, or both. "That's not bad. It's not like you've been doing this since you were a kid. You can do it when there's danger. You just need to find a way to trigger your ability without the danger component."

Scott scrubbed his face with his hands. "I know, but it's boring as hell. I just stand there with Highlight staring at me. Shinzo was there too, recording everything. No pressure, right?"

"It'll get easier with practice. It can't be all that different from bloodsurfing. One day it'll just click and the next thing you know, you won't have to struggle. You'll just go *poof,* and what you want will appear right in front of you."

His smile grew, his brows opened up his face so she could see his gray eyes, still stormy and intense, but not so troubled.

"It would be nice to have a beer appear in hand whenever I want."

Hannah choked on her brisket. "Yeah. You could pull me right into the room with you with just a thought."

"Don't tempt me." He wiggled his eyebrows. He thought he was being funny, but her body took it seriously. *Calm down. You're not going to have phone sex. Not tonight.* She drank her soda instead.

"Seriously, though, how are you feeling? What happened with McNamara today?"

Nothing like talking about dissecting a human body to hold back the raging hormones. Blood and guts cooled her off, but she still wanted to give Scott an honest answer. "I'm angry, but I'm tired of being angry. I didn't even realize how angry I was until Jimmy's mother slapped me."

"Betty. Her name is Betty Chung. You have every right to be angry with her."

"I don't want to be angry, though. I don't want to be…" She hesitated, struggling for the word. "Unforgiving." Yes, that's it. *Unforgiving.* It fit Miranda perfectly. She didn't want to follow in that woman's footsteps. Could she forgive Ms. Chung? Just a little bit to save herself from falling down that path? "I just want to know what happened to her son. If I focus on Jimmy, then maybe his mother won't bother me so much."

Maybe thinking about Jimmy Chung rather than Miranda would help her get through today. Tomorrow the evidence of her crimes in the quarry would be staring her in the face.

"I spoke to Betty Chung this morning." Scott reached off screen for his own drink.

"You did? What did she say?"

"Not much. She showed me videos of Jimmy taken before his surgery."

"What did you see?"

Scott shrugged. "He was an active, energetic kid. Nothing like what we saw at the hospital."

"He could still be reacting to the surgery. I asked McNamara about it and he said he can't think of any reason for a surgery like that."

"Huh. Well, the man is a pathologist and not a surgeon. He can't know everything."

Why not? Hannah bit her tongue. Scott was just making a general observation. She pushed away the defensiveness, because Scott was still talking.

"I'm going to talk to Betty's sister as soon as the harbor operation is finished. I'll talk to Nik, too. He's the detective in the family. Maybe he could give us a hand. What did you see inside Jimmy, anyway?"

And just like that, her emotions were back to normal. "It looked like someone had cut through his spine, but even McNamara couldn't tell me why anyone would need to do that. I need to know more. I need to see his medical records. I need to understand what happened to that kid. McNamara said I could get access to his records once I'm officially working at the hospital, but that isn't going to happen until after tomorrow."

"Sounds like you'll be spending a lot of time with McNamara."

His tone of voice carried the low, suspicious tones she'd heard from Miranda. She hadn't imagined his earlier dismissiveness. Just what she didn't need: a jealous boyfriend. Well, Scott wasn't the only one who could deflect and distract.

"I need to do something, Scott. Every time you talk about your training, it sounds like they're following a protocol set up for third graders. No one has bothered to tell me *how* they plan to train me."

"They've never had to train anyone with your abilities before. They don't know what to do with you."

"Yeah. No one knows what to do with me." The food on her plate lost its appeal. "Miranda didn't know either."

"Don't talk like that." Scott put his drink down with a thump. He leaned toward the camera, the intensity she loved so much back in place. "Miranda had an agenda, she was never supposed to be anyone's mother. She couldn't handle a bright, willful child with Alt abilities."

Hannah shrugged. Willful sounded accurate, but bright? Sometimes she had to wonder. If she was as smart as someone like McNamara, would she have tried to run away? No, she would have found a less disruptive way to fight the Committee. "Anyway, if the Committee has a problem with me working with cadavers, they can take it up with McNamara. If anyone can put the Committee in its place, he can."

"You're probably right." Though he agreed with her, Scott looked away from the screen, as if he wanted to hide his doubts. "T-CASS has been around long enough to become entrenched in its ways. Everyone is too scared of Catherine to suggest changes. She's too busy to notice."

"Yeah." A familiar buzz tickled her backside. She'd forgotten to turn her phone off, damn it. Her time with Scott was precious, even if she was still annoyed with him, so she ignored it. "Catherine assumes I'm going to join T-CASS but I just don't know if it's what I want. I mean, it's not like I'm not thinking about it, but every time I do, I see people having their lives disrupted because of one emergency or another. Maybe I want to explore what it's like to be a Neut? I could set up my own medical practice. I could have a schedule, control how many people I heal in a day. Have a life after hours — "

Her phone buzzed again.

"Scott. I'm sorry, it's my phone. I'm going to check to see who it is."

The recorded message icon flashed. She double checked the number. It was McNamara.

Hannah hated to leave Scott hanging out in chat, but the faster she returned the phone call, the faster she could get back to Scott.

"Hannah?" McNamara answered on the first ring. He'd been waiting for her.

"Yes. I'm sorry, I was eating dinner. I'll arrange for a ride to the hospital tomorrow morning."

"The earlier, the better."

"Did something happen?" Her panic picked up

speed with McNamara's clipped tone. Her imagination grasped onto the worst case scenario. "Did the Oversight Committee tell you I couldn't work with you?"

"No. I haven't told them yet. I received a call from Star Haven, though. They asked me to arrange to have you down at the harbor when the bodies arrive."

"Me? Why? I mean, I'm going with you to the harbor anyway." More horrible scenarios played out as her stomach rebelled against her dinner.

"True, but I never told Star Haven that. I figured we'd keep you hidden in one of the warehouse's offices until after the bodies were delivered and the delegation had left."

She shouldn't have been surprised, but McNamara telling her didn't help. "I don't understand. Are they going to try and arrest me at the harbor for breaking the anti-Alt ban?"

"I don't think so. There are too many legal loopholes and they'd be fools to try with so much security in place. They wouldn't have the resources to follow through on your arrest and they know it. The interim mayor claims there's a package waiting for you in his office. His phone was also ringing off the hook, so he didn't elaborate. He insisted that you be at the harbor, nothing more. Do you know what this package might be?"

Her throat closed up, fear snatching away her ability to talk.

"Hannah, are you there?"

"Yes." She could barely talk over the tight throat muscles. "I'm here. No, I don't know what the package could be."

McNamara sighed. "I'll contact T-CASS and let

them know. They'll want to double up security if you're around."

"I can do it. I live with the Blackwoods, remember."

"Yes, but let me make the call anyway. This isn't like me hiring you and springing it on the Committee later. I can outmaneuver the Committee about that. This has danger carved into it and my report should go through official channels. They'll want to send someone to ask me questions."

He made the whole thing sound like a done deal, but her inner rebel leaked through. "You make it sound like I have no choice."

This time McNamara kept quiet for a minute. "I can't force you, but I need to let Star Haven and T-CASS know one way or the other. You do have a choice, but it took a lot of politics and negotiating for me to get Star Haven to agree to bring the bodies here instead of me going to Star Haven. Telling them you're not willing to join me at the harbor could torpedo this agreement to the bottom of the Bay."

This whole arrangement screamed of a set-up. But if she wanted to get a look at Jimmy's records, she couldn't afford to piss off McNamara.

"I'll go. It's just...I'm the one who disabled those guards, left them unable to defend themselves. I'm the one who killed Joe Austin."

Tears blurred her vision. Would Scott see? Damn it, why did she have to do this at all?

"Hannah, I promise. I'll be right beside you the whole time. I won't let anything bad happen to you. You won't be alone."

She took a deep, calming breath. The tears receded. "Thank you. I'll be there. I'll meet you at the hospital in the morning."

"I'll see you then." McNamara disconnected the line before she could.

"Hannah, what's wrong?" Scott asked.

She'd forgotten to mute the chat, so he'd heard her side of the story. She explained McNamara's side.

"I don't like it. Any of it. You should have said no. Call him back. Tell him you can't do it. You can't go to the harbor and you can't work for him."

Her tears might be gone, but the rebel remained. "Why would I do that? It's not like the harbor isn't going to be blanketed in security. And there's no good reason not to work for McNamara. He can help me with Jimmy's case. He can protect me from the Committee."

Scott leaned closer to the camera, his face tight with worry for her. "Working for McNamara is only going to throw you into the middle of the quarry investigation. You don't need to be dragged through that again. Let me handle Jimmy Chung and his mother."

Her rebellion turned to cold fire. Despite his worry mirroring her own, he didn't understand her need to make her own decisions. To grasp this one tendril of freedom she had. If she didn't, she might as well surrender her soul to the Committee.

"I'm not being dragged anywhere. I want to do this." *I want to see Miranda's body. I want to see her dead.* "McNamara is going to help me maneuver around the Committee. They already control too much of my life. He can give me some space to call my own."

"I can help you with that."

"Oh, Scott. You're in the same situation I am. I thought you would be more supportive."

"It's dangerous."

"More dangerous than turning myself over to

Miranda? More dangerous than fighting a rampaging mutant Alt? More dangerous than getting shot at?"

"That was different."

"No, it wasn't."

"Hannah— "

She cut him off. "Don't. Just don't. I made a decision. You might not like it, but you will respect it."

They both stared at each other. She could see he wasn't about to change his mind and she wasn't going to back down. Not on this, the first decision she'd made for herself without seeking permission from the Blackwoods. She was ready for a change, no matter the danger.

"I respect you, Hannah, but this is a mistake. There are other ways to find your freedom."

"It might be a mistake, but it's my mistake to make."

She could see his eyes narrow. Those storm-gray eyes she usually found comfort in. If he were standing in front of her, her determination might have weakened. Maybe not being near Scott wasn't a bad idea. He was not about to change his mind and she was not going to back down.

"I think we're done for the evening." Before he could argue, she pulled off the headset and ended the chat. The abrupt change created a vacuum in her heart before all her pain and anger rushed in to fill the void.

As if he were listening in, Eight-ball appeared at the corner of the couch. Hannah patted her lap and the all-black cat jumped on command. He rubbed her chin with his face. Hannah pulled the cat closer, her fingers finding the sweet spot behind his ears.

"Oh, Eight-ball. Today was so horrible."

Eight-ball started to purr, the loud rhythm bringing back her tears. "I hate my life right now. Everyone wants to lock me up to keep me safe. I won't let them."

Eight-ball continued to pace on her lap, his tail flicking her chin.

"Now Scott is pissed at me and I just want to go to bed. What do you say we go upstairs and forget today ever happened?"

Eight-ball allowed her to scoop him up into her arms and march upstairs.

Wind from the sea whipped Hannah's hair into a tornado twirl as she watched the cargo ship dock at the port on the south end of Thunder City's harbor. Scott was here, somewhere. She knew, though he never said anything about it when he texted her during breakfast. He didn't have to say anything, but she knew. His unrelenting need to protect her had calmed her raw soul when they were on board the *Elusive Lady,* but ever since she'd started spending time with McNamara, she found his caution irritating. He cared, she cared, but some things had to be risked or she'd never achieve the freedom she craved.

The Committee didn't want her here either, but at least McNamara had smoothed over those ruffled feathers for her. He was the only one who understood what she was going through. Somehow he managed to break through the logjam of everyone else's concern for her safety and give her a space to call her own. Her confused feelings of wanting her own life and wanting to make her own decisions didn't bother him in the least. He let her work out for herself what she thought was best.

Not that she didn't have her own doubts. She'd gotten very little sleep last night, her thoughts weaving around her feelings for Scott, anger at his overprotectiveness, and anguish about how much she cared for him despite their spat. If Eight-ball hadn't leapt into bed with her and purred in her ear, she might not have gotten any sleep at all.

The boom of a lowered plank echoed, followed by the grind of motors as cranes swung around, prepared to lift the containers of evidence off the ship. McNamara had let her listen in on a number of phone calls he'd made to work out the last minute details. The remains of Joe Austin took up at least three containers. McNamara speed-read the numerous forms and contracts he had to sign, promising everything short of his first born to keep Star Haven in the loop about every aspect of his investigation. She didn't even think he had kids. At least, he hadn't mentioned any to her. They'd both been pretty quiet after he picked her up this morning to bring her to the harbor. The rest of the Blackwoods had already left for the morning.

The last time she'd seen Joe Austin, he'd had her in his meaty grip, King Kong style. She'd been so small he hadn't managed to crush her bones, but he'd still managed enough pressure to bruise her up something fierce. Miranda hadn't just destroyed his body. She'd destroyed his mind. Hell-bent on killing everyone in his way, Joe had intended to slam her onto the quarry floor before continuing on his path of destruction. Before he could, Hannah had bloodsurfed through his head and blown up his brain from the inside.

She would have to testify to what she had done, but saying it out loud was different than actually seeing it. Once McNamara began his examination of Joe, the world would see her not as a healer, but as a destroyer, too. She understood how people thought, and she knew that there were those who would use her as a weapon. It was inevitable that there would be more Mirandas out there.

The face of Doctor Johnson interrupted her thoughts. Yeah, he was a Miranda wannabe, but she knew how to handle the Mirandas in her life. She'd make sure he regretted trying to cage her.

The longshoremen, with the assistance of a few Alts, used cranes to haul the normal-sized containers off the ship. Rumble and Roar flew above the ship. The twins created an air cushion under the extra-large container carrying Joe. The cushion grew in size until the oversized container floated in mid-air.

Despite the hostility toward Alts from Star Haven, T-CASS hadn't bothered hiding their presence. Their colorful outfits were bright and obvious in the harsh sun. Rumble and Roar made quite a show for the Star Haven crew, working in tandem with their Norm counterparts. Thunder City police patrolled along the harbor boardwalk. Out on Mystic Bay, police boats zigzagged across the Bay. TV crews also lined the boardwalk, their cameras capturing everything from a distance, including her. Especially her.

There were other Alts around, she was sure, not in uniform, but still ready to jump if even the slightest problem arose. Thomas would have his equipment set-up nearby as well, monitoring all of the electronic surveillance he'd put in place over the past week.

Hannah moved closer to McNamara, grateful when he looked down at her, but didn't comment. In her heart, she wished Scott stood beside her, despite their argument last night. Where was he? So far she hadn't seen him, but given his wardrobe of t-shirts and jeans, he didn't stand out like his family when they were in uniform. Had he managed to make it past the Thunder City security? She hoped he hadn't picked a fight with them. Maybe he'd sneaked in from somewhere? Had he told anyone what he'd planned to do? Warned his brothers, at least?

No, of course he wouldn't. If something did go wrong, no one else would know he was here, but Scott wouldn't care about that. He only cared about her.

There was nothing she could do about it now. While Thunder City took care of removing the cargo from the ship, the Star Haven delegation disembarked. She recognized the interim Mayor, who had been the Attorney General until Miranda died. He led a tight group of men and women, all of whom looked like they'd rather be elsewhere. One of the men scanned the crowd until his dark eyes locked with Hannah's. A shiver ran up Hannah's spine. He motioned for Hannah to meet him closer to the edge of the boardwalk, away from the small crowd.

Hannah hesitated. *Don't be an idiot. Star Haven may want all Alts dead, but they're not going to do it in front of the world. It's not just Thunder City watching. The whole state is watching.*

She closed her eyes for moment and remembered Scott holding her tight right after he killed Miranda. The thought gave her courage. If there was one thing Scott had in spades, it was courage. Shoving her gloved hands into her jean pockets, Hannah noticed McNamara watching her again, even as another Star Haven official addressed him. Hannah ignored it all and broke away from the crowd. The man led her over to one of the larger pylons near the docked ship.

He didn't spare any words, but had to shout over the grinding of the machinery. "I'm Detective Juan

Costenaro. The Mayor asked me to give this to you."

He shoved a small cardboard box at Hannah, forcing her to pull her hands out of her pockets to accept the box. His name sounded familiar. Maybe she'd met him at one of Miranda Dane's functions? His sharp cheekbones, wavy hair, and smooth complexion would have had her admiring him if she wasn't so damn scared.

"What's in it?" Her voice choked on the words. *Calm down. Just stay calm. You'll get through this.*

"Roger Dane's ashes." He bowed his head toward her a little, offering a hint of sympathy. "No one else wants them and you're his only living heir."

Stomach acid flushed her throat, burning, hurting. Roger, her stepfather, who had been shot to death by one of Miranda's thugs. Hannah's fingers flexed as if scorched, but the detective shoved a tablet at her. "I need you to sign at the bottom."

"Who told you to cremate him?"

Detective Costenaro shrugged. "I'm not a lawyer, just a cop doing his job."

Hannah tried to read the fine print on the screen, but she couldn't see through her grief. "That's it? Just his ashes? Roger Dane was worth millions. He had an art collection. A sailboat." *He had me. He loved me.* Hannah lost her voice with that last thought. What should she do? What else could she do? She couldn't recognize her own signature, but it was the best she could do with the gloves.

Costenaro snatched back the tablet. "Whatever he had, someone else has it now. I'll need an email address for the receipt."

The only email Hannah had was the one she used for school. She hadn't accessed it in over six months, but her brain kicked in with an automatic recitation of the letters. Costenaro typed out the information then tucked the tablet into his back pocket.

Instead of walking back to the delegation, Costenaro crossed his arms and stayed put, forcing Hannah to do the same.

"The news says you and Scott are a couple."

Why would a Star Haven detective care? Since the news speculated about it anyway, she couldn't think of a reason to deny it.

"Yeah. So what?"

"He's — was my partner. I don't know what you did to him, to make him an Alt, but he doesn't deserve this."

He doesn't deserve you. Costenaro didn't say it, but she heard him loud and clear anyway.

"I didn't make him an Alt. He already was an Alt, he just didn't know it. All I did was — "

The sharp crack in the background sounded all too familiar to Hannah.

"Gun!" Costenaro yelled.

It must have been instinct that caused the man to shove Hannah behind him as he pulled his own gun, because why would a Star Haven cop, Scott's former partner, who thought she had turned Scott into an Alt, care if she died?

"Stay behind me," he shouted at her again as he started to move south of the crowd, toward the media and away from the ship.

She did exactly as he said because chaos had broken out around her. Costenaro kept close even as the Thunder City police corralled the Thunder City delegation and dragged them off the boardwalk toward the warehouse. Star Haven security did their best for the Star Haven side, corralling their delegates as best they could as their people rushed toward the ship. Costenaro grabbed her hand. He might hate Alts, but he still kept himself between her and the sound of the gunshot as he led her back toward the Thunder City delegates. Back to McNamara.

"Go!" Costenaro shoved her into McNamara's arms. "Get out of here."

"Wait." She tried to keep her grip on Costenaro. "I don't know where Scott is. He's here somewhere."

"Scott can take care of himself." Costenaro let go and ran for the ship.

McNamara gripped her arm and pulled her in the opposite direction, toward the warehouse where there were steps leading to the parking lot. "We need to — "

The explosion knocked her into McNamara, with the people behind her falling onto her. Black smoke blanketed the air. Piercing screams rose in pitch. People shoved at her, scrambling to get away.

McNamara had wrapped his arms around her as they fell over. In the background, an all too familiar sound pounded out a rhythm.

Automatic gunfire. Scott had been right. The anti-Alts were going to shoot them all. She should have listened to him.

CHAPTER TEN

Even from the fourth floor of the warehouse, Scott couldn't escape the waves of tension riding the Bay breeze as the ramp from the cargo ship hit the dock. From the observation deck attached to a bank of admin offices, he had a near-perfect view of the dock and the ship at the southern end of the boardwalk. The construction scaffolding on the north side would hide him from the view of the police and T-CASS patrolling the area — if he didn't do anything stupid.

The handguns he'd strapped under his windbreaker wouldn't do him much good from up here, but there was no way he would risk bringing a rifle to the harbor, even if the Blackwoods owned one. The Thunder City police had refused him entry to the boardwalk, daring him to use his Alt ability and give them an excuse to arrest him. He wasn't a cop anymore, but he wasn't a member of T-CASS yet. His only protection came from his frayed family ties. It had taken no small amount of subterfuge for him to get this close to the action without getting arrested.

From the edge of the boardwalk, Scott could easily pick out Hannah with her hair blowing in the breeze. She stood among the dignitaries waiting to receive the dead. McNamara stood next her, his own red hair standing out in the crowd. Occasionally, McNamara would lean down to talk to Hannah, or just look at her. The more Scott watched, the more he didn't like it. In such a short time, the doctor had become her confidant.

Did she tell McNamara things she didn't want to tell Scott? Or couldn't tell him? It made their spat even worse. His jealousy returned. He recognized the ugly emotion after having grown up with it. He'd been jealous of his brothers for having Alt powers when he didn't. Jealous of the attention they got from their mother, when she couldn't even look at him. Jealous of their father, Demitrios Economopoulos, alive and healthy and wanting to be with them when all Scott had was a single picture of his own biological dad.

He tried to put his emotions in their place. Resenting Hannah's relationship with McNamara was stupid. The man could guide her career in a way Catherine couldn't. Maybe even guide her away from T-CASS. Wouldn't that stick in Thunder City's craw. It would be no small amount of self-satisfaction for both of them to make it appear as if the Committee's bullies had driven her away.

She wouldn't do that, though, no matter how much McNamara influenced her, Scott was sure. He was the petty one, gathering his grievances and holding onto to them like old friends. Hannah had a much more mature outlook on her life. He needed her to keep him grounded, keep him from doing something stupid.

If he could just get past his distrust of McNamara.

Scott continued to watch Hannah while the first representatives from Star Haven filed off the boat. His focus lasered on her, until a movement to his right caught him off guard. The Shield, carrying his rifle, stepped out onto a second observation deck. No one below could see him, only Scott.

Getting into position to fire, the Shield gave Scott a glimpse of familiar sunglasses.

"What are you doing here?" Scott called.

If the Shield was surprised to see Scott, he didn't look it. "My job."

"You think someone is going to attack McNamara? Here? In front of news cameras and the Star Haven dignitaries? With most of T-CASS around to stop them?" It would be a stupid move, but one not unheard of, for the anti-Alt organizations.

"I know they are. Why don't you?"

The Shield turned away from Scott to look at the boardwalk. Did he see McNamara? Or, did he see what Scott saw? Hannah moving away from the Thunder City delegation toward the edge of the boardwalk following a man from the Star Haven side. Scott almost choked. He recognized the man's swagger, his uniform. It was Juan, his partner. His ex-partner.

"Why don't I what?" Scott asked, but he was no longer watching the Shield. He watched Juan talk to Hannah, then shove a box into her hands.

"Why don't you know that the anti-Alt movement doesn't give a shit about dead bodies from the quarry raid? All they care about is dead Alts. This is a prime opportunity to take out Alts and traitors at the same time."

Scott kept watching Juan and Hannah. The Shield said exactly what Scott had been saying, but no one would listen to him. Hannah wouldn't listen to him. The Shield believed what Scott believed. "I know that. How do *you* know that?"

"It's my job to know. It's your job, too, if you're going

to be of any use in this war."

Hannah in danger crowded out the demand to repeat the question he'd been asking since the beginning: *what war?* "It's fine to know it, but if no one believes you what good does knowing it do?"

"It's also your job to make people listen, even if they don't want to, by any means necessary."

Threats. This guy was all about threats and violence. "So you're here to protect Hannah, not McNamara?"

The Shield raised the rifle to fire. "No. I'm here to protect McNamara. If that means killing your girlfriend to make him less of a target, so be it."

Cold instinct overrode Scott's panic. Even if he wanted to believe Juan would protect Hannah despite being an Alt, there was no way in hell he would stand by and let the Shield shoot her.

Without a second's delay, Scott knew he didn't just want that rifle, he needed it and he needed it now, before the would-be assassin killed Hannah. He wanted it like nothing else he'd wanted in his life, other than Hannah. Scott locked onto his desire for the rifle and yanked.

The rifle disappeared from the Shield's hands and appeared in Scott's. Scott swung it into position, ready to fire. The Shield looked at his empty hands before he saw Scott with his gun pointed at him.

Give me a reason, you son-of-a-bitch. Just give me a reason to fire.

The Shield appeared amused rather than worried, even as he pulled out his own handgun and pointed it toward the ground. "You're getting better. You pulled the gun into your hands instead of to the ground."

At this range Scott couldn't miss, even as he realized that the Shield would have his barriers in place. Had he pulled the rifle through the Shield's barriers?

"No, you didn't. My shield wasn't raised then. It is now. Grab the handgun."

Scott knew he was telegraphing his thoughts through body language. But how the hell did you control yourself so as not to give away your thoughts?

The Shield raised his handgun. "Grab it!"

Scott lowered the rifle. He focused on the handgun and tried to pull.

Nothing happened.

Scott turned to look for Hannah, but she was still talking to Juan. T-CASS zipped about the ship, helping to unload the containers holding the bodies. Overhead, Alek and Evan used an air cushion to raise one of the larger containers, the one that held part of the mutant Alt who had attacked Hannah.

Other T-CASS members helped from the sidelines, their colorful uniforms making them easy to find. Everything was peaceful. Everyone worked in unison, like they were supposed to. McNamara was busy shaking hands.

"Grab the damn gun!"

Scott turned back to the Shield to snap at him that he couldn't do it.

The Shield sighed, then raised his gun and fired at Scott.

Scott ducked. *What the hell?*

Shouts rained down from the roof. The shot had drawn the attention of the SWAT team topside. It wouldn't take them long to locate the source of the gunshot. They'd be all over him in a minute.

"Grab the damn gun."

Below, panic sent both sets of dignitaries running in opposite directions, Thunder City for the parking lot and Star Haven back toward the ship.

Hannah would be in the middle of the Thunder City group heading toward the parking lot, but he couldn't see her.

The Shield didn't appear concerned, forcing Scott to choose between detaining him for the cops and praying the police would believe his story, or running down four flights of stairs into the crowd to look for Hannah.

No choice. Hannah came first. Always. He lowered the rifle and turned to run back inside the building.—

The explosion rocked the building, knocking Scott into the door before he could open it. A cloud of debris smacked into either Alek or Evan, whichever one was closest to the ship, sending the black-clad body tumbling into the fiery explosion. From the back end of the cargo ship, a mushroom of black smoke rose in the air. The entire ship listed to one side as a wave of water hit the boardwalk, sweeping some of the Star Haven delegation into the Bay.

Scott froze in agony. He could do nothing from where he stood, so far away. His brother, he didn't even know which one, could be dead and he could do nothing from up here.

Hannah! Evan! Alek! He searched the crowed below, knowing one of his brothers was burning on the ship. He needed to pull them out of there.

"Don't you do it!"

Scott ignored the Shield, desperate to find Hannah and his brothers.

"Scott, listen to me. You don't know which brother fell. You risk pulling the wrong one. T-CASS will find him."

Scott heard, but couldn't process the words. He

couldn't see them. Any of them. Where was Catherine? Where was Thomas?

The crowd scattered as more T-CASS teams converged on the danger.

"Back up!"

"What?"

The Shield stepped backed to the farthest end of his deck, then ran toward Scott. Scott realized what the Shield intended to do and pulled back, just as the Shield's foot hit the railing and propelled him over to Scott's deck. He landed with a light thump.

"Give me back the gun."

"Why? So you can shoot Hannah?"

"Don't be a jackass. My shot was a warning to get everyone off the boardwalk."

"You knew this was going to happen?"

"I made an educated guess. Give me the gun or I'll take it from you, and your arm with it."

"My brother is burning. Hannah is getting trampled."

From inside the building he could hear SWAT checking all of the offices on this floor. He had a minute, maybe less, to get this situation under control.

The Shield grabbed the rifle and yanked but Scott couldn't unclench his fingers. He couldn't let the rifle go. "Fine. Keep the gun. I'll get us back to ground level."

"Did you know about the bomb? Did you know what the anti-Alts were going to do?"

The Shield reached around the rifle and grabbed Scott's arm, ignoring Scott's question. "If SWAT catches us with that gun, *you* will be arrested and *you* won't be able to help Hannah or your brother. Now follow me."

The Shield slipped a leg over the railing. The door

to the office that led to the observation deck rattled. Scott had jammed the lock, but cops would have no problems kicking the door down. He had no choice. For Hannah, he lowered the gun and followed the Shield over the railing.

The Shield slipped his arm around Scott's waist. "Jump."

The fall awakened the sick, twisted sensation of free-falling to his death when he'd hit the hospital roof two weeks ago. The memory hurt more than the sudden jarring sensation of hitting concrete four stories below.

Instead of releasing him to fall, though, the Shield tightened his grip around Scott, waiting until he recovered his senses. He hadn't died. He was upright and unhurt.

"Do exactly what I tell you to do."

His life flashing before his eyes for the second time in his life had turned Scott into a puppet. Still clutching the rifle, he followed the Shield, blind to everything except what was right in front him.

They stayed behind the scaffolding until they reached the northeast corner of the building. The Shield stopped, peeked around. "Shit."

"What?"

The Shield pulled back from the corner. "The explosion was just a diversion. This part I didn't anticipate."

Before he could say anything else, automatic gunfire erupted from the parking lot.

"Set an explosion on the ship, kill as many Alts as possible, drive the survivors to the parking lot. The stragglers would be caught between the explosion and the death squad heading from the harbor entrance. They didn't count on us firing first, warning people away from the ship. They won't be expecting this crowd."

"T-CASS — "

"Half jumped into the Bay to save the ones who fell in. The rest are trying to save the ship's crew and protect the delegation." The screams reached a fever pitch.

Hannah!

"Grey, listen to me."

Scott looked at the Shield, still unsure of his agenda. "We have one goal: Keep McNamara and Hannah alive. Understand?"

"Now you want to keep her alive? You were ready to assassinate her five minutes ago."

"And I still will if you don't do exactly as I say for the next five minutes. No joke, Grey. She will die if you don't follow me."

He spared a thought for his brothers, Alek and Evan as he followed, not sure if he was rescuing Hannah or helping this man kill her.

Hannah could barely hear the screams over the blood rushing in her ears. Hot wood burned under her cheek, her breath harsh under the weight of McNamara on top of her, the box holding Roger's ashes crushed under her chest.

"Doctor McNamara?" Oh, God, what if he was dead? She didn't want to roll over and find out. The members of the delegation were running around her, and security was running toward her. Either would trample her underfoot if she couldn't get up and run herself.

Hannah pushed up onto her knees to shove

McNamara off of her. Over her shoulder, a black cloud billowed upwards. Shouts echoed from all directions. In the sky, she could see only one Blackwood twin struggling to keep the largest container from falling onto the crowd. Where was the other? She couldn't see above the crowd stampeding around her.

McNamara came to his senses. A break in the crowd gave him the opportunity to yank her to a standing position and push her to jog ahead of him, putting distance between her and the burning ship.

"Where's the Shield?" she yelled, her voice muted by the ringing in her ears.

"He said he was taking the high ground. He's got eyes on us. We should be okay, but we need to get back to the car."

Sirens started to wail, and more T-CASS teams dashed past her. Some jumped into the water. Others soared into the air as the boat tilted with a harsh screech of metal against metal. More smoke made her eyes water. The crowd ahead of them blurred into a mass of color and panic. More gunfire erupted. The crowd ahead of them surged backwards.

"Ow, ow, ow!" A huge guy carrying a news camera stepped on her sneakers, crushing her toes. McNamara pulled her closer to the warehouse wall and away from the stream of bodies.

The Shield rounded the corner, arms pumping. He saw them. Next thing she knew, he had grabbed her and pushed her against Scott, who crushed her to his chest with one hand. In the other, he carried a rifle.

He'd been right and she'd been wrong. She should have listened to him. Hannah closed her eyes, a thousand apologies ready to spill if only he wouldn't let her go.

"Behind me." The Shield motioned with his handgun. "I can shield all of you, but you have to stay close together! There are gunmen in the parking lot."

Scott tucked her head under his chin. Sharp bits of wood, metal, and blood rained down from above.

"Alek? Evan?" she stuttered.

"I don't know." Scott's grip on her shoulders tightened.

A bullet winged overhead. The crack of wood splintering tucked her even closer to Scott as the debris landed about two inches from her face, then bounced to the ground.

So that's what the Shield meant by "shield." The flying debris couldn't touch her, at least as long as she stayed pressed against Scott.

"Come on!" The Shield motioned them forward, away from the building. "Hannah's one of the targets. We have to move."

Hannah didn't want to leave Scott's arms. Instead, she matched his stride, keeping her head low as they made their way around the building to the parking lot. McNamara staggered beside her. Was he hurt? She didn't see any blood. She didn't have time to take a closer look. The Shield led them toward the nearest row of cars. McNamara stumbled into her again.

"Keep your heads down! Get behind the SUV!" The Shield pointed to the second row, and a red SUV parked between two pickup trucks.

The Shield motioned for Scott to watch their backs. "I'll drive. You use the rifle," he ordered.

"Lean on me." She reached for McNamara. She was the only choice if he was going to make it to the car.

They shuffled as fast as they could. McNamara favored his right ankle. Nothing she could do about it now. They had almost made it to the SUV when another bullet whizzed by her head, bounced off the Shield's shield, and punctured the SUV's window. The glass shards sprayed the Shield, covering both of them. More gun shots followed. This time Hannah pulled McNamara behind her until they crouched next to a tire.

"How bad is it?" Hannah reached for McNamara's ankle. She only wanted to look at the damage, but McNamara knocked her hand away.

"Not here," he said, but before she could correct him, he pulled her into his arms as another barrage of bullets fired in the background. "It's nothing serious. We'll worry about it later."

He lied. He was hurt. At least he didn't deny he was hurt at all. Should she risk bloodsurfing? She could outmaneuver McNamara if she had to. Could a bullet hit her if she was inside his body? No, McNamara was right. Not here, not now. No matter how fast she was, she would be putting them both at greater risk.

In the meantime, Scott fired the rifle while the Shield used his handgun to fire back. They worked in sync, the Shield firing until he'd spent his magazine, then pulling back while Scott fired the rifle. They created a wall of gunfire around her and McNamara, but she couldn't see how many terrorists they hit.

"What's happening?" she shouted. More gunfire spat past the SUV before Scott could answer. Instead, he rounded the corner of the SUV to start firing again.

The Shield swung around the opposite side. He released a spent magazine from his gun and slapped in a new one, while Scott continued to fire.

Scott pulled back. "I'm out."

Hannah assumed he meant bullets for the rifle. He

reached into his jacket. She knew he always carried at least two hand guns with him.

"There are four heading in this direction, two from the south, two from the east," the Shield shouted to Scott. "The car is three rows back, fifth car from the end. Silver Cadillac. I can extend my shield in all directions but you need to stay within six feet of me for maximum effect. You cannot shoot through my shields if I cover your whole body. Wait until I tell you to shoot and I'll uncover your hands and the gun."

Scott slipped the rifle over his shoulder. "I'll take the east."

The Shield nodded, his handgun and sunglasses still in place. "On three...two...one...Go...Go...Go!"

This time, Hannah helped pull McNamara to his feet. With Scott and the Shield flanking them, a steady stream of bullets firing from their guns, they made their way three rows back, five cars from the end. Sparks flew as the bullets hit metal. Hannah kept her eyes forward, so she wouldn't trip with McNamara leaning one her, but she could hear the Shield shout at Scott every ten or fifteen steps, telling him to fire.

The return fire became erratic, slower, as if there were fewer gunmen firing at them, but Hannah didn't dare turn around to check. They made it to the car. McNamara fumbled with the keys from his pocket, until Hannah grabbed them and clicked the fob to open the doors. By the time she had shoved McNamara through the back door, the Shield had made his way around their group to take out the last attacker on Scott's side. He grabbed the keys from Hannah's hand before she could protest.

"You, get in the back with McNamara." He pointed at Scott. "You, get in the passenger side."

By now, cars had started to clog both the exit and entrance lanes. Horns honked and everyone yelled. The Shield slammed the driver's side door closed just as Scott did the same on the passenger side. Sitting next to Hannah, McNamara pushed her head down into her lap as he leaned forward over his own.

The Cadillac jerked backward as the Shield pulled out of the space. Then it slammed forward with tires squealing in protest. Hannah reached up to pull McNamara's hand off her head. She needed something secure to hold. He squeezed her hand, his head bent low close to hers. His breath pulsed against her cheek.

"We've got company!" the Shield shouted again.

"Stay down," Scott ordered from up front.

The car swerved, sending her body into the door. Branches scraped along the car's sides, scratching it. She suspected the Shield was making his own exit from the parking lot. Scott rolled down the window from his side.

"Not yet!" the Shield called.

"I don't see them," Scott said.

"You will. Ambush once we hit the asphalt. Hang on!"

The car spun a nausea-inducing one hundred eighty degrees, then sped faster. McNamara groaned.

"I see them!" Scott shouted this time.

"Not yet. I'll get you closer."

Closer? Wasn't the Shield supposed to keep them as far away from the terrorists as possible?

"Fire!"

Scott did, and kept firing even as the car hit what was either a pot hole or a speed bump. Either way, Hannah's head hit the door despite her crouched position.

"Got two, maybe three," Scott said.

The Shield didn't reply and he didn't slow down. Seconds ticked by.

"I don't think they're following us." Scott rolled up the window and looked back at both her and McNamara. "Are you okay?"

Hannah could only nod, her heart beating too fast for her to speak.

Another minute passed before she could sit up and talk. "What about the others? Evan and Alek...Spritz? Highlight?"

Scott leaned against the head-rest and rubbed his neck. "I don't know. I saw one of the twins fall into the middle of the blast. I don't know which one. I was going to translocate him out, but I don't know which one to pull."

Fall into the blast? "Can you call Thomas? He must know if they're okay or not."

Scott pulled his phone from his pocket.

"Do not use my name," the Shield said. Hannah peeked between the seats. The Shield didn't even have to take his sunglass-covered eyes off the road to let everyone know there would be consequences if he wasn't obeyed. "Do not tell them you are with me. That's an order."

Scott said nothing. With his thumb he speed dialed a number, then activated the speakerphone. "T-CASS dispatch."

"This is Scott Grey. I have Hannah Quinn and Doctor Russell McNamara with me. We've evacuated from the harbor area. We're fine."

"What is your current location and where are you headed?"

In the background, Hannah could hear lots of voices. Thomas's worker bees must be fielding hundreds of calls at this point.

McNamara squeezed her hand again and said, "Harbor Regional. I can bring Hannah to my office. It's as safe a place as any. We'll have access to my computer. We can follow the news reports."

Scott repeated the information in case dispatch couldn't hear McNamara.

"Acknowledged, Scott Grey," the tinny voice replied. "I'll let Hack-Man know you've evac'd and are on your way to the hospital with no reported injuries."

"Can you give me a status update on the harbor situation?" Scott asked. "Can you tell me if Rumble and Roar made it out of there?"

A slight pause. "I have no further information to give you at this time, Scott Grey."

It could mean anything, Hannah told herself. Scott was probably telling himself the same lie. "Thank you, dispatch. Please have Hack-Man call me directly at his earliest convenience."

He disconnected the line. Hannah pulled her hand away from McNamara's to reach around the seat. Scott grabbed her hand. They held each other despite the gloves for the rest of the ride to the hospital.

CHAPTER ELEVEN

Scott didn't want to let go of Hannah, but when the Shield swerved into McNamara's spot at top speed and stomped on the brake, the Cadillac jerked forward and Hannah's hand slipped out of his. Thank heavens for reserved parking.

"Everyone out," the Shield shouted.

Scott scrambled out of his seat and ran around to Hannah's side of the car pulling the door open for her. She threw herself into his arms. Needing to hold her close again, he pulled her tighter, his cheek lying on top of her head while he rubbed her back, his gloves rough against her cotton shirt. He didn't want to waste a moment with her in his arms.

Out of the corner of his eye he could see the Shield pull McNamara out of the passenger side.

"We'll get you to the Emergency Department," Hannah said, pulling away, but keeping a hand on Scott's chest.

McNamara grimaced as he put weight on his ankle. "No. Leave the ED for the real emergencies. All I need is RICE: rest, ice, compression and elevation. I can do that in my office. We'll be safer there."

"I still have to go to the Emergency Department. They need me," Hannah said.

What? The determined look in her eye scared him more than it reassured him. He touched her shoulder, gloves on shirt. For the first time, he noticed she clutched a small box to her chest. What was in there that was so important she hadn't dropped it when she started running?

"No, they don't," Scott said, gripping her shoulders so she would have to pay attention to him. "If you get caught down there, if the Committee sees you bloodsurfing — hell, if they even suspect you of bloodsurfing, they'll have you arrested. You can't help anyone from jail."

Her face turned manic. She heard him, but she wasn't listening. "I managed to get away from Miranda. I escaped her prison. Do you think Thunder City can stop me?"

Fear. It was just her fear talking. "Yes. Why do you think we have Rocklin Prison? Why do you think no Alt has escaped from there in ten years? You think Chaos Alts like being locked up? You think you're more powerful than Rocker or Black Hole?"

"But the wounded...I could heal them. I can heal all the others too. Alek...Evan...what if they're down there?"

"They will be fine." Her face crumpled as his own stomach froze. He'd avoided thinking about what might have happened to his brother — whichever one it was — who fell into the explosion during their mad escape. When had he started to care so much? There was a time when he would have shrugged off the loss. "T-CASS had the entire boardwalk covered. Someone would have dived in to find him. Have a little faith, okay?"

He started to pull her close again, to offer comfort

and gain some comfort for himself, but McNamara pulled her away with a yank on her collar. He'd managed to hobble over while leaning on the Shield.

"Enough of that. There are security cameras all over the garage. The two of you are going to destroy whatever future you think you might have if you keep this up."

Scott stood toe-to-toe with the Doctor, ready to slug him. This was the second time in as many days the man had come between him and Hannah.

"You know I'm right," McNamara said, not intimidated in the least.

Scott glanced at the Shield, who just stood there and watched. The guy looked relaxed, as if he wanted to stay out of the squabble, but Scott knew better. If he took a swing at McNamara, the Shield would have him pinned on the ground, maybe with a bullet in his head, before Scott took his next breath. No wonder McNamara didn't back down, with the Shield at his back.

"Guys." Hannah forced McNamara's hand off her shirt. "This isn't helping anyone. Least of all Alek or Evan."

McNamara hopped back half a step. "Hannah, listen to me. If you're seen anywhere near any of the patients in his hospital, the consequences will be severe. You want people to respect you? You want people to have faith in you? Then listen to Scott. Have faith, not just in T-CASS to save the day, but in the doctors who are, as we speak, working to heal the wounded. Even if you were down there, we would still be needed."

Scott could see the change in Hannah. She listened to McNamara, even though the man praised Scott's response, she paid attention to what McNamara said over Scott. The rebellion left her eyes. She lowered her gaze to the floor and nodded. So simple. Whereas Scott had only reinforced Hannah's rebellion, McNamara had deflated it.

And that pissed him off more than anything else, because it gave him no other option than to back down.

"We can't stand here in the parking garage all afternoon," McNamara continued. "Let's get inside and figure out what to do from there."

Only then did the Shield step away to grab the rifle Scott had left in the car.

Great. Even with his hospital ID, the Shield looked like a terrorist on his good day. "You can't bring the rifle into the hospital."

"Watch me."

Fucking hell, why did everyone think he was an idiot? Why did no one ever listen to him? Scott risked another fight and grabbed the other man's arm. Maybe he had a death wish. Maybe he just wanted someone to challenge him.

"You can hide the handguns. You can't hide the rifle. Even if the hospital allowed you to use one before, if you go in there like this now, you'll trigger a lockdown. The hospital is already receiving casualties from the harbor. We don't know if the anti-Alts will try to sneak in here. This will make things worse. This will only bring more attention to McNamara and Hannah."

Maybe the Shield could see his logic, because he didn't attack. Scott had expected him to put up a fight. Instead, the Shield looked over Scott's shoulder to McNamara.

"Do as he says." McNamara sighed, but motioned toward the back of the car. "Put the rifle in the trunk."

The Shield jerked his arm away from Scott, but did as asked, his expression as unreadable as ever. They made it into the hospital without further incident.

"I have a first aid kit in my office." McNamara put his hand on Hannah's shoulder. "I think Hannah could use some quiet time. No one will look for her down there."

Scott looked at Hannah, but she looked at McNamara, not him. McNamara was right, but Scott ground his teeth in frustration anyway. She would be safer in Pathology than where he was going.

"I'll go to the Emergency Department." He reached out to touch Hannah's cheek with his gloved hand, not caring who watched. "Just in case Alek or Evan. . . ."

Saying their names snapped her back to look at him. "I could still go with you and not bloodsurf."

"No. Like the doc said, the last thing we need is for the Oversight Committee to *think* you're bloodsurfing down there. Even if you're not. Even if Thomas's security is back online and we can prove you're not. All it takes is one accusation and you're back to square one with them. Stay with McNamara for now."

She at least kissed the tips of her gloved fingers, and blew the kiss to him. His heart eased its worry. "Find me later," she said.

He nodded. He overheard the Shield tell McNamara that he was going to keep an eye on Scott. Good. Scott had a few questions he needed answered.

No sooner had they gotten Hannah and McNamara on an elevator headed down, than the Shield shoved Scott against the nearest wall.

"Why the hell didn't you grab another rifle?"

Scott pushed back against the Shield, but the man didn't move. So much for his chance to ask his own questions. "What are you talking about?"

The Shield stepped nose to nose with Scott. "You're out of bullets, your men are down, your girlfriend is helpless, and you had people to protect. Why didn't you translocate another rifle from your enemies so we both had one?"

Scott's heart sunk. "I never even thought —"

"Stop thinking like a Norm. Stop thinking about control. Stop thinking like a cop who has rules and laws that need to be obeyed. That's what T-CASS wants from you. That's what your mother wants from you. Start thinking about what you have to do to get the job done."

Before Scott could answer, the Shield spun away from the bank of elevators toward the main desk lobby. He stopped near a tall potted plant next to a couple of couches already filled with people waiting. The people stared at them. No, they stared at the Shield. Scott was just an accessory.

The Shield paused behind the plant, his voice just low enough so no one else could hear. "Do you see the receptionist?"

"Can't miss her." The poor woman tried to keep up with the phone calls and answer questions from the line of people standing in front of her. The entire hospital buzzed with controlled anticipation. This was going to be a very long day and the harried look on her face said it all.

The Shield pulled back from the plant and leaned against the nearest wall, trying to adopt a casual pose, but not quite getting it right. Scott pulled back too, shielding the Shield. The last thing they needed was more attention. "Remove her earring."

"What?"

"Remove her earring. Call it to you."

"Why?"

The Shield reached under his jacket. "Bring me the earring or I'll shoot her."

Scott panicked, certain the Shield would do it. After the day they'd already had, after all the people they had killed, Scott didn't doubt for a second that the Shield would go through with his threat.

He was reaching for the Shield, desperate to stop him from pulling out his gun and creating chaos, when something dropped from his left glove. A fishhook earring hit the floor at his feet.

"And you didn't even have line-of-sight." The Shield pulled his empty hand from his holster.

"Your point?" Scott stooped to grab the earring, missing because of his bulky gloves. So he pulled an earring out of a woman's ear. Frustrated, he yanked off the glove and picked it with his bare fingers.

"You're bored." The Shield shifted his hands behind his back. More casual, but still failing to look less dangerous. If he would just take off the damn sunglasses, he might be able to pull off normal. "T-CASS hates you, and you hate them. You hate that they're not taking you seriously. You hate that you have to prove yourself all over again. You hate that you've become what you've hated. When Highlight tells you to pull one of those damned beanbags, you'd rather be anywhere else than where you are. That makes you sloppy and you miss."

How the fuck did he know about Highlight? How could he better understand Scott's emotions than even Scott himself? This guy had him targeted long before he showed up in the Arena. Not to mention there was a big difference between an earring, a beanbag, and a gun.

"So, what? You're saying I can't get the job done unless someone's life is threatened?"

"I'm saying you need motivation and respect. Without both, there's no point in staying with T-CASS. You might as well leave town because you're not going to be able to satisfy their desire to control you."

"They don't want to control me. They want me to control my ability so people don't get hurt."

"People get hurt regardless. You have control. You need to loosen your control to let your ability work for you, not for anyone else. Just you."

Scott didn't respond. Everything the Shield said was the exact opposite of what T-CASS was trying to teach him. "So what do I do?"

The Shield motioned toward the earring. "Put it back."

Was he crazy? "How. I mean, it's so small."

"So was the bullet you put in Dane's forehead. Small, fast, and dead center. This is no different."

Scott choked at the casual reference to his killing Miranda. Yet, Scott had to wonder why he reacted more viscerally to killing Dane than he had to the people he'd killed less than half an hour ago.

"Do it." The Shield reached for this gun again.

Scott turned toward the desk. This time he would use line-of-sight. He focused on the receptionist.

"I can't see that far. I don't even know which ear to aim for. What if I miss and put it in her nose?"

"It could only improve her looks."

No help, and no more excuses. The Shield's hand was still on his holster. Would he really do it? Would he really shoot the receptionist? Scott hadn't seen him miss a target in the parking lot, even with one hand on the steering wheel and aiming out of the car window.

Not sure what else to do, Scott pictured the earring, then the receptionist. He imagined an empty hole in the ear that wasn't pressed against the phone's handset.

The earring disappeared. The receptionist didn't flinch.

"Did it work?" the Shield asked.

"How should I know? I can't see that far."

The Shield let loose a long suffering sigh. "Go find out."

Scott mimicked the Shield's sigh, but headed for the desk. He bypassed the long line of people and pretended to search the desktop. The receptionist put down the handset to the phone. "Sir, I have to ask you to wait in line."

Two earrings, one in each ear. He'd done it.

"Sorry. I was just looking for a spare pen."

She shoved one at him.

"Thank you."

He walked back to the plant. "I did it."

"Good job."

It was a good job. Those two simple words from a man who thought nothing about taking a life made him feel so damn good about himself. For the first time since he'd pulled the comb off his dresser at Hannah's insistence, he'd used his power twice in a row. He was in control — or was he?

"You're not always going to be here to threaten murder and mayhem to make my ability work." Scott didn't know what else to say. The whole situation was crazy. Who was this guy who threatened the lives of people so easily, and yet made Scott feel as if he had hope?

"You don't know that. Now you can go to the ED and make sure your brothers are still alive."

The shaking stopped when Hannah remembered the package in her hand. Her arm ached from clutching the cardboard box for so long. McNamara limped over to his chair and sat down with a sigh.

"This was not what I had in mind for your first day on the job."

She didn't reply. All her fear blocked the anger grinding away at her heart. She had no voice. With Scott, she had tried to show her love, but the second he left all she had was her fear and her rage. Both needed an outlet, but here in McNamara's office — the VIP level — wasn't the place. She didn't know where that place was. Nothing about Thunder City gave her the comfort she needed.

Only Scott could give her what she needed and he seemed really chummy with the Shield. The way they worked together during the attack appeared to her as if they'd trained together for years. Or, maybe that was just Scott's police training and not anything special. She didn't know. She didn't know a lot of things about Scott. Things she wanted to know. She needed more alone time with him.

McNamara motioned toward the package she kept close to her heart while he hobbled around to his chair. "Care to tell me what that is?"

"Roger Dane's ashes."

He looked surprised. She couldn't blame him. No one talked about her most recent stepfather. Everyone wanted to talk about Miranda, but not about Roger. It was as if he didn't exist, and yet, if it weren't for him, Miranda would still be alive, and Hannah would be trapped inside her lab of horrors doing Miranda's bidding. The sad part was, that Hannah wouldn't have thought of herself as a prisoner. She would still be calling Miranda "mom."

"I'm so sorry, Hannah." McNamara sat down in his chair with a groan.

Hannah sighed, put the box on McNamara's desk, and slipped off her gloves. "I won't say anything if you won't."

McNamara didn't object as she rounded the desk.

She should have knelt down and placed her hand on the ankle itself, but the idea of kneeling in front of McNamara...the image alone sent a flash of foreboding through her consciousness.

Her stomach heaved, so she ran from the image before she became sick. He remained still as she placed her hand on the side of his cheek.

Inside. She had to travel from one of the interosseous veins to the subclavian vein and into the heart. Without stopping, she transferred into the thoracic aorta, rode down until she found the femoral artery. She had no idea what part of his ankle was injured, so she guessed and transferred into the anterior tibial artery for the last leg of her journey. Any other day she'd grin at her own pun, but it barely registered as she stopped at the calcaneo figural ligament.

The ligament had quite a large tear. McNamara must have turned his ankle while tackling her after the bomb exploded. Either way, healing the ligament would require a lot of stitching. For her it felt like half an hour, but if she guessed it only took half a minute on the outside. She repaired a few smaller tears in the other ligaments, then inspected the talus and calcaneus. Both looked fine. It took a little more work to disperse the histamine in the nearby capillaries so they would stop dilating and leaking plasma. She decided to leave the phagocytes alone to munch on the dead cells. Once she had absorbed the extra plasma, the swelling disappeared and she was done.

The reverse journey back to her body seemed to take less time than getting to the injury itself. A moment later she stepped away from McNamara.

"You are extraordinary." The reverence in his voice might have made her blush yesterday. Today, she didn't want to be extraordinary. She just wanted to be free.

"You're going to be busy regardless if any of the cadavers survived the attack intact," she said. "Thunder City is going to want to investigate. Star Haven will want an explanation too. Either way, you'll be on your feet a lot. It'll be easier to manage the investigators on two feet instead of one."

McNamara must have realized he was staring at her because he shifted his chair to face his computer, waking up the screen so he could type. "I applaud your attitude. You will make a fine doctor someday, Hannah. I'm very proud to be your mentor."

Such simple words, yet they cut her inner pain in half. If only everyone talked to her the way McNamara did. "I wish I could feel some pride. Right now — "

"Right now, what?" His fingers paused on the keyboard. She had his full attention again. Her despair receded even further.

"Right now, I'll settle for comfort. I'd prefer love, satisfaction, and happiness, but comfort will suffice."

His eyes narrowed, his look knowing, as if he read her mind. "You're thinking of Scott."

Was she? She guessed she was because until she met McNamara, Scott was the only person who made her feel special and not in the *oh, your powers are so cool show us how they work* sort of way. "Why wouldn't I? I love him. He gives me the comfort that I need." Yet, thoughts about their tiff yesterday threatened to destroy the hope she'd clung to whenever she thought of Scott. "Most of the time," she added before she could stop herself.

"Most of the time," McNamara repeated. When he leaned toward her now, she doubted he even noticed his ankle had stopped hurting. "Hannah, you have such potential. Your Alt ability — I don't think you realize just how much we can learn from you."

"What do you mean?" she asked — not that she didn't already suspect the answer, but deep down she hoped for an answer less about her ability and more about her as a person. She should get used to it. One thing she'd begun to notice about Thunder City was that even though Alts were welcome, that welcome came with a price. At first, she'd thought all of the Committee's rules about proving you had control over your power were practical, but Hannah had to wonder if for the Norms it had a second benefit: It forced Alts to prove their usefulness before they were allowed to stay.

For a moment, Hannah wondered what would happen to an Alt whose power proved to not be useful. Did any such Alts exist? If so, what had happened to them?

"Healing is just the tip of the iceberg," McNamara said, interrupting her inner philosopher. "Your Alt ability could revolutionize medicine as we know it. Can you imagine the research into new therapies and medicines you could jump start just by showing us how you do what you do?"

She could see how excited McNamara got as he

talked. His eyes, at one time soft and sympathetic, became larger and brighter as he let loose his zeal.

All she could do was shrug. "Everyone wants a piece of me. I can guess what the Oversight Committee has been saying. It's why they want to keep me isolated. It's like they want to keep me for themselves. I won't let that happen. After everything I've been through, after everything Miranda did to me — "

She paused, her gaze going to the box on his desk.

"After everything she did to me, I finally have had a glimpse of what a normal life would be like. With Scott." If she said it with enough strength, maybe the ugly doubts nagging her would disappear.

"You mean with someone you love. That person might not be Scott."

Why did she suddenly feel so cold? "Why do you say that? Everyone knows about me and Scott. Even Ms. Chung knew that we love each other."

McNamara sighed. "Betty Chung repeated what the news rags advertised. Everyone enjoys a romantic story. But, Hannah, you need to understand. Very few high school romances last through college. Even fewer survive med school. I don't think you quite understand what you and Scott are up against."

Hannah sat back down in her seat, but couldn't stop the small sneer of disbelief. "After the past two weeks, I think we have a pretty good idea. I ran from the Committee for a reason. I won't let anyone try to lock me up again."

"No." McNamara shook his head. "What you've experienced is life or death situations. Your emotions are running high; you've spent your life in the midst of an acute stress response. That's why you ran instead of relying on the law to defend you. You didn't trust

Thunder City to do right by you. Thunder City is much bigger and far more complex than just the Oversight Committee. You still see the world in black and white."

Her rage broke loose, damn the consequences. "If I had waited for Thunder City to defend me, I'd be locked up in the hospital room with a guard at the door. Acute stress response or not, they have no right to do that to me. I've made enough concessions to the Committee."

McNamara waited for her to finish. Damn his patience anyway. She had a lot more she wanted to say, but all her words got tangled up in her throat. McNamara saved her the trouble.

"The Committee knows this. You don't know how to act any other way. Even if Star Haven can tame the anti-Alt organizations, even if another terrorist incident never happens, the pressure you'll be under to perform will be enormous. Not special, not different, maybe even normal for any other doctor. For you, it could very well overwhelm and crush whatever dream you have of living a normal life with Scott."

The tears started before she could stop them. "Isn't that that the point of Thunder City? Isn't that what Catherine has worked so hard to achieve here? Normalcy for alternative humans."

McNamara's eyes hardened as they locked with hers. "You've never experienced normal. You saw Scott and the Shield this afternoon. That is not a typical day for them. You don't know what Scott would be like on a random Wednesday. He craves action, he needs an adrenaline high. He's not all that different from the Shield. His needs might not...will not support yours. Not if you're going to study medicine. Not if you're going to endure the crushing hours, constant phone calls, endless rounds of paperwork and committee meetings. There's more to being a doctor than healing people. Just like there's more to being a police officer than shooting people and Scott isn't even a police officer anymore.

"You talk about Thunder City trying to isolate you. Yet, from everything you've told me, you're bound and determined to isolate yourself. By refusing to entertain the possibility of love from someone other than Scott Grey, by clinging to the first man who says he loves you, by mistaking gratitude for saving your life for the deep and abiding love you deserve — Hannah, you're going to become exactly what Miranda wanted you to be: a slave to someone else's needs."

The cold shattered into shards. "Miranda didn't need me. The — " She stopped. No one else knew about the Court of Blood except the Blackwoods and Thomas's elite team of analysts. Even with McNamara she couldn't break the trust Catherine expected of her, to keep the information to herself. "Miranda was a slave to her own ambition. She wanted to control Star Haven. She thought she could use me to make Star Haven dependent on her. If she could control the health of the city, she could control the city. People would worship her just to get access to me."

"Is what Miranda wanted so different from Scott?" McNamara relaxed back into his chair. "He has no control over his own life, but he sees you moving forward with your own. You stood up to the Oversight Committee when they crossed the line. Scott could only follow in your footsteps. You have a job, you have ambition, you're building a life separate from the Blackwoods. Scott hasn't accomplished half of what you have in the past two weeks. Don't let him drag you back down to his level. Don't let him limit your possibilities."

Hannah sat, stunned. Scott had risked everything for her, yet he'd been cut down by a doctor she'd only known for less than a week? She opened her mouth to argue.

Nothing came out. Not a sound. The whole day became far too much for her.

"I need to be alone." She snatched up the box containing Roger's ashes and held it close again. Her throat tightened and the tears blurred her vision.

McNamara, thank God, didn't fight her. "I'll close the door. If you need me, I'll be meeting with my staff upstairs."

She didn't hear the door click behind him.

CHAPTER TWELVE

The Shield disappeared before Scott reached the Emergency Department. How the hell did he do that? One moment he was there keeping pace with Scott, and the next he was gone.

Maybe it was one of the lessons he wanted Scott to learn. Scott couldn't focus on that right now. He wanted to find out which one of his brothers had fallen into the fire. He kept his phone clutched in one hand as he entered the Emergency Department through the internal doors leading to the first floor ward. Thomas hadn't tried to call him back. The fact that his father hadn't called didn't bode well for the status of T-CASS.

A nurse rushed past him as a new patient arrived. Scott could see the man's clothing, dress slacks and an oxford shirt covered in blood. Not one of his brothers. Scott made his way to the curved desk manned by two nurses in blue scrubs tracking the action.

"I'm looking for either Alek or Evan Blackwood. Rumble or Roar," he clarified.

One of the nurses pulled a handset away from her ear. She looked at him, probably recognized him from the news as a Blackwood. Who said fame didn't have its privileges?

"They haven't come through here, yet," she said

before returning to her phone call.

Scott backed off to the side, trying to stay as far out of the way as possible. Fifteen minutes and six ambulances later, EMTs charged through the doors with a man dressed in a skintight black uniform.

Scott rushed over. Even with black ash smudged all over his pained face, Scott knew it was Alek.

"Sir, please stand back." One of the EMTs pushed Scott out of the way.

"He's my brother — "

Before he could say anything further, the EMTs raced the gurney toward the first empty room available. Scott knew better than to follow. He pulled out his cell phone to text Hannah.

Alek in ED. Alive, but hurt.

How hurt?

Scott thought back to what he saw.

Brace on his leg. Maybe broken.
Lots of soot, but didn't see blood.

I could fix him in seconds.

I know. So does he. Not now. Not yet.

Was he the one who fell into the fire?

I don't know.
Thomas hasn't contacted me yet.

I'll stay here with Doc M.
Maybe once he's in a cast,

they'll let me visit him.

McNamara again. Why did that guy always seem to be in the right when Scott needed him to be in the wrong?

I'm going to try and talk to Alek if they'll let me.

Stay with Alek. Visit me when you can.

She sent him a crying puppy emoji.

Scott stood outside of the exam room. He could sense, more than hear, the commotion inside. Another fifteen minutes passed, then twenty. More ambulances arrived. More commotion, as off-duty doctors showed up to cover their already overwhelmed colleagues. Shouting drowned out the controlled chaos.

The door to Alek's room remained closed. Scott resisted the temptation to call Thomas. He tried not think of what might have happened to Evan. Another two minutes, then he hear the howl.

"GET OUT."

Something loud and metallic hit the door. Scott shoved off the wall he'd been leaning on. Screw the rules.

Before he could force his way into the exam room, the nurses pushed their way out, followed by the doctor. One of them ran right into Scott.

"What happened?" He stopped one of the nurses.

"He was in shock. Not communicating. Then...the equipment just went flying."

"He's using his Alt ability to drive us out." The doctor wiped something off her scrubs before she straightened out to talk to Scott. "We need to get security."

"No security. Not yet."

Another loud crash thudded against the doors. Alek must have been tearing the room apart.

"I'll take care of him." Scott moved around the nurse but found himself blocked by the doctor.

"He's in distress. He called out to his brother. If something happened to his brother, he might not respond to you. He could hurt you. We don't want to hurt him, but even with Alt powers, security has ways to immobilize him so we can finish. If his brother is dead, you might not be able to get through to him."

Scott could see the doctor was an ally, someone who respected Alts. Maybe she just didn't recognize him. "He's my brother, too. I'll get through to him."

Scott pushed past the doctor. The exam room was a mess. Equipment was scattered all over the floor. Alek lay heaving on the gurney, his leg immobilized, but little else holding him back.

"Alek?"

A bedpan flew off a counter, right at Scott's head. Scott batted it away. Alek wasn't looking to hurt him, just to drive him away. Drive everyone who wasn't Evan away. He hadn't talked to Alek man-to-man in almost a decade. His heart leapt in to his throat. What could he say now to calm the brother who had never apologized for almost killing him?

"Enough, Alek. The doctors are ready to call in security. Do you really want them to hit you with a sedation dart?"

"Won't let them."

Nothing else came flying at his head, so Scott stepped closer. Despite his broken leg, and what must have been a shit load of pain, Alek had managed to twist his body so his face was buried in the poor excuse of a sheet.

Scott dug deep into the memories he'd tried to forget. "Sort of like how Patty Elwin shoved your face in the dirt when you tugged her hair. Yeah, your big, bad Alt powers really helped you there. Some Norm girl got you all messed up in no time flat."

Still nothing happened. Scott moved closer.

"She was my girlfriend," Alek whispered.

"Fifth-graders don't have girlfriends."

"Evan and I did." Alek let go of the sheet and lay back flat again. His face blank, no trace of pain or guilt. "He was dating Chrissy Olsen. We would carry their books for them, get them food from the lunch counter. They let us hold their hands. Evan and I did everything together. Patty didn't like it when I offered to carry Sonya's books too, even if I just floated them over to her. She shoved me first."

"Patty didn't know how good she had it." Scott risked standing right next to the bed. Alek wouldn't look at him.

"What are you doing here?" Alek finally asked.

"Staying out of trouble. Why did you attack the doctors?"

"They were pissing me off."

"Your leg is broken. They were doing their job."

Alek said nothing.

"Did something happen out there?"

"Evan fell into the fire." Scott had to bend closer to his brother's lips to hear the quiet voice. "He's gone."

No. Scott pulled away. Denial wrapped around his already wounded heart. "You don't know for sure."

"Our air cushion held the container from below. It was balanced and ready to transport to the warehouse. The explosion bounced it off the cushion. It hit my leg. I couldn't focus fast enough. Evan had to double up the air cushion, but the debris from the ship hit him too. He fell. I grabbed the container before it hit the harbor. I couldn't focus...couldn't rebalance the container fast enough...I couldn't grab Evan. He fell and kept falling into the fire." Alek lifted his head and slammed it back down. "I chose to save the coffin of a dead man over my brother."

"You saved the delegates who had run under the container."

"Fuck the Star Haven delegates. Bastards. Should have let them die. Should have saved Evan."

"You don't know that he's dead. You somehow got here to the hospital. You couldn't have seen everything."

Alek's face twisted. "Why the *hell* do you care?"

Scott winced. He'd been expecting an attack, but it still hurt when it hit. "Evan and I have been working on our relationship. Just like Catherine and me. We're not close, not even remotely as close as you and Evan. Or even you and Nik. But I care, Alek. Don't ever doubt that I care."

"It's all a lie, you know."

"What's a lie?"

"That we have a special telepathic connection. Me and Evan. Because we're twins. If I hadn't seen him fall into the blast, I'd never know if he were dead or not."

"You still don't know." Scott said it more to convince himself than to comfort Alek. For reasons he'd never understand, he grabbed Alek's smudged hand with his gloved one. "Until you see a *fucking* body, you don't *fucking* know."

His luck still held. Alek didn't pull away. That's when Scott realized what had been tickling his nose: A scent, sweet, like sugar cookies and ice cream, soft and cool and calming.

Cory. It's Pathia.

Pathia. T-CASS's telepath. Her telepathy had briefly touched him right before Miranda had ordered her mercs to knock him out. She had touched him again before they started torturing him.

I can't reach Alek. He's too angry. He can't hear me. He won't hear me. Tell him Evan is alive.

"Alek, listen to me."

"Fuck you! Why are you even here? You ignored us for a decade."

"Evan is alive."

Alek's glare didn't soften, but turned suspicious, tinged with hope. "How do you know?"

"Pathia. She can't contact you because you're crazy."

He's alive, but in trouble. He's still in the middle of the inferno, but wounded.

"He's still in the middle of the inferno," Scott said.

"Where's Flame?" Alek demanded.

Scott didn't know the T-CASS member so he thought the name. *Flame?*

Her orders are to rescue the ship's crew. There are groups of them trapped throughout the ship. T-CASS is divided into either rescuing the crew, rescuing those who fell into the Bay, or stopping the gunmen.

Scott repeated what Pathia told him.

"Where's Mom?" Alek asked.

Scott imagined an image of his mother.

She's under the ship, keeping it from sinking and drowning those still trapped.

Scott again told Alek what Pathia had said.

"Hang on." Alek started to push himself up, but stopped as pain overwhelmed him. Scott forced his brother to lie back down again with a firm hand on his shoulder. "I know what Evan is doing. He's lowering the oxygen levels to dowse the fire around him. If he lowers the oxygen level by at least seven percent by pushing the oxygen molecules away, that will stop the fire from spreading toward him and still give him enough air to breath. You have to pull him out before he exhausts himself from the lack of oxygen. Look for where there's a gap in the fire and direct the water toward the gap."

Scott couldn't come up with an understandable image of what Alek suspected Evan was doing, so he repeated his brother's words in his head. Pathia must have understood because the sweet scent disappeared while she relayed the message, probably to Thomas. It took a minute, but her voice and the scent returned.

We have two fire boats already on the scene. Spritz and Gilly are directing the water from the pumps. We're concerned that in his weakened state, more water could startle Evan. He could lose what little air he's using to keep himself conscious. We risk drowning him or burning him.

He relayed that information to Alek, too.

"No. Do it. Listen to me. Evan will be in the middle of the gap. If Gilly and Spritz can direct the water around the gap while Evan pushes away oxygen molecules, any water near him will split into hydrogen and oxygen before he can drown."

"But won't the hydrogen and oxygen molecules make the fire worse?" Scott asked.

"Hydrogen is lighter than oxygen. It will rise. As long as Evan keeps pushing the oxygen away and he's cleared his immediate area of flames, he'll be fine."

"But if he's not pushing away oxygen molecules at all, and doing something else instead, he could still burn in a second or two." Scott realized Alek was betting on

Hannah healing Evan. "Alek —"

"Tell her, damn you."

Scott again had to use words to describe Alek's plan to Pathia.

I'll let them know.

The scent of sugar cookies disappeared again. "Pathia is passing along the message."

Alek must have realized his hand was holding Scott's and released him. "It'll work. Once the gap around Evan is big enough, someone will fly in and pull him out."

Scott fished out his phone. "Anything else they should know?" He could text Thomas, at least, and hope Thomas read the message.

Alek shook his head. They waited. If T-CASS was still busy rescuing people on land and stopping the gunmen, they wouldn't contact either Scott or Alek until the situation was handled.

"You don't have to stay." Alek was back to staring at the ceiling. "I'm in control now."

"I've got nowhere else to be. Everyone's at the harbor except Hannah. She's with her new mentor." He tried to add a low chuckle, but even tone-deaf Alek could hear his cynicism.

"It won't take long." Alek glanced at him. "Hannah's tough. She'll prove her control next time around. Mom won't let her fail again."

"She didn't fail this time. That Chung woman screwed her up." This was the most Alek had said to Scott since he'd returned home. His relationship with Evan had improved because they had one thing in common: Hannah. Scott cared about her, but Evan had sworn to protect her. Alek hadn't made the same oath, but he'd follow his brother's lead.

"Chung's nuts. She'd been pestering Mom since before you brought Hannah here from Star Haven."

"About what?"

Alek shrugged. "Claimed the doctors messed up her kid during surgery. Says her son isn't her son anymore. He's someone else. No one listens to her."

"Maybe if someone listened to her, she wouldn't have attacked Hannah."

Alek didn't sneer at his brother's bitterness. "You have to admit, though. It does sound crazy."

It did sound crazy, but Hannah had said she'd found something. If she could talk to McNamara about it, maybe she could find a plausible reason for Chung's behavior. For her son's behavior.

"Maybe." Scott pulled over a chair so he could sit by his brother's bed, but he swallowed a groan as he lowered himself into the plastic seat. Everything ached all of a sudden. "Hannah's a big disrupter in the Alt community. No one can do what she does. Everyone wants a piece of her. Even you."

Damn it. Wrong thing to say. Alek tensed, his old anger making his eyes squint against the fluorescent lights.

"I'm not expecting her to heal me."

"No, but you're expecting her to heal Evan." Scott pulled his chair closer to the bed, his accusations sounding harsh, but he knew exactly what Alek was thinking. "If this scheme works, he's still going to be hospitalized. He could be burned, or oxygen deprived, or worse. Don't tell me you didn't imagine Hannah healing him. And you."

"Yeah, okay, the thought did cross my mind." Alek kept staring at the ceiling, not meeting Scott's eyes. Scott didn't need to see his brother's eyes to understand how much pain he was in. "She's an asset. She belongs with T-CASS."

"She's a person with her own goals. She won't let herself be used. Not by T-CASS. Not by Thunder City."

"We're not trying to use her," Alek insisted, his fists clutching the sheets.

"You're all trying to use her the way Catherine uses all of you. Don't tell me Catherine doesn't use you and Evan as publicity. How many flyovers have you two done for no other reason than Catherine wanting to remind Thunder City of how important Alts are? How powerful we are. How much they depend on us for their security."

He'd hit a nerve. Alek was the quieter of the two twins. The more private one. Even as a kid, Scott had known not to bother Alek when he didn't want to be bothered.

"You said *we*." Alek gave him a sly look.

Scott winced again. Leave it to Alek to use Scott's own words against him. He had say *we*, hadn't he? Had he reached that turning point? Did he now consider himself one of the Thunder City Alts? A member of T-CASS even if it wasn't official yet? The Shield thought otherwise, said he could teach Scott what T-CASS couldn't. Wouldn't. Scott thought about Highlight and the beanbags. He thought about this afternoon, shooting terrorists in tandem with the Shield.

"Yeah, well. We'll see. Maybe."

Alek returned to staring at the ceiling. Evan was still in danger. Neither of them would leave the other until they knew for sure.

Hannah watched the news streaming on McNamara's

computer. Numbness had taken over her limbs, so she melted into the leather executive chair and let the rapidly shifting scenes across the screen lull her into a state of mindless ease. So mindless that even when she heard the odd sound of dogs barking or the wind rushing through the walls, she didn't react.

She still clutched the box containing Roger's ashes.

The scene shifted to the hospital. Harbor Regional earned its name because of its proximity to the harbor. Ambulances lined up outside carrying the wounded, most of them from Star Haven. The Star Haven delegates had been closest to the ship when the first gunshot had been fired. They had been the ones to run toward the ship, not away from it, their fear of Alts making the horrible decision for them. Now, they were entering a hospital that had a clinic dedicated to Alt medicine attached to it. The Star Haven victims wouldn't appreciate the irony.

McNamara appeared in the doorway without warning.

"Will you be okay for a little while longer?"

Hannah could only nod, her vocal cords too tight to speak.

"I may have to head to the ED," he explained. "Everyone's being called in from all departments. We're trying to shuffle the non-emergencies to other hospitals. Air ambulances are being diverted.

"Star Haven is already demanding my head because I arranged this whole debacle. I'll have to make a statement at some point, but I will come back to bring you home."

Hannah nodded again, still not ready to speak. The scene changed again on the computer screen to the activity outside the hospital. All she could do was watch. McNamara disappeared, leaving the door still open.

Between the open door and the news, Hannah imagined she could feel the frenetic energy running through the hospital. Everyone had a job to do. Everyone knew where they had to go and what to do. Everyone except her. She had nowhere to go and nothing to do.

A tremor shook her body, her own pent up energy loosening its power. The box shook in her hands. She had to do something, so she opened the box. Inside was a simple brass urn.

Roger. Her stepfather. The man who had sacrificed himself to make sure she survived. The man who had warned her to run so she could escape Miranda's clutches. What had he figured out right before he died? Had he learned of Miranda's secret prison? Had he known that she murdered all of her previous husbands? Had he suspected he was next?

Maybe he had, but not that it would happen quite so soon. Hannah had heard the glass break from the gunshot through the phone.

Roger had never stopped fighting for her. Even before he discovered whatever it was that had tipped him off to Miranda's true nature, he'd fought for her. He maneuvered his life in such a way that he shielded her from the bulk of Miranda's abuse.

He kept trying to save her, when he didn't have to. He put himself in harm's way and didn't care about the consequences to himself.

Hannah looked back at the computer screen as the first air ambulance arrived. Scott was up there, trying to find his brothers. The newscasters didn't have any information on Rumble or Roar, just that one of them had fallen into the fire and the other looked as if he had a broken leg.

Hannah brushed her fingers over the smooth surface of the urn. No engraving or anything. Star Haven hadn't cared about Roger Dane after he died. Miranda no doubt had stolen all of his money to support her prison operation. Did the Court of Blood take control of her accounts?

Determination stopped the wobble in her legs, the involuntary shudder of indecision. Damn them all. She couldn't sit here when she could do something. If Roger could sacrifice everything for her, then she could sacrifice her right to remain in Thunder City. She could save people, even if no one else thought she should.

No one was in the hallway, so she figured the voices she heard were through the vents from the floor up above. She used her card to bring the elevator down to the VIP level and take her one floor up.

McNamara had a cluster of young women and men around him near a row of offices. Hannah marched right up to him, the urn still in its box, and didn't wait for him to give her permission to speak.

"I'm going to the Emergency Department. I'm going to use my ability to save the victims of this attack." She made certain to look McNamara in the eyes before she turned to look at each and every one of McNamara's staff as she continued. "Anyone who has a problem with that can lodge their complaint with the Oversight Committee tomorrow. I'm done waiting for them."

She turned and marched back into the elevator. In the background she heard McNamara say something to the others before he joined her just before the doors slid closed.

"Are you sure you want to do this?" he asked.

"Yes." Hannah punched the number for the floor she wanted.

"They won't let you leave, you know? The law is very clear and very specific. It's not like before, when you ran away before you committed yourself to training. You're making the deliberate choice to break the law after you'd been warned. They *will* put you in jail."

The elevator headed up one more floor. She didn't shake in fear for the entire ride. "They'll try. If you want to return to your office, I'll understand."

McNamara laughed. "Oh, no. I'm not missing this for the world. Watching you use your ability is a privilege Hannah. Too bad the rest of the Committee can't see it that way."

The elevator doors opened, and Hannah turned toward the swinging doors leading into the Emergency Department. Inside, the noise slapped her with urgent need. Doctors, nurses, orderlies, all milled about in the controlled chaos. She looked around for Scott, but didn't see him. She didn't see anyone she knew.

"I'll need you to triage for me," she told McNamara. "The worst first. And if you can get me a bottle of water, I'd appreciate it."

McNamara kept his hand on her shoulder. "Fine, but let *me* do the talking."

Hannah was okay with that. Despite the talking she had already done, her throat still felt tight with the sick feeling of loss. She had lost Roger. She'd lost any sense of security she had in Star Haven. Now she was going to lose Thunder City. So be it. She was done being dictated to by people who did not understand her. She laid Roger's box with the urn in the corner behind her.

McNamara had a way with words. She could hear him speak, using a combination of subterfuge and lies of omission to negotiate her first patient into the back corner of the ED she had staked out for herself. Most of the Committee was comprised of various specialists who didn't work in the emergency department, which made things a lot easier. In less than a minute, she had her first patient.

Lots of shrapnel embedded in the skin. First, push the shrapnel out, stitch closed the cuts. Now stitch up the bones, clean up the leaking blood, and keep the heart pumping and the blood flowing. Then rebuild the skin of the third degree burns, refill the oil glands, realign the collagen fibers to prevent scarring. Patient one done.

She reemerged. Folks had taken notice of her by now. McNamara handed her a bottle of water, keeping hospital security at bay.

"Let her do her job," he said. "She knows what she's doing. Let the second patient through."

The guards looked undecided.

"Let's do this," she forced herself to shout before gulping down half the bottle. *Just keep them coming. Don't stop to think of what you're going to lose.*

The first patient pushed himself off the gurney. He looked at her, then down at himself. He must have been from Thunder City because be turned to the crowd. "Let the Blood Surfer heal!"

Someone else from deep in the crowd echoed the words, followed by a third. Maybe the guards realized they were on the verge of a riot because one of them motioned the others to back away.

"One at a time." McNamara directed a second gurney in front of her. "Worst cases first. Do not crowd her. Do not touch her. Do not wait for her if you need immediate attention, let the other doctors help you — "

She didn't wait to hear what he had to say about other doctors. Her second patient was rolled in front of her.

She's pregnant. Four, maybe five months. Did she know that before she went to the harbor? I've never worked on a pregnant person before. All right. I can't save the baby if I don't save the mother first. Heart, lungs, brain, then baby. After the baby, then back to handle the bones. One last check. All systems normal.

Hannah emerged. "Done. Who's next?"

McNamara had moved to the middle of the crowd, directing traffic. Another gurney rolled in front of her. Other patients streamed past her into the exam rooms. Nice, neat, and in the order McNamara demanded of them. If anyone had protested, she didn't see the evidence. Another water bottle was pushed into her hands. She drank without thinking. In the background, phones rang while equipment beeped and sirens screeched.

Back inside. Third degree burns. Easy enough to fix, but also diabetes, type one. She could handle that too while she was in here. It wouldn't take too long to fix, but it the future she'd have to establish her own protocol. Fix it all, or stop and move on so she could save someone else who might be in danger of dying. She'd figure it out another time.

She emerged again and demanded another patient. Then another, then another. A polite crowd stood across the room, held back by security. Cameras flashed. She was being recorded. Whatever, as long as no one interfered.

She worked on three more patients before Scott

stood before her, his brother stretched out on the gurney he pushed. She stopped just to look at Scott.

"We waited until the emergencies were done," he said. He didn't sound angry, even though he knew what she had done. What McNamara had helped her do. Maybe he thought McNamara should have talked her out of it. Maybe he didn't. Whatever he thought, he kept it to himself. She had a job to do. She looked down at her newest patient.

"Hey, Alek. Looks like you're all banged up."

The smudged face turned toward her. The doctors must have pumped him full of painkillers because his hazel eyes looked glassy and lethargic.

"Hey, Hannah. Evan is alive. They're going to get him out."

A relief she didn't know she'd been waiting for loosened the last few remnants of shock holding her back. She touched his cheek, but didn't surf. "Oh, Alek. I'm so glad."

"Yeah."

"I'll heal him, too. I promise. No matter what."

He nodded, his eyes already closing. "I know you will."

She looked up at Scott. He reached over his brother to caress her face. She didn't even mind the glove, but leaned into the cool fabric. How long had she been at this? Scott had said he'd waited for the emergencies to go first. Which could only mean the crisis had passed. At least as far as this hospital was concerned. For her, the crisis was just starting.

In the background, the cameras still rolled, people still witnessed her touch Alek. Witnessed Scott touching her. Were any of them from Star Haven? Had she only poured more fuel on a smoking fire?

She pulled her face away from Scott's touch. Somehow blood had smeared her fingers and her clothes. When had she gotten this sloppy? It didn't matter. What mattered was making a difference. What mattered was that people would live. She couldn't guarantee a happy life, but she could guarantee they would live.

She touched Alek's cheek again and surfed. His broken leg was fixed in less time than it took her to sneeze. His uniform had kept the worst of the shrapnel and flames at bay, but he still had some minor damage, which she repaired in no time.

When she emerged again, the guards were back. Surrounding her. Doctor Johnson stood to the side.

"Arrest her."

Scott turned on the guards. "Don't you even think about it."

The guards hesitated. Maybe it was the look in Scott's eye or maybe it was just the rumors they'd heard about his own wild power.

"You have no authority here." Johnson pushed his way past the guard to challenge Scott. "I can have you arrested, too."

Scott opened his mouth, but once again McNamara intervened. "Gentleman, this is not the time or the place."

"You are not on the Oversight Committee." Johnson pointed a finger at McNamara. "You have no authority here, either."

"I have sufficient authority." McNamara stepped closer to Johnson, using his height to intimidate, though it didn't appear to have any effect. "Hannah works for me. I filed the paperwork yesterday. I gave her permission to be here. I escorted her here myself."

Johnson stepped back. "What do you mean by this?

Do you have any idea of the danger in which you've placed us? How many laws she's broken? I'll have you arrested, too."

"Yes, yes, fine. Have us all arrested. Make a spectacle of yourself." McNamara waved to the all-seeing media. "Let's put on a fine show for Star Haven about how Thunder City treats its Alts. Let's show them how small, and mean, and uncompromising we are in the face of — "

"Hey, assholes."

Hannah looked to Scott, but he appeared as surprised as she did at the profanity. He wasn't the one who'd spoken. Alek sat up, rubbing the back of his head.

"Could you take this somewhere else? You're giving me a headache."

"You think this is funny?" Johnson turned his ire on Alek. This time both Scott and Hannah stepped back as Alek slid off the gurney. Scott knew his brother better than Hannah. Hannah had seen Alek's sometimes funny, sometimes gentle, sometimes awkward side whenever he was around her, but she also knew he had a temper and held grudges. Scott knew that better than she did.

"I think you're forgetting this hospital is full of patients who need help. You want to arrest people. Go get a warrant. I'm taking Hannah home."

Alek held his hand out to her. Hannah scooped up Roger's urn, then walked around the gurney and let Alek hold her ungloved hand. She didn't bloodsurf. She had witnesses. Then Alek motioned for Scott to join them. Scott stepped closer to his brother, the three of them facing down Johnson. From her peripheral vision, she could see a change in McNamara's face. This, he wasn't happy about, but it was too late to change her mind.

"If you want to arrest me too," Alek continued, pushing his way past both doctors, pulling her and Scott with him. "You know where I live."

Hannah looked around Alek to Scott, but he didn't try to stop his brother. Hannah's heart squeezed. She followed Alek as he worked his way through the knot of guards toward the exit. The cameras followed them. Once outside, Alek held both of them close by the waist before he launched them into the sky.

CHAPTER THIRTEEN

Scott stood in his usual place, leaning back on the parlor doors, except this time both doors were wide open to keep Hannah from panicking. To his left, Hannah's translucent self sat on an ottoman while she healed Evan, who lay on the sofa.

Evan had done exactly what Alek said he would — he lowered the oxygen levels until the fire around him died. All he had to do was keep breathing until Hopper leapt over the remaining flames to lift him out the same way. Catherine had let the ship sink once the crew had been rescued. Then she carried Evan home after the paramedics stabilized him for transport. She had known by that point what had happened at the hospital and where Hannah would be.

The whole family had gathered in the parlor, just as they had when Scott had first brought Hannah here. Scott had never thought much about this room when he was a kid. In those days, his mother had used it to entertain guests or meet with city officials. The couches and chairs could handle a half dozen or so guests, while they sipped their drinks from the small bar in the corner or warmed themselves in front of the fireplace. He'd never thought of it as a war room, but ever since Hannah had dropped into their lives, that's what it had become.

Except this time there was another newcomer. Daniella Rose stood next to Nik near the picture window facing the front yard, her bare arm around Nik's waist.

Alek stood with them instead of with his twin, giving Hannah the space she needed to bloodsurf. Catherine relaxed against Thomas near the cold fireplace, waiting for Hannah to reemerge. Scott figured that by this point, Hannah had healed so many people no one would notice if Catherine ignored her own law again.

"He's fine," Hannah said, turning from near-nothing translucency back to her normal, solid self. "Concussion, second and third degree burns, and a few broken ribs were the worst of it."

She looked around the room at all of them, her eyes searching for a respite from what she knew was coming: a long, involved discussion about what had happened this morning and how to handle the fallout. Evan sat up and gave her a hug, which was as much refreshment as she would get.

Scott yearned to hug her too, but kept his gloved hands behind his back where they belonged.

All of the Blackwoods were still in uniform, including Thomas, with his black slacks and red polo shirt. Catherine started to pace, as she always did when forming a strategy, but this time not even deep thinking could erase the weary look on her face, which was still smudged in black. Thomas let her go. He didn't have a drink in his hand this time. Alek returned to the couch to sit next to Evan.

Poor Daniella. Nik had given everyone in the room a brief overview about Daniella's run-in with the Committee while Hannah worked. There wasn't time for details, or why he had called a red alert, but it sounded as if Hannah wasn't the only Alt to kick the Committee in the teeth this week. No wonder Johnson was in such a rage.

Still, Nik assured them that Daniella had passed her preliminary test, but the Committee had delayed making a final decision because Johnson insisted on consulting legal council first. Scott would have to get the full story later.

No one else seemed inclined to ask the question, so Scott decided he would. "What happens to Hannah now?"

Out of the corner of his eye, he could see Hannah's posture stiffen. In front of him, Catherine didn't stop pacing. "She'll be arrested."

"Can't you stop Johnson?" he asked, though he knew the answer.

"This isn't about Johnson. He's just a mouthpiece. I'm the one who started this. I'm the one who advocated for such a strict policy." She paused, closed her eyes and rubbed her temple. It was such a Norm gesture, a learned one, because as far as Scott knew, his mother didn't get headaches. "It seemed like a good idea at the time. I thought the threat of arrest would force the more resistant Alts to fall in line."

"They have, for the most part." Nik glanced at Daniella who rolled her eyes, a teasing grin on her face.

"And the law has worked up until now." Evan cuddled Cue-ball, who, in a rare show of affection, had jumped onto his lap with a quiet meow. "We've had no reports of accidents due to an Alt not being able to control their ability since we implemented the testing. Your school programs have worked wonders. The time-out rooms have worked as well." He glanced at Scott. "With a few modifications."

When you don't have assholes for brothers, Scott thought, but kept his mouth shut. He'd made too much progress to backslide now. His brand of sarcasm wasn't what his mother needed from him. She needed his support. He needed her to support Hannah. They all wanted to keep Hannah out of jail.

"Maybe the law needs to be updated," Evan continued, his fingers rubbing Cue-ball's ears. "I can call for a review, but our immediate problem is how to help Hannah without creating a bigger problem down the road."

"We'll need to get her a lawyer," said Alek.

"It's not a trial that's the problem." Hannah stood and stretched, the day's events etched into the shadows under her eyes. "It's incarcerating me at all. When I said I wouldn't allow myself to be locked up, I meant it. I can barely tolerate riding in an elevator. I'll fight. There has to be another way. You'll have to talk Johnson down. Give me some space."

Space. Where on this planet would someone like Hannah find space? It wasn't the physical location that mattered, it was peace. Peace to live and to love. Scott held his gloved hand out to her and Hannah left Evan's side to hug him, let him hold her close as Nik held Daniella. No one protested. Holding Hannah in his arms had never felt so perfect, so natural.

Thomas's phone buzzed. He pulled it out of his pocket while Scott held Hannah. He cleared his throat.

"You're also forgetting the growing support she's getting from the Norms. They don't want her locked up any more than we do. The count for the crowd outside the hospital during Hannah's testing reached over four hundred. After today, if the Committee continues to prevent Hannah from healing the sick and injured, the Norms might champion her. They want Hannah in a hospital doing exactly what she did today."

Catherine stopped pacing. "I can't supply Hannah with a lawyer or bail her out. It's a conflict of interest. If I did, it would look as if I have no confidence in a law I helped craft. Evan is correct: The law works. If I can't stand by my own law, Thunder City will lose faith in me, in my objectivity. They already suspect I let Hannah heal Nik, and the media is demanding to know why I'm not letting her heal Kavenaugh. I can't risk losing more of their faith now."

"Let McNamara hire the lawyer and bail her out." Scott couldn't believe he'd just made the suggestion, but he couldn't deny McNamara's influence. "I would bet he'd do it if she asked him. It solves the conflict of interest problem. Norms will like the idea that Hannah has a Norm mentor who's a respected doctor and not a Blackwood."

"They'll still know you have a hand in this." Daniella flipped her lock of brown wavy hair over her shoulder as she looked around, locking eyes with every single Blackwood. Clearly, she wasn't someone who was afraid to speak her mind. Scott liked her already. "Her personal life is front page news. Trying to deny it is only going to annoy the Committee and I've already annoyed them enough for a lifetime's worth of annoyances. I think the best course of action we can take is to keep the Committee distracted as we build a stronger support system for her within both the Norm and Alt populations. The attack on the harbor will keep the Committee busy for a while. I can distract them more by moving up the date of my transplant, something my brother has been yammering about since my Alt status became public."

"Cory's still right about not giving the Committee more ammunition than they already have. It would be better all-around if McNamara bailed her out." Thomas tugged his wife's arm and pulled her close.

Alek raised his voice. "There's still the risk of the judge not setting bail for her in the first place. She's already run once. She's a flight risk. They'll also be watching Cory. They didn't go after him for helping Hannah escape the first time because of McNamara's intervention. They won't look away a second time."

Alek was right. Both he and Hannah were at risk. "She can't stay in jail. She needs help, and she won't get it in jail."

Even as he spoke, a thought wormed its way into his head. *He* might not be able to break Hannah out of jail, but the Shield could. So far no one had noticed the Shield. The guy had a way of remaining invisible. Maybe his barrier made him invisible? Maybe not. If Hannah needed a jailbreak, the Shield would be the guy who could pull it off — but would he?

He would if you promised to break off your relationship with Hannah and follow him into this war of his.

"Scott, what's wrong?"

Scott looked down at Hannah, beautiful and secure in his arms. "Nothing, why?"

Her frown knitted her pale brows over her eyes, the eyes that shone even when she bloodsurfed. "You had a look on your face, as if you were in pain."

He really needed to work on not projecting his thoughts. "I was thinking about how I could break you out of jail, and about everything that could go wrong with my plan."

She patted his chest. "My hero."

"How long do we have?" Daniella asked. "Before the Committee gets a warrant for her arrest?"

Everyone in the room looked at someone else. Catherine returned to Thomas's arms. "Harbor Regional is overflowing right now. Sixty percent of the Committee works there. They're going to be busy until most of the victims are either taken care of or transferred to hospitals where the other Committee members will be waiting. They'll find out about Hannah's intervention soon enough. We might have a day or two." She looked at him. "I'm sorry, Cory. I wish I could do something to prevent this. In the meantime, you can stay here through dinner, but then…"

Scott nodded his understanding. He'd have to return to Thomas's penthouse downtown, but he wouldn't stay there. He only had a day, maybe two, of freedom for Hannah. They would have a plan in place before then. He needed to find the Shield.

Hannah stayed in Scott's arms as the meeting broke up, warm and secure. Alek pulled Evan off the sofa, neither twin showing signs of their injuries. Nik brought Daniella over to her and Scott.

"Cory, Hannah, this is Daniella Rose."

Hannah remembered to not reach out to shake Daniella's hand.

"Please, call me Dani. I'm so happy to finally meet both of you, but I'm also sorry about what happened this morning."

Scott's hand felt its way up to rub her shoulders. "Thanks. It sounds like you two had your own adventure together."

Dani's smile turned into a mischievous grin as she

looked up at Nik, who towered over her. Nik looked down at her with unabashed reverence, while he toyed with the curls in her long hair. Hannah couldn't help the twinge of envy. Dani wasn't just gorgeous. She exuded a confidence Hannah needed right now, but couldn't quite grasp.

"It's quite a story, but at least Fredek Varga is dead. He won't be selling blitz to anyone ever again." Nik looked over his shoulder at Catherine and Thomas. Even stuck in between two giant men, Hannah could peek in between to see Thomas whispering in Catherine's ear. Catherine leaned into her husband's embrace.

"The four of us should go out to dinner together." Dani elbowed Nik and brought his attention back to her. "Once we clear up your little legal situation."

"Not so little." Hannah didn't want to burst Dani's bubble, but she didn't think that Dani could appreciate just how much of a threat the Committee was. Had Nik told her about the Court of Blood? "Johnson doesn't like me. I've defeated him twice — with help from Scott and Dr. McNamara — but he does have the law on his side. Like Catherine said, there's only so much she can do to protect me."

"Oh, don't worry about Johnson." Dani threw back her head and laughed. "Believe me, if there's one person he wants to lock up more than you, it's me. And, Thunder City won't protect me the way they'll protect you."

"Really? Why?" Scott maneuvered her away from the parlor doors to let Alek and Evan leave the room. Both twins patted her shoulder on their way out, so she smiled at both of them, even though she really didn't feel like it. "What happened to you two?"

"Oh, let's just say, I have an unsavory past." Dani

wiggled her eyebrows. "Not to worry. If I can distract the Committee with my nefarious ways and give you some breathing room, all the better."

Hannah could see what Nik saw in Dani. She had a way of making you feel as if she were your best friend without even knowing you. "Don't get yourself into trouble on my account. Scott and I — we'll make this work, somehow."

If Dani was confused by the Scott/Cory name change, she didn't indicate it. "Oh, honey, not to worry. I relish causing trouble. Don't I?"

Nik rolled his eyes. "Yes, you do, but I love you anyway."

Love? Did Nik just say love? Maybe her feelings for Scott weren't too new after all? The look on Nik's face told her all she needed to know: He meant it. He loved Dani and Dani returned the same look with her own teasing variation.

Maybe she should tell Scott she loved him? What would his reaction be? Was he ready for her to love him? Did he feel the same?

Dani stood on tiptoe, but Nik still had to bend down so she could whisper something in his ear. Swear to God, Nik blushed to his ear tips.

"Dani and I are going to take a walk outside," Nik said while he straightened.

"Are you spending the night here?" Scott asked. "I was hoping to ask you a few questions about a case."

Nik wrinkled his nose. "A case? Um, sure. Dani why don't you wait in the sunroom? I'll show you where it is. Scott and I can talk while Garrett gets you a snack."

"Sure thing, sweetheart. I feel like I'm about to waste away."

Hannah guessed the questions Scott wanted to ask

his brother had to do with Jimmy Chung. Nik guided Dani out of the room, with Scott following them. Hannah was about to follow when Thomas let go of Catherine and made it to door before she could leave.

"Hannah, Catherine would like to talk to you."

She didn't mistake his light tone for a request. Neither did Scott. He paused, already on the other side of the door. The kiss she wished she could press to his lips landed on her gloved fingertips instead. He mimicked the gesture before closing the door.

Thomas had a very close relationship with Scott. Father and son hadn't had a lot of time together since they rescued her from Star Haven, so maybe it was a good idea to let the men talk together, even if it was about Jimmy Chung.

From across the small room, Catherine pulled one of Thomas's favorite brandies off the shelf and poured herself a drink.

"I shouldn't contribute more to your delinquency, but — " she held out the bottle to Hannah.

Hannah shrugged. Why not? Catherine poured her two fingers in a shot glass. Hannah wandered over, trying to appear casual. She tested the liquid with a small sip. The evil taste burned going down, but once it hit her stomach, the warmth relaxed her.

Catherine sunk into the sofa. Hannah sat next to her, but kept a respectful distance between them. She admired Catherine, even when they disagreed, but Hannah never thought for a second that the two of them had anything in common that would create a closer relationship. Catherine was not her mother. Hannah had no mother, and didn't want one. So what do you say to comfort a woman who for the third time in two weeks had almost lost a son?

"I'm sorry I wasn't there for you this morning." Catherine set her drink aside, and laid her head back, her eyes closed. "I'm glad Cory was. I know the Oversight Committee's rules can be burdensome. I just wish we could finish this process and be done with it. I wish we didn't have to hold you back from the world."

Hannah's heart squeezed tight. Catherine felt exactly as she did. "How do you do it? How do you live with all of this uncertainty?"

Catherine picked up the glass again, sipping more brandy. "I won't lie and tell you I don't have a choice. I do have a choice. I've always had choices. I could leave all of this behind at any time, take my family to a far off mountain somewhere and keep them safe. With all of my strength, all of my money, it would be easy."

She paused, her focus on the glass, but her eyes distant. "The temptation is always stronger when one of my sons has been hurt. It's stronger now, having you so close and yet so untouchable. You've saved all four of my sons. It would be so easy to tear down the conventions I put in place and have you join us on the mountain and become our personal healer."

She paused again. Hannah waited a beat, then two. "I would do it if you asked."

Catherine's gaze turned on her, hardened. "I know. That's a problem. You idolize Captain Spectacular and you shouldn't. It makes resisting the temptation to misuse you all the harder."

Hannah sipped her own drink. Did this stuff really make you more confident, or did it just make you louder? "I resisted you before. I'm the one who insisted on returning to Miranda. You damn near had me cowering under the table, but I resisted. I fought back. In the end we won. We saved Scott...Cory."

Catherine let a small smile crack her anger. "Yes, we did, but we almost lost you instead. I'm sorry, Hannah. I didn't mean to imply that my weakness was your problem. It isn't. You have an inner strength all of your own."

The taste of the brandy remained on Hannah's lips. She licked the taste before deciding it wasn't so bad. She took another sip. "I don't feel strong. I'm scared. I thought the fear would go away once I arrived in Thunder City, but I'm still scared. Not of the terrorists, not even of Star Haven. There's always this fear of...I don't know. Making choices? And anger. I'm always angry these days." It all made sense to her. Or, maybe it was just the alcohol talking. "I'm angry that I'm forced to make these decisions that I don't think I'm ready to make."

"Welcome to adulthood. Only the very foolish and the stupidly arrogant are never afraid to make choices."

"When have you ever been scared?" The idea of Catherine not staring down fear was unimaginable.

"The first time I became pregnant."

Hannah's shot glass slipped from her fingers, but she caught it before it hit the floor. Instead of yelling about the near accident ruining the carpeting, as Miranda would have, Catherine laughed. "Do the math. Nik's twenty-eight. I'm forty-five. Thunder City put on blinders when it came to my teenage dalliances."

Seventeen. Hannah hadn't given Catherine's age a thought, but she'd only been seventeen when she gave birth to Nik.

"Of course, I wasn't Captain Spectacular then. I was just a stupid teenage girl who didn't think she'd get pregnant the first time. I wasn't sure I could even get pregnant. My father had warned me early on, when I first got my period, that even if I had the same biological functions as Norms, pregnancy might not be possible. How could a baby grow inside a womb surrounded by muscle capable of withstanding a speeding bullet?"

Catherine stood to pour herself another drink and refilled Hannah's glass. It didn't appear as if Catherine were paying attention to the alcohol.

"Nik proved stronger than my body, though. He survived. Alek and Evan survived. Then Cory. No matter what the Chaos Alts tossed at me, the boys survived while inside of me."

"You fought for Thunder City even while pregnant?"

"I didn't want to. My father had other plans and I wanted to please him. I found out much later he'd been testing me. He hadn't cared about my sons as a grandfather should. He wanted a family of Alts, but he wanted them only if their abilities proved useful for him. He encouraged me to keep having babies to defend him and Blackwood Enterprises. He would have used us, used me, to increase his wealth and power. He thought of Thunder City as his personal playground. Alts were his tools, his weapons. Norms were nothing but wage slaves."

Hannah swallowed more of the warm, smoky liquid. Her head spun a little, but her body sank further into a cushion of pleasure while she listened to Catherine's horror play out. She craved the attention Catherine paid her. She didn't want to break the connection.

"Scott told me you kicked your father out of the house."

"So much evil committed right under my nose and I never even saw it. We'd been fighting, always fighting. T-CASS wasn't born on a whim. Truth be told, I'd been inspired by Demitrios — my first husband. He was the one who wanted to unite the Alts, he was the one who wanted to protest the restrictions Norms placed on us."

"What happened?"

Catherine sighed, another swallow disappearing down her throat. Hannah followed with a sip of her own, the taste no longer distracting her. "He never saw it as something as formal as T-CASS. He never wanted the Oversight Committee. He just wanted it written into the law that Alts could live their lives however they saw fit within the general rule of law set out for Norms. He never wanted a set of rules set aside just for us. He fought me, too. Daily. All through my pregnancy. He was supportive of our marriage, but — "

"You're Catherine Blackwood. Your marriage isn't separate from your job."

Catherine closed her eyes. "I saw myself as an example. I thought if I led by example, other Alts would follow. Some did. Others didn't. The schism between T-CASS and Neuts started because some Alts threatened to leave Thunder City if they had to become a part of T-CASS. Other's threatened violent protest."

"Nik's father?"

Catherine hesitated. "I don't believe Demitrios would have hurt anyone to get his way, but I couldn't say the same about a few others. They were good people, not Chaos Alts, but they didn't believe they should be forced to join T-CASS if they didn't want to. I had to compromise or I risked losing my dream. I didn't want any Alt to feel as if they had to leave Thunder City and the security we offered for freedom somewhere else. I didn't want to lose all of their talent, their drive, their ambition. Demitrios was right. You can't force people to live good lives. You can only inspire the ones who choose to join you and hope the rest will respect the ground on which you stand."

Hannah had always watched Captain Spectacular from the distance of Star Haven. The Captain could inspire her even from across the Bay. Catherine was different — at least this Catherine, the person, not the Alt. "Nik turned out okay. So did Alek and Evan."

Catherine smiled. "Yes. Demitrios and I divorced, but he stood by our sons. I have no complaints. He loves them as much as I do. Without him, I couldn't have undone the damage my father inflicted on them, especially the twins."

"And Scott...Cory?" Her head buzzed. It was getting harder to remember only she called Scott by his assumed name.

"Yes, and Cory. If Cole — his father — had lived, things would have been very different."

"He would have loved Cory even if he hadn't been an Alt."

Catherine opened her eyes again, but she didn't look at Hannah. Hannah wondered if Catherine even remembered who it was she was talking to. "I loved Cory, but he reminded me too much of Cole. I had already lost my mother to cancer and my husband to my own ambitions. Cory looks just like his father. Seeing him grow reminded me of my failure to save him."

"What happened to Cole? Cory told me he only knows what he read in the paper and what his brothers told him."

Catherine leaned over and kissed Hannah on the forehead. "There isn't enough alcohol on the planet for that story." She stood up to leave, but paused at the door. "Get yourself a glass of water before you go to bed."

Then she was gone. Hannah didn't even hear the sounds of her footsteps on the stairwell. Maybe she flew, low to the floor, her feet not quite touching the carpet?

Hannah contemplated the rest of her drink, still a finger left in the glass. She swallowed the rest of it. Why not? If Catherine had served it, there was no reason why she couldn't enjoy it along with her hero. With renewed purpose, she scooped up the box with Roger's urn and left the room.

CHAPTER FOURTEEN

Eight-ball greeted Hannah in the kitchen with a meow before threading himself between her wobbly legs. After Catherine's talk about husbands and fathers, Roger's ashes took priority over cuddling the cat. She would scatter his ashes tonight, giving him peace, before anything could happen that would delay his return to the earth.

All of her plans for food and a shower melted away. The ashes weighed heavy in her hand, all of her emotions boxed behind a wall of control leaking brandy through ever widening cracks. Garrett, the butler, more than likely had retired for the evening. Dani wasn't out in the sunroom, so maybe she'd decided to explore the rose covered trellis at the end of the walkway.

The cat followed Hannah outside, but disappeared to hunt as she made her way toward the dock out back. She didn't see Scott, Nik, or Thomas, either, so they must have disappeared elsewhere inside the mansion. Hannah chose the path leading in the opposite direction from the trellis. The *Elusive Lady* floated in the shadow of the lanterns lining the wooden walkway. The *Lady* belonged to Thomas, and Hannah needed to be as far away from the reminder of the Blackwood family as she could while living in their home, so she made her way along the border toward the neighboring estate.

The breeze from the harbor picked up, with just a hint of autumn chill in the air as the sun set. Where the shore curved to hug the Bay, neighboring estates turned on their evening lights, twinkling in the growing dark. The silence opened its arms to comfort her.

She wasn't sure how long she sat there before Scott's heavy steps found her. Funny, how she could recognize his gait from all of the other members of the household after less than two weeks.

He sat next to her, his arm wrapped around her shoulders and his gloved hands on her knit sweater, keeping her warm against the cool breeze.

"What's in the box?" he asked.

"Roger's ashes," she said. *What's left of my heart*, she wanted to say but didn't. What she really meant was, what was left of the only man who had ever made her feel like she belonged, like she was normal, as if she were special enough to care about. Roger had cared for her, enough to die for her. How did you honor something so precious?

Scott didn't reply right away. He kept his thoughts to himself, while the water lapped against the pylons underneath them. After a long while he said, "There's a cemetery about ten minutes away if you'd prefer."

Hannah shook her head, but realized Scott wouldn't see the subtle motion in the growing darkness. "I want this done. I loved Roger, but he was Miranda's husband before he was my stepfather. No matter how much I cherish my memories of him, I can't think of him without thinking of *her*. I don't want Miranda lingering anywhere near Thunder City. She doesn't belong here. She doesn't belong anywhere. Her body might be lost at the harbor. I don't care about that.

I have to let Roger go here, now. I can't have him without *her*."

She still couldn't bring herself to open the urn and scatter Roger's ashes. She just sat there, huddled against Scott, her fingers growing numb from her death grip on the urn.

Scott let go of her shoulders to rub her back in slow circles. "Take your time. We're in no rush."

But she was in a rush. A rush against possible incarceration. A rush against the need to prove herself. A rush against an investigation that wasn't going anywhere fast.

There were so many unanswered questions. What had happened to all of Roger's money? Was there really nothing for Hannah to inherit except the urn and his ashes? Miranda had married Roger for his money, so Miranda's accounts, and Roger's by default, must have been tied up with building the quarry and paying Miranda's mercenaries. Or maybe it had been transferred to the Court of Blood. Not that the money would do her any good now, but what about her future? Did she even have one? Would the Committee let her have a say in her future at all?

"When I was eight," she said, leaning into Scott, "I won a science contest at school. A demonstration with prisms about light refraction and rainbows. Miranda's second husband had helped me pick out the prism and tape it to the cardboard box. I hadn't thought Miranda had noticed what we were doing, much less cared. But something changed that day. She got a phone call and became all excited. Out of the blue she offered to help me bring the project to school and even spell-checked my essay. She offered to let me use an old tripod we had out in the garage as a stand for the cardboard box. After I won, she took me out for ice cream, just the two of us. She let me pick out whatever flavor I wanted. I decided to try strawberry, though I'd never eaten strawberry-flavored ice cream before. Miranda bragged to the waitress about my science project and asked her to put extra sprinkles and whipped cream on top. When the waitress came back, the bowl had more whipped cream than ice cream."

Her tears softened the stars appearing in the sky.

"You had a good day with her," Scott leaned low, to whisper in her ear, still keeping his lips just far enough away to not touch her. "She introduced you to your favorite ice cream flavor."

"I had forgotten that." Her throat tightened, her voice became more ragged. "After her third marriage, I had forgotten about the ice cream. I had forgotten even after Roger took me out one day before he married Miranda. He offered to buy me ice cream and I asked for strawberry with extra whipped cream and sprinkles. I've always thought of Roger when I thought about strawberry ice cream, but it was really Miranda who bought it for me first."

Scott's arm tightened around her shoulders, pulling her closer, the pressure of his arm keeping her strong, keeping her tears in check.

"Why am I remembering this now? I hate her. I hate what she became, I hate what she did to you, I hate what she did to me, and to all the other Alts stuck in her prison. Why can't I dump Roger's ashes? I should be thinking of him. He used to take me out on his sailboat. Why can't I think about that without thinking of Miranda?"

Scott said nothing for a while, rocking Hannah back and forth in a gentle motion. Hannah closed her eyes, imaging herself on Roger's boat, and Scott's rocking motion was just like the Bay lulling her to safety and comfort.

"Miranda is all you know," he said, finally. "For better or worse, she raised you. She's your most dominant memory and you can't forget her so easily until you have other memories, better memories, to erase her."

Better memories. Yes, that's what she needed. Better, happier, memories. Memories she would build here in Thunder City. Hadn't she already started? With Scott? The Committee was ruining the memories she should be building, damn them.

Hannah inhaled the salty air, long and slow, but the brandy still kept her heart wide open. Scott had her back and she had his. He wanted her to build new memories. That would be her mission, her mantra. New memories and a new life with Scott by her side. They would make it happen, somehow.

With care, she unhooked the top of the urn.

"Go ahead, Hannah," he urged. "She can't hurt you anymore."

Hannah turned the urn over. The wind picked up with a burst, scattering the ashes far across the murky waters. Without a second thought, she tossed the urn into the water along with the ashes.

"Thank you for Roger, Miranda. Thank you for giving me the gift of a real father. I hope you only spend most of eternity in hell. Roger, you gave me hope, which was more important than what anyone else had given me."

She watched the urn bob in the waves for a moment, then sink beneath the surface. It was done. She owned nothing from her past and was glad for it. So why did her soul weigh her down like a wet blanket over a kicked puppy?

The tears started to spill then, because she couldn't see Scott, even in the light of the lanterns against the darkening sky. Her world blurred and her cheeks cooled with the wetness. Scott shifted, pulling his hand from her shoulder to run his gloved fingers through her hair.

She curled into him, wanting the contact, damning the Committee for taking human contact away from her. She need to touch someone. The feeling of skin, the warmth of a someone so close to you, you could feel their pulse, breathe the same air. If touch could be addictive, she was desperate for a fix and it had been so long since she last touched Scott on board the yacht. Touching skin to bloodsurf only teased her with possibilities. She had control when she healed Scott. If only she could dam up her pain and let it leak through more slowly, controlling the vicious sorrow that clawed away at her stomach, her heart, her mind.

Her tears slowed after who knew how long. She wiped her eyes. The stars shone across the sky, and the sun had set. Scott still held her, rocking a gentle rhythm in time to the water lapping against the dock.

"I want to spend the night with you."

Had she said that? She must have because Scott broke his rhythm mid-rock. "We can't."

"We can." Her determination overrode her grief. She needed to feel Scott, like she had oh, so briefly in his bedroom before his arrest. Nothing had made her feel more blissful than having Scott's whole body pressed against her, all hard muscle, except his lips, which were soft and playful. The memory of his fingers touching her between her legs sparked a slow burn where her jeans pressed into that same juncture. Skin-on-skin contact would lay the foundation for all of her new memories, and only having Scott's rough hands on her body could satisfy her. "I want you. I want this. No one has to know."

"My parents will know. It's their house. Nothing happens in there that they don't know about. Alek and Evan will probably stay the night too. You know those two will be snooping around getting up to no good."

Hannah couldn't stop the giggle at the idea of all Catherine's grown sons sneaking around the mansion. "Do you think Nik will stay? With Dani?"

Scott's shoulders lifted in a half shrug. "Maybe."

"I want to make love with you," she repeated. "For real this time. No bloodsurfing." Scott's arms were still around her, his gloved hands tucked around her waist. Instead of giving her comfort, it made her remember what his hands were doing when they were in his bed. The feel of his fingers touching her where she'd never been touched before, the orgasm he gave her without even entering her body. Yes, that was how she wanted to feel, to sweep away the pain, push it so far away it couldn't hurt her anymore. "If Nik and Dani can sleep together, there's no reason we can't. We have control right here, right now. Even if we didn't, no one is going to get hurt but us. We'll take responsibility if someone finds out."

Even in the low light she could see Scott lick his lips, temptation in his eyes. Good to know that despite everything, he still wanted her. She rested her head on his chest where she could hear his heart. He had a perfect heart because she'd made it perfect.

Without warning, Scott pulled his long legs up onto the dock. He stood and with one smooth tug, pulled her to stand next to him. Hannah took one last swipe with her sleeve across her eyes to keep her tears from showing. With firm resolve, she put Roger, and with him, Miranda, out of her mind.

Making love with Scott wasn't a mistake. She wouldn't let it become a mistake. The Committee might regulate everything else, but she wasn't going to let them control this. What she and Scott shared together was none of their business. They were adults who'd survived too many attempts on their lives to let others decide what was best for them. The Committee would call them selfish, but it was the Committee that was selfish. They wanted to keep the Blood Surfer to themselves.

Instead of bringing her back into the house, Scott led her onto the *Elusive Lady*. No one would see them here. He turned on a light but kept it low. Ignoring the master bedroom, Scott took her to a guest bedroom across the hall.

Like the rest of the yacht, this room had the warm, earthy colors of late autumn. Outside the porthole, Hannah could see the lanterns from the deck reflecting off the low waves from the Bay. The yacht rocked ever so slightly as each wave rolled against it.

Scott sat down on the bed and motioned for Hannah to join him. "We don't have to do this if you change your mind. Just say 'stop,' even if you're not sure."

She sat next to him, put her arms around his waist, her head, both heavy and light at the same time, on his shoulder. "I'm tired of just dreaming about you."

His gloved fingertips trailed light along her upper arms, eliciting a shiver. A cold calmness dropped her heartbeat from too fast to a slower, calmer rate, matching the rhythm he created. After running hot for most of the day, a more languid comfort wrapped around her. The slow weakening of her instinct to fight, to run, to save, made her legs wobble.

The light tickle disappeared. She opened her half-closed eyes to ask why he'd stopped. One finger at a time, Scott tugged at his gloves. When his hands were free, he placed the gloves on the night table next to the bed. He'd made his choice, his commitment, to her. "Wherever you go, even if it's only in your dreams, I will follow."

"You'll never need to follow me." She matched his decision, and tugged off her own gloves one finger at a time. When her own hands were free, she placed her gloves on top of his. "We'll walk together side-by-side."

Hannah watched Scott as he undressed, each discarded piece of clothing revealing more of his forbidden skin. First his jacket, followed by his weapons, which he carefully placed on a chair next to the bed. Then the t-shirt, sweeping up and over his expansive chest, each rib distinctly outlined. A few new bruises on his arms and shoulders distracted her from the rest of his perfection. She swallowed back the urge to ask him how he'd gotten hurt, but she placed the question into her mental box. If Scott wanted her to know, he would tell her.

His abs contracted as he sat down to tug off his boots, but he watched her watching him as he stood back up to remove his jeans. Adorably, he turned his back to her as he unzipped. His firm backside had no bruises for her to worry over, but he kept his back to her far longer than necessary, while he folded each article of clothing and placed them next to his weapons. She licked her lips in anticipation. When had her mouth become so dry?

"Now you decide to become a neat freak?" she asked. "Last time you tossed your clothes on the floor."

He looked over his shoulder. "Eager are you?"

"You're killing me, Grey."

He turned around and walked over to stand right in front of her, arms across his chest. He was built, just like she'd seen him last time. She cared about nothing else right now, other than Scott standing naked in front of her.

It took a few moments for her to realize he was waiting for her to undress.

"Sorry." What a dork she was, but she couldn't stop staring. Deciding to lose your virginity and acting on it were two different things. Last time she chickened out because emotionally she knew it wasn't the right time. Right here, with Scott standing in front of her, she had to wonder if she shouldn't chicken out because he was so damn big. "It's just — you're amazing and I'm not feeling particularly amazing right now."

"Let me give you a hand."

He knelt in front of her, and made short work of the knots in her sneakers. A second later, her sneakers slipped off her feet, followed by her socks. The shock of cool air caressed her toes, as she wiggled them. Firm fingers halted her mid-wiggle to massage the arch of her left foot, the warmth shooting along her nerves straight to her head. The light tingle of need mixed with the brandy. Her breath hitched, the rhythm of her heart followed the stroke of Scott's fingers as he abandoned her left foot in favor of her right.

"That feels so good," she whispered.

His gray eyes gazed directly into hers, low, intense, and aiming straight for the core of her being. She held his look, letting her need fall into a cloud of desire. His hands loosened, sliding up her calves, to the hems of her capris, where he paused to massage those muscles as well. It was a slow seduction, but her greed took hold and Hannah leaned forward to cup Scott's cheeks and pour all her unspent desire into her kiss. As she did, she widened her legs so he could slip his hips in between, his hands roaming higher, as she wrapped her legs around his waist.

"You are amazing." He stared down at her chest, as though he could see through her thin blouse. "I grow more in awe of you every day."

He leaned in for another kiss, warm and sweet, and she remembered the last time he had her in his bed. She'd bloodsurfed then, not sure if she was ready, but not wanting Scott to think she didn't care for him. From that experience she learned how much pleasure she could give a man. Stroking Scott to an orgasm, however, would mean she would have to wait until he was done for her to receive the same.

This time it would be different. She vowed not to let her inexperience get in the way of her desire. The brandy still sang a sweet song, caressing her soul, making her tingle.

Scott pulled his lips away from hers for a moment. "Music, classical, level four," he said.

The strains of a violin weaved a spell through the night air.

"Just remember," he said, his thumb reaching between her legs to rub the fabric separating them. "If you want to stop, just say 'stop' and I will."

His voice tangled with her mood, stroking her core. All the love she wanted during her life spelled out in just a few words. "I promise. I want this. I want you."

"Even if it means we have to run again?" he asked.

"Even then."

His fingers abandoned her core and reached for the buttons on her blouse, while his lips found hers again, distracting her from thoughts of tomorrow. She wanted his fingers back on her, but with nothing separating them. Emboldened, she unzipped her capris herself, shoving the material down to her thighs. They wouldn't go any farther unless Scott backed away from her.

Scott obeyed her silent command after a sweep of his tongue along hers. The capris fell to the floor, followed by her blouse, underwear and bra. Scott's lips returned, hungrier, more demanding. The buzz in her head eased as Scott lay her back, his hands everywhere at once. Her skin tightened under the onslaught, her nipples peaked the more he fondled them. She arched her back, pressing herself against him.

"Ouch." She froze with the sharp twinge under her ribs.

Scott's hands stilled. "What's wrong?"

The worry in his voice carried away her pain. He was so caring and considerate, the way he treated her like a treasure, desirable and beautiful.

"Nothing. It's fine. My ribs are still sore."

Scott didn't move to continue their lovemaking, but her body still screamed for more pleasure. "Really, I'm fine."

Her fingers brushed through the hair on his chest while she explored his body, ignoring his bruises and praying he wasn't in any pain either.

"If you're sure."

"I am." She lifted her hips up to rub against his hardness. His breath increased the faster she moved.

"See? Nothing's wrong."

Obviously he believed her, because he pulled the covers over both of them, returning most, but not all, of his weight on top of her. She'd seen his body before, but she'd never touched so much of him, she'd never tasted him except for his kisses. Her tongue found the nape of his neck and traced a path down to his right nipple, where she sucked just long enough to make him moan before she continued her path down to his abdomen. Turned out, he was an innie, which she took advantage of by lapping her tongue around the circle before delving inside.

His sharp intake of breath caught her unawares, and she didn't expect him to haul her back up so he could kiss her again, his mouth hard on hers. As he reclaimed her lips, his hand reached under one of her thighs, encouraging her to bend her knees, widening her legs and giving him more room. It still didn't satisfy, so she wrapped her legs around his again, letting his hand wander down to rub where he gave her pleasure the last time.

Her moan begged for more of the enticing friction, but his hand disappeared to touch her elsewhere, leaving her wanting. Her nipples, already hard, became more sensitive while he massaged her chest, his fingers dancing across sensitive skin before sucking one nipple into this mouth. She squirmed against him, silently demanding him to devour her. He responded by pulling away, trading his massage of her other breast with his tongue, lapping at her hardened peaks.

The need to pull him closer forced her to grip her hands on his backside. With her hands full, she urged him to move faster as he rocked against her. His fingers returned to stroke her between her legs and sent her spiraling again into a vortex of want and need. She wanted him and needed him, but not the way that triggered her ability.

The heels of her feet found his calves, so muscular, while she let go of his backside to run her hands through his thick hair. "I'm ready, Scott."

"Not yet." He nipped the tip of her nose.

"Why?"

He rolled off her in the opposite direction. Had she done something wrong?

Crinkling foil caught her attention, while she spooned herself against Scott's back, trying to recapture the closeness she had just moments before. Her hand slipped around his waist seeking his hardness, but he stopped her before she could touch him. Instead, he placed her hand on his stomach while he rolled on the condom.

He turned back to face her. "Are you ready?"

Instead of telling him "yes", she wrapped her arms around him, her kiss first finding his bottom lip, then the top, then together she poured all of her passion into him. Working with nothing but primal instinct, she left his lips and worked her way down his jawline, the five o'clock shadow scratching her tongue. He had a bruise the size of a golf ball near his shoulder, so she left that area alone, heading for his nipples to tease him the way he teased her.

"You feel so good." His voice hitched. She kept going, taking time to lap her tongue inside his navel. Her exploration didn't last long. Scott grabbed her upper arms and hauled her back up until she was eye level with him again.

"Not yet."

His kiss nearly stole her ability to breathe, while

he pushed her onto her back. The tangled blanket wrapped around her legs, which she kicked free. Scott moved lower, his lips finding her nipples, which his tongue played with until each one until she thought she would scream in frustration. He moved lower, slowly paying her back for her exploration of his belly button. She thrashed, trying to create more contact, but he pinned her hips with his hands until his mouth reached between her legs. The heat he created burned away all resistance. She melted into him, thrust upwards, but it wasn't enough. It would never be enough, while he teased her body.

The friction she craved stopped as Scott moved back up her body, slowly retracing the path his tongue had created, while his hand remained below, his fingers replacing his kisses.

"Now." Did she say that?

"Are you — "

"If you ask me that one more time, I'm going to bloodsurf and make you finish this."

Clearly, he needed nothing else. She opened herself wide and arched her back, ignoring her sore ribs, as Scott pressed himself into her. She gasped at the contact and forced herself to relax, secure in the knowledge he would be as gentle as he could. Scott moved slowly at first. There was pressure, a ping of pain. She groaned when his fullness entered her completely, her hips arching to meet his.

"Are you okay?" he panted.

While the lower half of her body adjusted to the new sensations, the urge to *move* set her rocking her whole body against him. "Yes. Keep going."

He rocked along with her, his arms keeping his torso from crushing her. She matched his rhythm, pulling him back down, rubbing herself against him as best she could. The tension within her was like nothing she'd expected. From the inside, she'd seen Scott's body react to her touch, the dance of the nerve signals across his skin, the rush of blood as he came during her stroke. She had no guide here except for the expression on his face. He was close, eyes half closed, brows knitted in both concentration and ecstasy.

His body sped up and she matched him, the friction tugging her into a world of new sensations. There were no words, just sharp gasps followed by frenzied groans until she spilled over, her cry of pleasure washing over in a wave of satisfaction.

Scott joined her a moment later, his own orgasm speeding up even as hers slowed down. She didn't have to wait long until he thrust one last time into her, then stopped. She captured a mental picture of him at the moment, eyes closed, tension gone, free of the world around them. He lowered himself back onto her his breath soft as he cradled her in his arms.

CHAPTER FIFTEEN

The sun woke Scott the next morning. Hannah was already looking at him, tucked up against his chest, eyes wide and unblinking. Music still played in the background.

"How do you feel?" he asked.

Hannah shifted against him, her skin so soft, but he had to make sure she had no regrets. She inhaled deeply, her chest now rubbing against his, tempting him to repeat their lovemaking.

"I'm not sure. Having an aria in the background sort of made it like the movies, but — " She shifted, and winced.

"You're hurt."

"No, no. I'm fine. Just a little sore. I stretched a bunch of muscles I haven't used in a while. It'll go away."

He ran his fingers through her long and messy hair. "There are pain killers in the medicine cabinet. Feel free to take what you need with breakfast."

She propped herself up on one elbow to look around the room. "I guess we shouldn't stay here. Thomas might need the yacht."

Scott pulled the blanket off himself and swung his legs over the side of the bed. "I shouldn't be here at all. If we're going to get busted, better they find us far apart."

"Then what?" Hannah stayed in the bed, tucking the sheet around her chest. "If they really do go through with arresting us?"

Scott stood and Hannah gasped. "What?" he asked.

"I saw some of your bruises last night, but not all of them. What's Highlight doing to you at the Arena?"

He didn't want to lie, so he turned to look out the window. He'd tell the truth, but leave out the details. He'd been doing that a lot lately. "It's not Highlight. It's McNamara's bodyguard. We've been sparring."

"It looks as if he nailed you more than once."

"He's a challenge, that's for sure." He looked back to see her face. To his relief, there was no condemnation there, no judgment. She knew he needed this, he needed to feel useful. He loved her, but he needed more in his life than just love. So did Hannah, which to his mind is what made them perfect for each other. Still, he wanted to confirm that she wasn't putting on a brave face for his sake. "You're not angry, are you?"

A confused looked crossed her face instead. "Why would I be?"

"You've literally rebuilt my body from scratch twice. You must be getting tired of seeing your handiwork destroyed."

She slipped out of bed, leaving the sheet behind. They both stood nude, as if it were the most natural thing in the world. "If sparring with the Shield makes dealing with Highlight's training easier, if it keeps you in shape, then I don't care how many times I have to heal you." She touched one of the bruises on his left shoulder. "That doesn't mean I'm going to leave you this way."

With that, she disappeared, leaving behind only a

vague shadow of herself. Scott stood still, trying to feel where she was in his body, but unlike when she'd stitched up his broken bones, all he could sense was an odd tingling in various spots. Less than a minute later she reappeared.

"No more bruises."

He leaned down and kissed her hard. "Thank you."

"Do you have to train today?"

His frustration escaped in a growl before he could stop it. "Yes, this afternoon. But I'm going to swing by to see Rita Han this morning, Betty Chung's sister. Nik agreed with me last night that I should talk to her too. He said I could get a different perspective on both Betty's and Jimmy's behavior. He suggested a bunch of questions I should ask. After I pick up fresh clothes at the penthouse, I'll head over there."

"Good. I'm going to go back to the hospital. McNamara said I would have access to Jimmy's records, now that I'm an official employee. It'll keep my attention off the Committee."

He couldn't resist one more kiss. "Call me tonight after dinner. If we're not in jail, we can talk about what we find out."

"And if we are in jail?"

She was so dear to him, how could not pull her back into his arms? "I'll translocate you to me and then translocate us both to somewhere safe."

Her sigh broke his heart, as she laid her head on his chest. "Is there such a place?"

"I'll find one. I promise." He stroked her hair one last time. "Shower here. I'll head inside, grab something to eat, and see if Evan will fly me downtown."

She stepped away, picked up her clothes off the floor, and headed for the bathroom. He washed up in the bathroom across the hall before he dressed, and grabbed his gloves off the chair. Back at the house, he found Garret in the kitchen.

"Alek left you a note on the table." The butler handed him a plate already filled with eggs Atlantic. "Will Ms. Quinn be joining us for breakfast?"

If Garrett guessed what he and Hannah had been up to the night before, he used his best butler's discretion to keep it to himself. Besides, the smell of the salmon was making Scott's mouth water. "She was showering last I saw her."

"Very good, sir."

Scott shoved a bite of drippy eggs into his mouth as he made his way to the dining room. Alek's note lay at the head of the table. He could have texted, but then, maybe Alek didn't have the number to the phone Scott had taken from Thomas's vault? He'd have to make sure everyone in the family had it before the end of the day.

Brought your Harley back from the harbor before the Committee could confiscate it. It's in the garage. Filled the tank. Will be at Thomas's this afternoon. I have a plan. I'll give you the details when you get here.

What was this plan? And why did Alek, and not Evan, bring back his Harley? Maybe Evan had asked him to? Was Evan not feeling well enough?

No, Hannah would have been thorough with her healing. Alek's attitude toward him might be turning slower than Evan's, but Scott knew better than to make a thing of it. He finished his breakfast and headed for the garage.

He kept the cycle at a slow pace until he turned onto the main road. Traffic was lighter than usual. It was as if Thunder City was holding its breath. He turned down the next street. Betty Chung's sister also lived in the Fargrounds.

He made it to the West Ashland Park, which separated the Bayview neighborhood where the Blackwoods lived from a mixed-use area with a denser population. The park had about fifteen acres open to the public, but he hadn't walked its trails since elementary school. He remembered enough about the park to know where the back entrance was located. He could take a short cut through on the dirt trail and find a good hiding place in case he needed to translocate himself and Hannah away from the estate. Maybe even stash some supplies there ahead of time.

His memories were the only thing that saved his ass when the Shield stepped into the middle of the road, rifle raised.

Scott skid his motorcycle into the short driveway just as the Shield fired. Son-of-bitch was using live ammo. Scott made it twenty feet, only to discover his escape route stymied by the guard arms chained shut.

He could see from the rearview mirror the Shield rounding onto the drive, his arms cradling the rifle. Scott ditched his bike, dove under the guard arms and hit the grass to the left.

What had gone wrong? What had he done? Why was the Shield trying to kill him after they'd worked together at the harbor?

He could hear the Shield in his head as he ran. *Wrong question, Grey.* The Shield wouldn't waste time planning to hunt him. It was a perfect set-up for a live-fire exercise with Scott as the target.

Scott hid behind a generous oak to catch his breath. He had his own weapons with him, of course. He reached for his Ruger.

Wrong answer again, damn you. You failed to pull the rifle yesterday.

The Shield wanted him to use his Alt ability, not his guns. He pulled his hand off the holster.

The birds chirped their early morning song. The small river rushed over rocks. Did he hear a twig break to the west?

The river ran diagonally across the park. Was the Shield herding him in that direction? Could he pull a gun from a moving target?

Wooden picnic tables and barbecue pits lined the river. What could he use besides his guns?

What the fuck is it with you and the wrong questions?

Fine. The Shield used barriers to protect himself. If the Shield used a full body barrier, how long could he hold it? A full body barrier would cut him off from oxygen. If he kept his barrier lowered to breathe, he wouldn't raise it until he had to. Right now, the Shield more than likely didn't think he'd need a barrier because he didn't believe Scott could find him.

Scott closed his eyes and covered his nose. He imagined the dust from the nearest fire pit — small, dirty, damaging — and yanked.

The dust slammed around him, the cloud covering a solid ten feet in all direction. A short, sharp half-sneeze, half-choke gave the Shield away. So close. How had the man gotten so close?

Didn't matter. Scott charged forward, using a kick to get his point across. Then he pushed his advantage, his fists busy, not holding back.

The Shield recovered after Scott's second punch. They were practically on top of each other. Not bound by police rules, not caring much for T-CASS's restrictions either, Scott let loose with his fury. That didn't stop the

Shield from fighting back, hard and mean.

Voices traveled up the river, growing louder. The brief distraction was all the Shield needed to sucker punch Scott in the head, driving him to his knees. His ears ringing, he could only watch the Shield as the Neut jumped back and ran.

More voices. The Shield's and someone else's. Scott forced himself off the ground and moved away from the cover of trees to the path.

Fucking hell.

The Shield had taken an early morning jogger hostage, his handgun to the woman's head, his rifle still on his back. He was actually smirking. Scott's fury burned hot. What did that son-of-a-bitch think he was doing?

"Okay, hotshot. Save the hostage, if you can." The Shield whispered something into the woman's ear.

"Help. Help," she called, not terribly convincing with a giggle. How the hell had the Shield convinced her that he wasn't really a threat? He looked like a threat without even trying.

Role-play or not, Scott reached for the Shield's hand gun and pulled. Nothing happened. He pulled again. Shit, he couldn't pull the gun through The Shield's barrier. But, if he couldn't pull the gun, how could The Shield shoot? How had he done it during the harbor attack?

"I could have killed her and ordered out for breakfast by now," the Shield taunted.

Scott's face burned, the fire in his belly raged. In the blink of an eye, the hostage disappeared and reappeared in his arms.

"Oh, my." The woman looked up at him. She had short, snow-white hair, with a grandmother's kind face.

"I'm so sorry, ma'am." He couldn't stop the stutter. "I meant to pull his gun away — "

Before he could finish, the grandmother patted him on the chest. "Oh, don't worry. There's nothing to get this old heart pounding than to have a couple of young studs fighting over me. You did a fine job. Keep up the good work."

She gave him a flirtatious wink and a wave to the Shield, who actually waved back, before jogging off.

The Shield's smile had disappeared by the time he walked over to Scott. "You were supposed to pull the gun."

"No shit. I couldn't from under your barrier."

"I didn't have my shield raised. You caught me off guard with the dust." The Shield holstered his gun. "Maybe you just didn't want it bad enough."

Scott burned with failure, and yet it wasn't quite as bad as when he was with Highlight. At least the Shield admitted he'd been caught off guard. The partial victory heartened him. "Maybe you're just an asshole."

"I'm always an asshole. You knew she wasn't in jeopardy, so when pulling my gun became too hard you took the easy way out. If I really wanted to kill her, I still had the gun to shoot both of you. You need to think ahead. Stop panicking about death. People die in war. They die in our line of work. You need to accept that you can't save everyone and sacrifices have to be made."

Scott looked away from the accusations. "If I'd pulled the hand gun or the rifle, you still could have broken her neck."

"You're damn right I would have broken her neck, but *you* would still have the ability to fight. You need to think ahead and stop being a pussy about killing people."

Scott recoiled. "I've killed people. I killed at least six yesterday. Even before Dane, I killed two people. It's not something I celebrate."

"Well, congratulations. I don't celebrate my kills either. That doesn't stop me from doing my job."

"Which is what, exactly? You mumble about a war, you dragged me through this bullshit training exercise. Why don't you just tell me what you're getting out of this?"

More voices echoed in the background. The Shield grabbed Scott by the arm and yanked him off the path and into the woods.

"It's about the Court of Blood. It's about what they're doing to Alts."

"How do you know about the Court of Blood?" The only people who knew about the Court were the Blackwoods and Thomas's elite team of hackers.

"I work for them."

Scott tripped over the pronouncement. "How? Why?"

"*Why* is not your damn business. *How* is what I'm teaching you."

"You're grooming me? You're recruiting me into... whatever it is they're doing." Scott tried to stop, but the Shield was unstoppable.

"Grooming you, yes. Recruiting you, no. The Court of Blood needs to be stopped, but it has to happen from the inside. I want to bring you into the organization. I'm trying to train you so they can't corrupt you."

They reached the entrance to the park, where Scott had ditched his bike. The Shield let go of Scott's arm.

"Why me?"

"You have potential, Grey. You can make the tough

shots when you need to."

"How do you figure that? Yes, I'm a good shot, but there are others who are just as good as, if not better than, me. Ask the SWAT commander. Or, hell, just go down to the shooting range near the Fargrounds."

"They're not Alts. Alts don't carry guns. Your mother saw to that."

"You mean T-CASS doesn't carry guns. You're an Alt, and you carry a gun. You even have clearance for the Arena. How do you know there aren't any other Neuts who are good shots?"

"Maybe there are, but they're not you. You have the combination of police training, Alt power, and a history of getting the job done. Neuts with guns only use them on the range. That's the only place they're allowed to use them."

"Legally." To believe all Neuts kept their guns at home while freelancing was a naïve belief.

For a second it looked as if the Shield was going to yank off his sunglasses in exasperation. Scott's breath hitched, hoping he could finally look the other man in the eyes. There was a secret there, but at the last moment the Shield only rubbed his forehead. "If I thought for a second that there was another Neut in this city who could kill two Alts and an agent of the Court of Blood, I would be training them, not you. You're what I have to work with."

Scott chuffed his disbelief. "You sure know how to build a guy's confidence. For a moment I thought I was the chosen one. Now, I'm just the least worst of all the possible terrible solutions."

"The chosen one is a myth of twisted magical thinking. You're real, Grey. Your skills are real. Your power is real. I don't have any more time to waste explaining myself. If you're in, I'll teach you what you need to know. If you have doubts — if you think this is all just a joke, then tell me now and I'll find someone else."

"You just said there is no one else." Scott leaned against the guard arm, the wood rough under his backside. This clandestine meeting with the Shield made him feel alive again. Hannah gave him comfort and solace, and a reason to get up in the morning, but the Shield offered him a destiny with instructions on how to get there. He hadn't realized how much he needed that until now.

T-CASS looked down on him. It would take more than a few parlor tricks with bean bags to gain their respect, and even then, he didn't know if he wanted their respect. He didn't care about T-CASS and they only tolerated him because of his family, because of Hannah.

She would join T-CASS eventually and they would take care of her. If he wanted to be a part of her life, he needed to be a part of T-CASS. He wanted what Thomas had with Catherine, but maybe T-CASS wasn't the only way to make it happen. Maybe The Shield could offer him an option.

"Okay, I'm in. I'll help you take down the Court of Blood."

The muscles at the very tips of The Shield's lips relaxed. Not even close to a real smile, but a damn sight closer to any other emotion Scott had seen.

"Where do we go from here?"

"You go nowhere. You use T-CASS to your advantage. You hate playing with beanbags, but use the access you have to build your other skills. The ones I'm teaching you. The ones you will need once you're undercover."

Scott was already making a mental list of things he could do from within the Arena. "What about my family? They're going to want to know why I'm suddenly nose-diving into training."

"You *cannot* confide in them. You're tempted to tell Carraro what you're up to. Forget it. He can't help you with this. And ditch the girl. She's a liability you can't afford."

Scott bristled at the order. "No. I won't give up Hannah. She's the only reason why I'm even considering this. The Court of Blood wants her. I want to protect her. Dumping her isn't an option."

"Keeping her isn't an option either. You think the Court is going to allow her to slip through their fingers? Why do you think they let Dane raise her? Her power is a game changer for the Alt community. Healing is a half-step short of resurrection. Entire religions are built around what she can do."

Scott's heart screamed. *It can't be the only way.* What had he just stepped into? Yesterday he was thinking of asking the Shield to rescue Hannah if Thunder City arrested her. "I'll..."

"No, you won't think about it. You'll do it. You don't have a choice. You're a part of this now. A part of the solution. Back away from me, and Hannah will be in more danger than when she was trapped inside the quarry."

He had to find another way, a way where he could protect Hannah and still...what? Love her? Live with her?

He was going to make sure Hannah lived. Thomas often called him stubborn, but loved him anyway. Scott's heart clutched at his father's words. Hannah was almost as stubborn as himself. -

Scott nodded to let the Shield know he'd agreed, but what he had planned couldn't be further from the truth.

Hannah pushed open the door to the video room with her hip, her breakfast balanced on a large plate, but stopped short when she saw Alek on the floor in front of the coffee table, fiddling with a new device. She looked around for Evan, but didn't see him. Evan had been the first twin to talk to her after she'd arrived in Thunder City.

Alek, she didn't know so well. The only reason she knew this was Alek and not his brother was because he was the techie of the two. He always had a gadget or tablet in hand, usually gaming, something she knew nothing about. Since Alek had his back to her, Hannah figured she could back out and return later when he was finished.

"You don't have to leave."

Caught in the act, Hannah stepped into the room. "Um. I can eat in the dining room so I'm not in your way."

"You're not." Alek stood up and brushed off his jeans. "I just got back a little while ago. I brought Cory's cycle back from the harbor. Now, I'm installing a new VR system for you and Cory."

"Both of us?"

"Yeah, hang on." He motioned Hannah to sit on the couch. "I'll go over to Thomas's place this afternoon. I need to install the same set-up there for Cory."

"What is it?" She put her breakfast down on the coffee table and took the headset Alek handed her.

"It's a standard VR set-up, but I wrote the software. It

runs on one of Carraro's private servers. Nothing fancy, but it's a way for you and Cory to be together without breaking any laws. You'll have complete privacy."

Hannah spun the headset around in her hands. "I don't understand."

Alek broke down a cardboard box. "I created a world as part of a gaming system I'm going to build and sell. Right now it's only world building — background scenes. It's not even close to beta-testing yet. No one else can get in there. You'll have a few options: strolling along a beach, there's a forest with bike paths, sailing on an ocean — you mentioned once you like to go sailing?"

Hannah nodded, her throat tightening up again when she thought of Roger. *He's happy now, floating in the waves of Mystic Bay forever.* The tightness in her throat eased.

"You're not going to be able to pick up a gun and defeat the evil empire or anything like that. I mean, eventually I'll finish writing that part of the program, but it'll take time —"

"This sounds perfect." Hannah clutched the headset to her chest as she sat down on the couch while Alek cleaned up the mess. "Thank you. How do I contact Scott through this?"

Alek sat next to her to walk her through the controls.

"Got it?" Alek asked.

"I think so." Hannah fiddled with the headset. "Alek, you're not doing this because I healed you, are you? I mean, it's not necessary. I heal people because I want to, not because I expect — "

Alek held up a hand, so she shut up.

"I'm doing this because Evan yanked my chain last night and told me to stop being an asshole. Not just to Cory, but to Thomas and well, anyone else who pisses me off. He's right. I hold grudges longer than he does. Cory was there when I needed family in the hospital. You healing me was just a bonus. I'm doing this because it's time I stopped being an asshole."

"I never thought you were an asshole."

Alek shrugged. "I think you've had to deal with a lot worse than just a run of the mill asshole in your life. You deserve much better."

Alek stood to leave, but then he turned back with the oddest look on his face. "Hannah, even though you and Cory will be operating in a virtual environment, that doesn't mean you can't be hurt. You know that right?"

"Of course." Hannah gave Alek her most confident grin, thankful his confession was over. Having someone sort of apologize to her gave her a weird feeling of worthiness that she wasn't used to. "I read an article about this while I was at Star Haven Memorial. A medical journal I borrowed from a break room. It talked about everything: people tripping over furniture, seizures, muscle spasms, eye strain — "

"No, I don't mean that." Alek sat back down next to her, reaching out to hold her gloved hand. His cheeks looked red, like he was blushing. "I mean, I don't know how close you and Cory became before the Oversight Committee told you that you couldn't touch, but if you two decide to try to get closer, um, physically, in this sort of environment — "

"Sex? You think Scott and I are going to have sex virtually?" Talk about being a day late and a hymen short.

"That's not why I wrote this program." Alek let go of her hand, as if he hadn't realized he had taken it in the first place. "I wrote it just to give you two some privacy to be together, but if things do progress — "

Hannah could hardly hear Alek's words as her own blush rushed to her ears. After last night, virtual sex couldn't beat the real thing, but if it was their only option until the Committee set them free, then — "I wouldn't do that. I mean, we wouldn't do that here in the house."

Alek paused. "I'm not judging, because it's not my business, but Catherine isn't always the best when it comes to talking about that sort of thing. I mean, I had my dad, and Cory had Carraro. Given your history with Miranda Dane I wasn't sure if you needed someone to talk to before you plugged in —"

"You guys were talking about me and Scott having sex?" Could this conversation get any worse?

Alek turned away from her. He looked like he was trying not to laugh. "No, but I've been using VR for quite some time now. I've seen what happens in there with people. Sometimes people mistake VR for reality and other times they mistake it for a safe place where anything goes without consequences. I'm just saying that if you make the decision to get closer to Cory, um, Scott, that being in a VR environment will protect you in certain ways, but in other ways, like emotionally, you could still get hurt."

Hannah wasn't sure what to say. Before last night, she might have been the least sexually experienced eighteen-year-old on the planet, but Alek was the last person she expected to have a birds and bees sort of concern for her.

"Thanks, Alek. I promise, whatever happens between me and Scott — I'll be careful."

He seemed relieved, patting her gloved hand once

more before he left the room. *What just happened here?* Hannah sat for a few moments, both touched by Alek's concern for her, but more worried that she'd actually managed to have a life-changing night with Scott and no one had noticed. Alek hadn't seen anything different about her. This was a good thing, right? Wasn't this why she'd fled to Thunder City in the first place? To disappear? Live a quiet life where no one took notice of her?

Miranda is dead. You don't have to hide from her. You shouldn't have to hide from the Committee.

A familiar buzz tickled her backside. She'd forgotten to turn her phone off. The recorded message icon flashed. She double checked the number. It was McNamara.

"Hannah?" McNamara answered on the first ring. He'd been waiting for her.

"Yes. I'm sorry, I'm eating breakfast. I'll be there as soon as I can get a ride." She'd been so flustered about talking to Alek about sex that she'd forgotten to ask him for a lift.

"The earlier, the better."

"Did something happen? Did the Oversight Committee tell you I couldn't work with you?"

"No, but if the Committee does try something, I think it would be better if you were here at the hospital. I can protect you if you're here."

Hannah had to figure he meant the VIP floor. It was so far underneath the hospital, it was the last place the Committee would look. It would buy her some time if she needed to escape, but Scott wouldn't have access. At least, he wouldn't have physical access. She wondered if he could translocate her from so far underground.

"Hannah, I promise. I'll be right beside you the

whole time. I won't let anything bad happen to you. You won't be alone."

She took a deep, calming breath. "Thank you. I'll be there soon. I just need to get a ride."

"I'll see you then." McNamara disconnected the line before she could.

Half an hour later, Hannah used her secret card to get back to McNamara's VIP level office. She still closed her eyes in the elevator, but her shaking wasn't quite as bad. Maybe she was getting used to closed doors?

This time when she stepped into the hallway, the Shield wasn't there standing guard. Without him, the hallway appeared incomplete, but far less threatening. She knocked on McNamara's door, but there was no answer. Her phone buzzed in her pocket again.

Meet me in the first autopsy room on the left ~ M.

The eerie quiet made the whole set-up creepier than it should have been. All the doors to all of the rooms were closed, so she knocked on the first autopsy room door.

He met her in the doorway, already wearing scrubs. Instead of inviting her inside the room to watch, he slipped into the hallway and closed the door behind him, as if he didn't want her to see what was in the room.

"How are you feeling this morning?"

Various song lyrics about being a real woman flittered through her mind, none of which she was going to repeat for McNamara. "I'm not sure."

He looked her over, as if searching for visible wounds. For a moment, she wondered if he could tell she wasn't a virgin anymore.

"Confusion is natural after trauma, and you've had quite a few traumas in the past few days."

"The past two weeks."

McNamara nodded, his sympathy obvious now and more welcome. His scrubs included gloves, so he was safe. She didn't flinch when he placed a soft hand on her shoulder.

"Since we lost the cadavers from the quarry raid, I suddenly find myself with more free time on my hands. I thought we'd try a few experiments with your Alt ability."

Experiments? The shadow of Miranda passed through her soul. How could this be? McNamara had saved her from the Committee. He'd thrown himself on top of her to protect her from the explosion at the harbor. He was nothing like Miranda. Experiment was just a word and she reacted to it like it was a closed door. It wasn't. It couldn't be. Not here, safe in the hospital with McNamara.

"Are you sure we should?" she asked, stalling.

McNamara moved past her to push open the door to another room behind her. "Why not? We're not working on the living, are we? It's not like we could cause a cadaver any harm or pain."

Not causing pain was true. Not causing harm, though? Everyone deserved some dignity after they died, didn't they? Even the cadavers transported from Star Haven would have been buried or cremated if their bodies weren't at the bottom of the harbor, including Miranda's.

Miranda's body polluted the harbor. Hannah pulled herself away from that morbid thought.

"You needn't worry about ethics," McNamara continued. "These folks donated themselves to further the cause of science. I can show you the paperwork if you wish."

Now Hannah felt foolish. Of course McNamara would make sure he had consent before experimenting. He was a doctor. Hannah never should have doubted him.

"Sorry. My thoughts drifted. I probably should get changed first."

McNamara motioned toward the counter. "I took the liberty of finding some scrubs for you. I had to guess at the size. Is medium big enough?"

Hannah hadn't been a size small since middle school. She snatched the scrubs off the counter.

"I'll leave you alone here to change. Come in when you're ready. Don't worry about your gloves."

Hannah changed as quickly as she could. When she entered the first autopsy room, she saw McNamara had a new cadaver inside, but this time, the cadaver was hooked up to an IV and a cardiopulmonary bypass.

"What's all of this?" She couldn't even guess why a cadaver would need a machine to replace the functions of the heart and lungs.

"Part two of what you started before the harbor attack."

"Are you not sure she's dead? Is that what I'm checking for you?"

"Oh, she's quite dead. Heart attack, poor thing. Only thirty-six and quite healthy. Not sure what brought the heart attack on, which is why she's down here."

"Down here in the VIP level, but not upstairs? Is she famous?"

"No. We're just borrowing her for a little while."

A niggle of doubt wormed its way into her heart. She wasn't as fluent in medical ethics as she was in anatomy, but this setup reminded her of a few horror films.

McNamara must have noticed her doubt. "Really, Hannah. I didn't select the cadaver easily or without the utmost reverence. Her family, if she has one, will only be grateful if we can solve the mystery of why she died. They'll be even more grateful if we can figure it out without slicing her open, wouldn't you think?"

It all sounded reasonable. The autopsy process was a barbaric way of solving mysteries, but so far no one had found a way of replacing it. At least, not until now. McNamara had no reason to want to harm a dead woman, and he was her mentor after all. Of course he'd want to push her to her limits. How could either one of them know what she was capable of if she didn't push past her boundaries? "Sorry. To the families, the autopsy process must look like a necessary evil."

"Is it, though?" McNamara pulled her closer to the body. "Does it have to be a necessary evil?"

Now Hannah could see what McNamara had done. He'd hooked up an IV to push blood into the body. The CPB machine was forcing it to circulate.

"You want me to bloodsurf through her?"

"You're a smart woman, Hannah. Your knowledge of anatomy is near perfect. Let's take it one step further. We now know that you can penetrate a dead body, but you still need blood flowing to surf through it. This one has blood flowing through it. Try to do what you did before. Try to surf to her heart and let me know what you find there."

It all sounded so reasonable. Saving lives, healing people. She didn't do anything different than your average doctor, nurse, or even paramedic. But this *was* different. The wrongness made her skin crawl.

"Hannah. This is just an autopsy. You're not doing anything more than what I would do. You're just not going to leave the scars on her body that I would. It's okay. You're doing the right thing."

McNamara's reassuring voice conquered her concerns. Of course it would be okay. She wasn't doing anything that McNamara hadn't done hundreds of times, but she could be cleaner about it. If it worked.

She placed her hand on the woman's chest, just over her left breast. Might as well start as close to her target as possible.

Inside. It worked. It actually worked, except the blood flow lacked the pulse of a beating heart. The smooth ride to the bicuspid valve didn't require any thought on her part to keep herself moving forward. She didn't have to fight the current. As fast as she could move in a living human, without a pulse she moved even faster.

She still had work to do, so she used her newfound momentum and zipped through the rest of the woman's body. When she reemerged, almost as quickly as she entered, she had figured out the mystery.

"You did it!"

McNamara sounded almost as amazed as she felt. Her whole body tingled with the joy of discovering an amazing gift.

"I did. And, I think I know why she died. Diabetes, possibly undiagnosed, and she smoked."

"Well, that does seem plausible and reasonable. I'll follow up on your findings." He started to disconnect the equipment.

"Wait. You mean you're going to autopsy her anyway?"

McNamara paused, but removed his hands from the switch. "Oh, Hannah, I'm so sorry. But, this was an experiment. An unauthorized one at that. I do have to perform the autopsy the normal way. It's still my job. Until the Committee is satisfied with your control, this has to remain between us."

Of course, dummy. She couldn't just break the laws of science, not to mention what she suspected were several dozen ethical standards, and expect the doctors on the Committee to overlook that. It could be years before they allow her to do something like this again.

"It'll be okay, Hannah." McNamara returned to disconnect the CPB machine. "I promise. Now that we know what you're capable of we can start working toward the goal of showing the Committee by using proper channels. It'll take time, but it will be done."

Yes, it would. McNamara would see that it would get done. She'd never met anyone who could navigate through the maze of rules with the slickness of oil like he did. He had a way of making you trust him, so when he did break the rules, no one would believe it — and even if they did, they would forgive him. Just as she did. Or, did she forgive him because he gave her permission to join him in his subterfuge?

At the end of the day, she was responsible for her actions. The Committee might say she was influenced by someone she trusted, but McNamara hadn't forced her to bloodsurf through the woman on the table. She did it herself. She made the choice. A poor choice by certain standards, but she'd been making a lot of those lately.

"Are you planning to call someone?" he asked. McNamara wasn't even looking at her, and yet he knew she'd pulled her phone out of her pocket. She hadn't even realized what she'd done until he mentioned it.

She put the phone back and slipped on her gloves instead. "Sorry. I was going to call Scott. I wanted to tell him about our success, but I guess I shouldn't."

"No, you really shouldn't. Have you given any thought to what we talked about yesterday?"

"About breaking up with Scott?" How could she answer a question like that after last night? "I haven't thought about it because I can't do it. He means too much to me."

McNamara brought the sheet up to cover the cadaver and motioned her to the door. Together they walked back to his office.

The Shield was still missing. Maybe McNamara didn't need as much protection down here? They appeared to be the only two people on the whole floor — and yet, who had helped McNamara set up the autopsy room? Who was going to bring the body back? It seemed odd he would do either by himself.

The oddness of the situation disappeared when McNamara motioned for her to sit behind his desk. Jimmy Chung's records had already appeared on the screen. McNamara was trying to help her, so she dug into the records as McNamara left, remembering to keep the door open. He might want her to break up with Scott, but Hannah had other plans.

CHAPTER SIXTEEN

Scott made a pit stop to change clothes and clean up at Thomas's penthouse. Hannah hovered on the edge of his consciousness the entire time he showered and changed. Last night wasn't what he'd had in mind for their first time. He'd wanted to take it slower, more careful, more romantic with flowers and a fine meal and all of the other things a man does to seduce the woman he cares about.

Instead, he gave into her command to speed things up, to give her what she demanded when she asked for more. The turn-on spurred him to keep going and hope that he didn't hurt her. She didn't appear hurt, but he'd call her later to make sure.

He checked his watch after his shower. Not even mid-morning and he already needed a second cup of coffee — black and strong. He'd have to grab a cup at the shop located on the first level.

All the coffee in the world wouldn't solve his problem with committing both to Hannah and the Shield. His conversation with the Shield circled his protective instincts, pecking at the weak spots, looking for a break in the barrier that would let loose all of his insecurities.

His training as a cop demanded that he let Thomas know that the Shield worked for the Court of Blood.

The Shield knew their secrets, their mission, their vision, their members, their locations. He claimed to want to bring Scott into the organization to bring them down, but did Scott trust the Shield enough to follow him?

If it weren't for the Shield, he, Hannah, and McNamara would have died at the harbor. They worked well together, in tandem, as if they were already a team. Scott knew he needed the kind of training he wouldn't get from T-CASS, but there were still too many unanswered questions about his new mentor.

And what about McNamara? Was he a part of the Court of Blood, too? Or, was he part of the Shield's subterfuge, keeping Hannah away from the Court without making it look as if he was protecting her?

Scott needed answers, but first, he'd promised Hannah and Betty Chung that he would help figure out what the deal was with Jimmy. Until he was sure about the Shield, he would focus on Hannah's report about someone slicing through Jimmy Chung's spine, a barbaric mystery that needed to be solved. He'd worry about the Shield and the Court of Blood later, after his training session at the Arena.

If Thunder City cared about his dilemma, morning traffic didn't show it. He hit every light between downtown and the row of factories bordering the Fargrounds. Nik had encouraged him to observe Jimmy himself; Nik wouldn't be able assist except to advise from the sidelines. If Dani was going to donate her kidney to her younger brother soon, Nik would stay by her side.

Scott had to wonder if Nik's new girlfriend had something to do with Highlight's attitude during their training sessions. Scott had only met Serena Jakes once when he had been a kid, maybe ten or eleven. Nik was already in high school, and Serena was his brother's first serious girlfriend. She'd been nice enough to him then, asking him questions about the new computer he'd gotten for his birthday, but she didn't really have much else to say to him.

He buried this latest train of thought, as he pulled into the driveway of a row of townhouses. He found the right number just as a woman opened the door. He could see the resemblance to Betty, despite the longer hair and stouter body. An older sister, it would seem, but not by much.

"Ms. Han, I'm Scott Grey."

"I recognize you from the news. Your mother was here this morning to check on Jimmy."

"Is she still here? My mother, I mean."

Rita shook her head. "No, she didn't stay long. She wanted to make sure Jimmy was adjusting. That's what makes Captain Spectacular so special to us Norms. She really does care about us. Please, come in."

Rita opened the door wider to let him inside. He looked around. Rita's home, unlike Betty's, was tidy. "I was wondering if I could see Jimmy?"

Rita sighed. "Betty showed you the video, didn't she?"

Sisters talked to each other. He should have expected no less, but after years of not talking to his brothers, the familial connection still caught him off guard. "Well, yes, she did."

"It proves nothing." Rita backed away from the door to let him inside. "Look, my sister means well, but this whole 'my kid is an Alt business' didn't start until after her husband ran off with another woman. He lives in Star Haven, but is fighting Betty for custody. He thinks...we all think...Betty is trying to fake Jimmy's Alt power to keep him from getting custody. If her ex insists on living in Star Haven, and if Jimmy is an Alt, Jimmy can't live there because of the Alt ban. If her ex wants to see his son, he'll have to move back here, or at least commute here every weekend or however the court sets up visitation rights."

It was a simple strategy, but only if Jimmy was truly an Alt. Betty had to know she could only keep such a charade up for so long. Since no one knew, except for Hannah, what caused Alt power, there was no way to prove that a child was an Alt until they used their ability in front of witnesses. Hannah had promised Catherine that she would never tell another soul, not even Scott.

He took a seat near the living room picture window. "I'd still like to see Jimmy, if you don't mind."

Rita left the room. A moment later, she returned with Jimmy in her arms. She sat the boy down in the middle of the room.

"Jimmy, this is Mister Grey."

The boy blinked at his aunt, then turned to stare at Scott. He blinked again, but didn't try to crawl or stand or fuss with the toy in his hand.

"Hi, Jimmy. I'm glad to meet you. You've had a couple of exciting days."

Still not much of a reaction. Jimmy sat and stared.

"He's tired." Rita reached down to pull Jimmy into her lap with a groan. Scott guessed Jimmy was of average weight for his age, with dark hair and eyes like his mother. "After the operation, he became lethargic. The doctors said it's just a reaction to all the trauma from the surgery and the drugs. It'll take time for him to come back to his usual self. It's only been six months after all."

"What sort of drugs is he taking?" Scott had no idea of what was necessary for transplants. Maybe he could ask Daniella Rose? With her transplant already in the planning stages, plus working in the biomedical field, she might be able to spot something out of the ordinary.

"Oh, too many for me to name. I can print off a list for you."

Scott held out his arms to take Jimmy, while Rita disappeared again. Jimmy's head found Scott's shoulder and he fell asleep without Scott having to rock him to sleep or anything. Was six months enough time for a child to return to his normal behavior? Did Betty's attack on Hannah really tire Jimmy to the point where he couldn't stay awake longer than a few minutes? Scott rocked back and forth despite Jimmy's contentedness. He knew nothing about babies, but even he could see that this was not the same Jimmy he'd seen in the video. Yet, everyone made excuses for the change in personality. Everyone except Betty, who would know her son better than anyone else.

Rita returned with the printed list of medications.

"Thanks, Ms. Han. I should go."

He shifted Jimmy back to his aunt. "You're pretty good at that," she said.

"What do you mean?" He picked up the paper and gave the list a brief glance.

"Handling kids." Ms. Han stroked Jimmy's hair. "You should try it with your own."

Scott raised his eyes from the paper. "You've been reading the gossip columns."

Rita smiled. "Well, it's far more pleasant to read about two young people in love than about all the nasty politics between here and Star Haven. I apologize if I was out of line, but even the Captain said she was happy that you were happy."

His mother had said that? Scott slipped the paper into his pocket. Nothing looked familiar to him, so he'd have to research the medications later. For now he put on his game face. "There are worse people to sound like than Captain Spectacular."

He waved so Rita wouldn't feel as if she had to stand up and show him out.

As he mounted his cycle, his phone buzzed. It was Juan.

I'm still here in TC if you want to meet.
Your stuff made it through the attack.

Scott let out his breath. Juan had survived the attack. He'd wondered, but his first priority had been Hannah.

Yes. I want to meet.
Been busy since the attack.
Where are you?

He hadn't given his stuff a second thought since he'd brought Hannah across the Bay.

At the harbor hotel.
We could meet out front,
on the boardwalk.

Scott checked his watch. He needed to book it if he was going to get to the Arena for his training session on time. As much as he'd prefer to blow it off and meet with Juan now, he knew there would be more trouble for him and Hannah down the road if he canceled.

Maybe this evening?
Have to keep an appointment
this afternoon.

Scott held his breath until Juan answered.

5:30?

Yes. I'll meet you at the hotel's
entrance to the boardwalk.
I'll see you then.

Scott wanted to keep the conversation running, but he didn't want to appear desperate. He tucked his phone away, and revved the Harley's engine.

Traffic still hadn't improved much. He had to detour away from Harbor Regional where the police had set up roadblocks so ambulances could have an easier time redistributing less critical patients to other facilities. Parking at the Arena was also an issue, with the planned soccer game going forward despite the attack. Never let it be said that Thunder City didn't know how to keep calm.

"You're late."

Scott bit back his sarcasm. The last thing he needed today was Highlight's criticisms. Instead he ignored her and walked to the other end of the room. If she wanted an explanation, she'd have to stand there forever. He could see the line of beanbags she'd created on the table, all new. Shinzo stood behind the screen with the camera, waiting for Highlight to give Scott the order to pull.

Scott decided not to wait. He'd learned more in the past few days from the Shield than he ever had from Highlight. His determination to keep Hannah safe and in his arms overrode his good sense.

One by one he pulled each of the beanbags into his left hand, dropping them to the ground beside him, not waiting for Highlight to comment. After he pulled the last one, he pushed instead of pulled and sent the beanbag back to the table, placing it where it had started.

"You've improved. What's changed?"

She sounded suspicious, as if Scott had managed to find a way to cheat. Except there was no cheat. He had motivation now. A desire to use his powers. His interest in sharing information, however, didn't reach beyond the fact that he'd shown up and passed the test.

"Nothing's changed. I passed the test. I'll see you tomorrow."

"Get back here, Grey."

Scott ignored her and left the room.

※

This time the groan wasn't an echo from the floor above filtering through the vents. Hannah leaned back in McNamara's executive chair, her eyes blurred, her headache blossoming across her frontal lobe, headed for the parietal and temporal. If she didn't stop reading Jimmy's records now, it would reach the occipital and cerebellum. Once that happened, she'd fall to the floor and spend the night staring at the ceiling of McNamara's office.

The rumble in her stomach protested the thought of another empty hour, so Hannah shut down the screen with Jimmy's records. She hadn't found anything out of the ordinary. He'd been diagnosed with a low-grade focal brainstem glioma of the medulla. Surgery had removed the entire tumor and further examinations had shown that follow-up radiation wasn't necessary.

The splice she'd found on Jimmy's spine was located below the medulla at the point where the spine began, but there was no reference in the records to such a splice. Not even a footnote in any of the post-surgical reports and follow-up exams. It was as if the splice itself had never happened. Except she'd seen it, hadn't she?

Hannah checked the time. She must be tired if she was beginning to doubt her own findings when she bloodsurfed.

Through the open door, the empty hallway beckoned her toward the elevators. McNamara hadn't returned. Neither had the Shield.

She needed one more minute. What she really wanted was a head massage. Not for the first time, she bemoaned her inability to heal herself. Maybe she could ask Scott for a massage the next time they were together? The thought of his hands on her body sent a tingle from her hippocampus to the phalanges in her toes.

Ugh. Nothing shut down a lovely thought of Scott's lovemaking like a perfect understanding of human anatomy. Another sigh and a moan, and she shoved herself off the chair.

"*Mommy.*"

She froze mid-push.

"*Mommy.*"

Nope. Not her imagination. But a child calling for his mom wouldn't echo from pathology upstairs either, unless she had fallen into a horror movie.

"Mommy."

I-will-not-freak-out. I-will-not-freak-out. A child telepath, maybe? The Alt clinic was right next door. Pathia had never contacted her directly, so she had no idea what it felt like to have someone else in her head. Scott would know, though. She pulled out her phone to call him.

"Mommy."

She hesitated. The word echoed exactly the same as the first time she'd heard it. Same tone, same pitch, same rhythm, and it sounded vaguely familiar.

"Mommy."

She knew that voice. How could she forget it? She'd heard it every year in a holiday movie about a boy who wished for a real family on Christmas. It was slow, sappy, appeared on more than one channel, and she watched it every single time because of the comfort of watching the deliriously happy child race into his new family's arms at the end, calling *Mommy, mommy, mommy*. That clip had become a popular meme over the years, one that she sometimes played on her computer when she couldn't shake her own depression.

She sat back down to check McNamara's computer. She had closed the medical record program before standing, and the browser was shut down as well. Just to be sure, she turned off the volume.

"Momm-"

The whine stopped mid-syllable. From over the top edge of the computer, she could see through the open door down the hallway. In theory, all cadavers were stored upstairs before they were autopsied. Where the freezers were. Like the one in which Miranda had locked her.

Cold iced over her headache. Her appetite

disappeared. *Out. Get out of here before Miranda returns.*

In order to get out she had to get to the elevators. Seen through the open door, the hallway looked a lot colder, emptier, and much longer than it had an hour ago. Despite her raging fear, she remembered to turn off the light in the office as she stepped over the threshold. Bright fluorescent lights overhead made her blink.

She didn't hear the voice again until she stood parallel to the elevator doors. She hit the "up" button and waited.

"Mommy."

"Stop it! You're scaring me!" The first stage to overcoming your fear is to acknowledge it, right? Okay, she was scared. She was hearing voices in her head. A voice from a stupid movie she hadn't seen since she'd escaped Miranda. This was Miranda's fault. Miranda was haunting her with hallucinations.

Auditory hallucinations. Like the kind Betty Chung claimed Jimmy could do.

The elevator door opened, waiting for Hannah to enter, but she didn't. If Jimmy could throw sounds, and he was separated from his mother, wouldn't the first thing he would call for be his mother? And if he couldn't call for his mother using his own voice, he would create a familiar sound clip to do it for him, wouldn't he? Could he?

But Jimmy was far away, living with his aunt in the Fargrounds. Could he throw sounds from so far away? Could his call reach her here, underground, through tons of concrete, metal, and earth?

Hannah turned away from the inviting elevator. What if Jimmy wasn't home? What if he was here, in the hospital? Had he gotten sick? She pulled out her phone. Her first instinct was to call Scott again, but she disconnected before she pressed his number. Even if she called him, anything she told him would set him to worry, and he couldn't get to the VIP level without a key card. She dialed McNamara instead.

"Hannah? I'm so sorry. I didn't realize how late it had gotten. You must be starving."

Her empty stomach growled. Just hearing a human voice calmed her down. The hallway became less bright, less frightening in the blink of a second.

"Yes, I am, but are you busy right now? Could you check something for me?"

"I could use a break from all this politicking. What do you need?"

She swallowed, searching for a way to make her request sound perfectly normal. "Could you see if for some reason Jimmy's here, either in the hospital or at the clinic? Maybe he had a check-up this afternoon or something?"

McNamara was quiet for second. "I can check, yes. Did something happen? Did you find something in his records that needs immediate attention?"

"No. There's nothing in his records. I just — " she couldn't get the words past the tightness in her throat. "I'm just really overtired and need to go home, but it would help if I knew he wasn't here in the hospital. That he's really safe."

It was a lame excuse, but it was the best she could do.

"Okay. I'm going to send the Shield down to escort you back up here. I'll have the answer for you when you arrive."

Oddly, the idea of the Shield escorting her made her feel safer. If anyone could scare away the irrational creepiness of her imagination, it would be the Shield.

"Okay. Thank you. I'll be waiting." She disconnected the call.

How tired she must be to also forget that there might be other Alt children who could produce auditory hallucinations. With the Alt clinic was right next door, it wasn't unreadable to assume another child was calling for his mommy. After all, there had been an Alt who could translocate objects before Scott arrived in Thunder City. Blockhead was as strong as Captain Spectacular. Both Looper and Pathia were telepaths, albeit with different ways of expressing their ability. Duplicate abilities were not unusual in the Alt community. She, alone, was unique.

Still, it wouldn't hurt to check. Just to be sure. She'd ask Doctor McNamara when she saw him.

Around her, the low hum of the hospital's air conditioning drowned out the silence, but there was no mysterious voice calling for a mommy. Her fear lessened, knowing the Shield was on his way, so Hannah wandered toward the autopsy rooms. There were three of them, two on her left, one on her right with a supply closet next to the single room. The opposite end of the hallway was closed off by an emergency exit marked with a huge red sign reading "Do not open. Alarm will sound."

"Mommy."

Damn it! The voice sounded quieter this time, but the cadence hadn't changed. She stood in front of the first autopsy room on the right. The room where McNamara first had her experiment with her ability to surf inside a cadaver.

Open the door. Go on. You know it's empty. You can't keep a cadaver on a table all day long with no one autopsying it. Open the door.

She slammed the door open, the bang challenging her inner voice. Nothing. As she'd expected, the room was empty. Neat, clean, with all of the equipment back in its proper places, the temperature a few degrees colder than the hallway. She closed the door and opened the next room. The same conditions there, and the same with the third.

She tried the maintenance closet. Inside, she saw an imposing block of metal instead of supplies. A backup generator, maybe, in case the hospital lost power? It emitted a low thrum, so maybe it supplied power to the lower levels of the hospital, and wasn't just a backup.

That left the emergency door. She closed the door to the generator's room, and put her hand on the push bar for the emergency door. The cold metal didn't entice her to open it, nor did the red sign right in front of her face. Should she? Did she dare open the door to see if Jimmy was on the other side?

"Don't open it."

She spun with a screech.

Son-of-a-bitch. She'd been so wrapped up in herself, in her imagination, that the Shield had managed to sneak up her. She couldn't even stammer an apology. His heavy hand on her shoulder yanked her away from the door.

"You'll set off the alarm for the entire hospital."

"Yeah, I know, but...."

He maneuvered himself between her and the door. "But, what?"

Oh, hell, the mirrored sunglasses did nothing to ease her confusion. "Nothing. I was just curious, and it went too far. It won't happen again."

To avoid any further questions, she spun away, intending to head for the elevators. As she did, she couldn't help but notice the Shield's reflection in one of the folder holders outside the nearest autopsy room. He'd turned away from her and was examining the exit door.

Instead of asking why, she broke into a run. The elevator was still open and waiting, so she entered. A moment later, the Shield joined her. He was the one who hit the floor button that would take her to McNamara. He had to because she'd wrapped her arms around herself so tight she couldn't let go. The closed elevator doors didn't help.

"You're not going to do it, are you?"

Hannah had to blink. In her frightened state, she had to look at the Shield to make sure he was the one who was talking to her, and not some imaginary voice.

"Do what?" She almost stammered, but instead dug her fingernails into her biceps.

He turned to face her, for all the good it did with the sunglasses. "Break it off with Grey."

Had McNamara asked him to pressure her? Oh, hell, now her anger rose up against her panic. The toxic mix damn near made her sick. "No. No, I am *not* going to break up with Scott. What the hell is it with people trying to talk us out of our relationship? Just leave us the *hell* alone."

Good Lord, did he actually smirk at her outrage? Damn him, anyway. The elevator opened and she stormed out into the next corridor, which was just as bright, but much larger and busier, with other doctors, interns, and orderlies milling about. McNamara stood off to one side, talking on his phone.

Leaving the Shield in her wake, Hannah stormed over to McNamara. He held his hand out to her, pulling her out of the department's foot traffic. She huffed, but waited quietly. It wasn't his fault that she couldn't decide if she was scared, crazy, or just pissed off.

He disconnected the phone. "Jimmy isn't here or over at the clinic. Want to tell me what this is all about?"

Hannah looked around. The open corridor, the bright lights, the Shield standing at her back. No, she didn't want to talk about hearing voices in her head or through walls or vents or anywhere where anyone else could overhear her.

"Not here. In fact, not tonight. I'm too tired and I really just need to go home and have dinner."

She could see McNamara look at the Shield. She imagined the Shield responding by not responding at all, or maybe by giving his boss a casual "she's an emotional kid, what were you expecting" shrug.

"Okay. Give me ten minutes and I'll — "

"No." She had to get out of here, and not with McNamara or his bodyguard. "You're busy. I'll get Alek or Evan to bring me back. It'll be faster and you can finish your job."

More eye contact between the two men. "If you're sure."

"I'm sure."

She didn't wait for their response. Pushing herself back into the flow of traffic, she returned to the hated elevators. Neither man followed her. She punched the number for the garage level. Her body shook during the entire ride, but once up there, she pulled out her phone. "Alek, it's Hannah. Could I bother you for a lift home from the hospital?"

CHAPTER SEVENTEEN

Scott parked as close as he could to the hotel at the harbor boardwalk. The extra-wide front steps led up to a wraparound porch with circular dining tables belonging to the interior restaurant. People milled about talking in low tones. He suspected many of them were survivors from the Star Haven delegation, left here until the investigators from both cities could interview them. They gave him the side-eye when he walked by, either because they recognized him or because they were suspicious of anyone not part of the delegation and assumed he was an Alt.

The front doors slid to the side, letting him into the well-lit lobby. More people gathered together in clumps, talking. A decorative fountain spraying water in the center of the room created white noise, drowning out what folks were saying.

Scott knew where to go, so he weaved his way across the polished floor, ignoring the security guards, whose eyes followed him as he headed out the back doors. Down one more set of stairs, and he was on the boardwalk.

He looked to his left, but the half-sunken ship docked at the warehouse was too far away to see. The sun had started to set early this time of year, but it wasn't quite dark enough for the lanterns to light the boardwalk.

The colorful shops on either side of the hotel beckoned to the tourists milling about with music and chalkboard signs. There weren't as many tourists as he'd expected. Either they had decided to stay away from the boardwalk voluntarily, or more than likely, the police had closed down the boardwalk farther north, closer to the warehouse.

Long wooden benches lined the handrail separating the boardwalk from the Bay. Juan sat on one of them, dressed in jeans and a light jacket instead of his uniform. He'd crossed one leg over the other, with a small brown box, not completely unlike the one he'd given to Hannah earlier, tucked under his left arm.

Scott walked up to his friend, his heart in his throat. Juan didn't stand, nor did he look at Scott. Maybe it was too much to ask for his former partner to remember the good times they'd had together? All Juan could see was a traitor to the Norms, a former friend who had lied about being an Alt.

Deciding to say nothing, Scott sat on the bench, far enough away to give the other man space. He chose not to say anything, letting Juan take the lead on this.

It took a minute of uncomfortable silence before Juan decided he was ready to talk.

"Were you there yesterday? Did you see the attack?"

Scott swallowed, taking his time to answer, keeping it simple. "Yeah, I was there."

More silence. Then Juan said, "The anti-Alts planted the bomb on the ship. They had people working from the inside. They were planning an attack all along. Not even working for Mayor — for Dane. They didn't care about the delegation. They didn't care about who they shot. They were just looking for a high body count."

"We know that." Scott knew Juan still wasn't looking at him, but he nodded anyway. "We've always known that, even if we couldn't prove it. We let this happen because they've only targeted Alts in the past. Now, they're targeting anyone who gets between them and the Alts. Dane's death hasn't changed anything. She just fueled the ideology of 'anyone not with them is against them and should die a traitor's death.'"

More silence, but Scott waited. He'd wait as long as he had to.

"Why didn't you tell me?"

There was the question he'd been waiting for. "I didn't know."

"How could you not know you were an Alt? Your mother is Captain Spectacular." Juan turned to look at him, but Scott couldn't return it. He didn't want to see the hurt, the disappointment in the eyes of someone he still thought of as a friend.

"Because I was broken. Something inside of me broke, either when or before I was born. I never had any Alt ability, ever. Not until Hannah healed me. When she was inside of me, rebuilding my body, saving my life, she fixed what was broken and my Alt abilities manifested." He'd had the opportunity to change it because Hannah would have broken what she'd fixed. He was the one who had changed his mind.

"Fixed you, huh. How did she do that? What did she fix?"

"I don't know." Juan's snort of disbelief triggered Scott's anger. "Why do you want to know? What difference does it make? Unless you're planning to go Dane's route and incarcerate me so that you can dissect me, experiment on me, or make me your slave, what possible reason could you have for wanting to know?"

"I'm all for locking Alts away from the rest of us. Just like you used to be."

Scott flinched. He'd voiced the same sentiment lots of times once he'd moved to Star Haven, but he also knew it would never happen. He knew how powerful his family was, and he had felt safe knowing they were across Mystic Bay and wouldn't bother him or anyone else in Star Haven.

Hannah's escape from Dane's custody had changed all of that. Juan had done his job as a cop; he obeyed the law, including whatever orders had come down through the chain of command. He had ambitions, just like Scott. Nothing had changed, except that Scott had lied to Juan about his name, his family, and his past.

"What will you do now?" Scott glanced at his friend, who still looked at him like a problem that needed solving. "You're in a city filled with Alts."

"Orders, man." As he talked, Juan flicked the air with his fingers as if brushing off an annoyance. "Star Haven is still in chaos. Our government is temporary until we can hold elections. The Left Fists are still running wild. The Anti-Alts are growing stronger, obviously. The Mayor says we gotta stay here until the investigators talk to us. We're still waiting because there's no one in Star Haven to lead the investigation."

"So, you're stuck here. At least for a few more days?"

"Guess so." Juan must have remembered the reason he wanted to meet with Scott in the first place because he shoved the box in Scott's direction.

"Thanks." The flaps hadn't been sealed, so Scott flipped them open. Two items lay on top of some t-shirts. He ran his fingers over the badge — a symbol of what he was and would never be again. He left it in the box — reminiscing was the last thing that would keep Juan talking to him. Instead, he pulled out the small four-by-six-inch picture in a simple black frame, fit for a nightstand.

"Your dad?" Juan guessed.

"Biological father." Scott had mentioned he had been adopted during one of their first few shifts together, but not by who.

"Was he an Alt too? Did he have the same powers that you do?"

"He was an Alt, but his abilities were different. Thunder City called him Shelter because he could protect himself and others from bullets and debris and whatever got tossed at him."

Scott really hadn't thought much about the picture since leaving Thunder City. He had kept it on his nightstand mostly to annoy Catherine, who refused to talk about her second husband, even with their son.

"You miss him?"

"Can't miss someone you never met. He died before I was born." Scott shrugged. "Nik — Ghost — told me a story once about how Cole would cover half the back yard with his barrier and let him, Alek, and Evan bounce along it like a trampoline."

"Sounds like fun. Alek and Evan, they were the ones in the air yesterday?"

"Yeah. Rumble and Roar. Evan was the one who fell into the blast. Alek's leg was broken when he collided with the container, but he kept it from falling."

Juan leaned over putting his elbows on his knees. "I would have died if he hadn't. I was trying to get everyone running for the ship to run in the other direction. Not that it would have saved anyone."

"Alek knows that. He watched his twin fall into the fire, but he still kept the container in the air."

"Is he all right?"

Was Juan really concerned or was he just being polite? "He's fine. They'll both be fine."

"And what about Hannah? I gave her a box from the Mayor's office."

"She's fine, too."

Juan didn't ask about the box, so Scott left it alone. Instead, Juan sat back up, his eyes finding the middle distance between the bench and the hotel. "Living without Alts — I chose that because I just couldn't see losing my job to folks with superpowers who could do it better, but after yesterday — maybe they're right. Maybe us Norms should just step aside and let the Alts take over."

"Don't say that." Scott scooted closer to Juan to press his point. "If Alts could do everything better, Thunder City wouldn't bother with a police or fire department. Alts have weaknesses. That's what Miranda Dane was trying to exploit in her quarry prison. The news media makes it look like Alts are all over the place, but in the past two weeks I've almost lost all three of my brothers — one of them because I fucking shot him in the chest."

Juan had to have known that. He must have seen the coverage on TV.

"There aren't as many Alts as you would think," Scott continued, "Even fewer of them are members of T-CASS. I still don't know what I'm going to do with my ability. I just need a fair shake to figure it out."

Juan shrugged. "Guess it helps when your family owns half the city."

No point in denying it. "It helps, but don't forget what my mother has lost in the process." Scott waved the picture of his father at Juan. "Money didn't save her first marriage and it didn't save my father. And don't forget, my brothers are her sons too."

Juan nodded. "Fair enough."

Scott dropped the picture back into the box. Maybe he'd leave it there, along with the badge that he'd never wear again. His need to annoy his mother had long passed. It's not like she'd be visiting his bedroom any time in the near future anyway.

"I know you can't leave until Star Haven can get its own investigators over here, but if you'd like see Thunder City beyond the boardwalk — "

Juan stood at the same time Scott did. "Believe it or not, Grey, you're not the only person I know in Thunder City. I've been here before. I know my way around well enough. I just don't want to live here."

Scott took a risk and held out his gloved hand for a shake. Juan looked at the hand, then shook it, just like the first time they had met.

"See you around, Juan."

"Maybe."

Scott headed back into the hotel and through the lobby, keeping his eyes straight ahead. If any of the guests noticed his meeting with Juan, they didn't challenge him. Neither did security. He was shoving the box into one of his saddlebags when a familiar buzz tickled his backside. He pulled out the phone. Hannah.

"Hey there," he said. "Are you okay?"

"Yeah. No. I don't know. Are you at Thomas's place?"

Her voice sounded rough, like she'd been crying. "No. Not yet. Why are you crying?"

"I'm not really. I'm overtired, but I really need to talk to you. Something happened at the hospital."

"Did McNamara hurt you?"

"No."

"The Shield?" He'd rip the bastard's heart right out of his chest if he'd laid a hand on Hannah.

"No. No. Nothing like that. I just — "

A voice in the background. Alek or Evan, maybe. He heard Hannah say "okay" before she returned to talk to him.

"Alek set up a VR system at Thomas's penthouse for us to use. We should test it."

Odd, but then Alek had been acting odd since the hospital. This drama couldn't be about Alek or a VR system, though. "Yeah, sure. I'll be there in about twenty minutes or so. I'll call you when I'm ready."

"Good. I miss you."

That made him smile. "I miss you too. See you in a little bit."

He disconnected the line and peeled out of the parking lot. Hannah wasn't in danger, but if the past two weeks were any indication, trouble was stalking her again. He needed to get home fast.

※

Hannah woke up with a start when her phone buzzed. She'd laid down on the couch in the video room, her dinner plate empty and the water glass half full. Her phone indicated only a half hour had passed, but already she felt less cranky and more annoyed with herself.

"Scott?"

"Yeah, I'm here."

"Do you see the equipment Alek left behind for you?"

"Yeah. Go ahead and log in. I'll meet you in there in a minute."

She disconnected the phone and put on the goggles, vest, and gloves. Flying with Alek had lifted her spirits, and he'd been sweet enough to bring her a tray of leftovers from the kitchen after he'd reviewed the VR instructions one more time. She followed those instructions, and activated the VR system.

Falling autumn leaves swirled around her, and the sun hovered near the horizon, leaving behind a clear late evening sky. The surroundings resembled a generic town green or park, with memorials and a gazebo, flag poles, a swing set, see-saws, and monkey bars. Maybe someday she and Scott would get to meet earlier in the program's day cycle with the sun bright and shining above, or maybe later under a full moon. For now, she'd settle for Scott showing up. She needed him.

The long grass tickled her ankles as she walked toward a huge decorative fountain with stone benches surrounding it. She sat there waiting for about three minutes until Scott appeared right beside her.

She could feel pressure on her arm. She leaned into his touch while he put his arm around her shoulder.

"It's not as perfect as reality, but it'll have to do."

She looked up at him. Alek must have programmed their images into the software. Scott's eyes were a shade too dark. The off-kilter color made it harder to connect with him, so she looked away. It wasn't how he looked that mattered, really. They were together and sort of touching. It was enough for now.

"What had you so upset when you called?"

The water spilling down the fountain created a soothing rhythm that lulled her into a sense of security. "I think someone faked Jimmy's medical records. I don't think he ever had a brain tumor. When I was bloodsurfing, I don't remember seeing a scar where the tumor was supposed to have been or any stitches related to a craniotomy — where the skull would have been removed to get to the tumor."

"Why, though?" Scott shifted next to her, getting more comfortable on the stone bench, or maybe on a computer chair at Thomas's place. "Surgery near the brain is pretty radical in the first place. Why would someone subject a child to unnecessary surgery?"

"I don't know, but — " Now that she could actually voice her suspicions out loud, the stupider they sounded.

"But, what?" Scott prompted with a quick squeeze.

Hannah licked her lips, tasting her dinner which wasn't even in front of her anymore. "Do you know if there has ever been any other Alt who could create auditory hallucinations?"

Scott didn't answer right away. "Not off-hand, but I haven't exactly memorized the current T-CASS roster, either."

"Yeah, me neither. Do you think we can find out?"

Scott pulled his arm away from her shoulders. "I don't have that kind of access to the Arena's database, but Thomas would."

"Can we contact him?"

Scott reached out to catch a falling leaf. A red one. The program allowed his long fingers to snag it out of the air. He flipped it around, so even she could see the details, the stem and veins. Then he released it to continue its lazy pre-programmed path to the ground.

"It's so real." She laid her head back on his shoulder, drawing comfort from the perceived closeness.

"Alek did a good job." Scott leaned down to kiss her on top of her head. "I wish we could stay in here where no one could find us."

"I've seen that movie." She looked up at Scott. "It doesn't end well for the program. Alek will get pissed if we mess up his work."

He laughed, but it wasn't Alek she wanted to think about. Jimmy and his hospital records slid away because he belonged outside. What she wanted sat next to her in this world. Here, she didn't need to wear gloves on her hands. She reached up to pull Scott's lips back down for a kiss.

It worked. She could feel the pressure on her lips. What would happen if she — oh, not quite. Once her tongue disappeared in between Scott's teeth, the sensation disappeared. It was like sticking your tongue through a doughnut hole, sweet at first, then nothing. Too bad. She'd have to try using her hands.

Scott was way ahead of her, his hands slipping across her chest, under her shirt. Did she want this here?

"Scott, maybe we shouldn't — "

"Why shouldn't we?" His hand changed direction, reaching for her jeans. Of course her zipper wasn't real, so there was nothing to really unzip. It was all in her mind. "We're not touching, not really. You want me to stop?"

"Yeah. I want you to stop."

He pulled his hand away. She bit her tongue to stop her groan of disappointment.

"Alek and I had had this conversation earlier and… it's not enough. I can't virtually make love with you after I've experienced the real thing. The difference between last night and me sitting here, with you cuddling me while you're on the other side of the city, is that it will never be enough. I need you and unless I can have you, for real, in a bed we can call our own, I don't want to pretend like we're making love."

He kissed the tip of her nose. "You're right. No more virtual touching. But one of these days you're going to have to tell me about this conversation you had with Alek."

Oh, that would never happen. Maybe he'd forget about it after today.

"So, let's try this again." She sat forward, just far enough to put some space between her and Scott. "Can we contact Thomas to get access to the Arena database?"

Scott ran his fingers through her hair, patting it back into place for her. "Sure, but we'll have to log out of the VR to do it. We can't access anything from an isolated server."

Good. After the half sort-of kiss with Scott and the not-quite touching he'd been doing, she was ready to leave. He disappeared first. She took one last wistful look around, then disconnected from the system and removed the equipment.

Her phone buzzed, so she answered using the TV's connection to her phone. Scott's face appeared in the corner. She could see his real eyes, smaller on the screen, but at least they were the right color. He was looking off to the side.

"I'm chatting with Thomas now. Give me a sec."

Thomas's image appeared next to Scott's, his headset in place and the mic near his mouth.

"Hello, Hannah. Sorry I haven't been around for you these past few days. The harbor attack has kept us all busy. Has Doctor McNamara been treating you well?"

"Yes, he's treating me just fine, but I'm really concerned about Jimmy Chung."

"All right. Let's start with what you know."

That's what she liked most about Thomas — he got

right to the point. He would have to, if he wanted to take care of T-CASS operations and handle his own security company at the same time. Hannah relayed as succinctly as she could what she had, and, more importantly, hadn't found in Jimmy's file.

"Do you suppose that Jimmy's name was accidentally entered into someone else's medical file?" Scott asked.

Thomas leaned back in his chair, a doubtful look on his face. "I would venture to say it's possible, but not likely. My company handles hospital security, but we don't deal with electronic medical records. I could find out who does, though. If there are any reports of errors in their system, I'll let you know. What else?"

Hannah jumped in with her own question. "Do you know if there are currently any Alts in Thunder City, either T-CASS or Neutral, that can create auditory hallucinations?"

Thomas looked down at his own screen. "I remember a guy from many years ago — before Catherine formed T-CASS — but I think he retired and moved south. I'm checking the database now to see if there's anyone else I'm not familiar with."

Scott threw Hannah a quick wink while she drummed her fingers on the coffee table and waited for Thomas to finish.

"I was right. He left Thunder City four years ago. There's no one else listed with that ability. Do you think Jimmy's mother was right? Did you see the tie linking Jimmy to an Alt power while you were bloodsurfing?"

"No. No, I didn't." Thomas knew a tie existed, he just didn't know what or where it was. "The thing is, I've been hearing things in the hospital that aren't there."

"That aren't there? Like what?"

Oh, boy, how to explain it? "At first it was rain

falling, but McNamara said it was water from the toilets above us, then I heard dogs barking, which McNamara said were probably security dogs. It was right after the harbor attack, so it sounded reasonable that there would be security dogs sniffing about for bombs. I've also heard the wind, like during a storm, but I brushed it off as the air conditioning blowing through the vents.

"This afternoon, though, I heard someone calling *mommy*. It took me a minute to figure it out, but it sounded exactly like a clip from a movie that airs on TV where a little boy calls out *mommy, mommy, mommy* at the end. I thought maybe Jimmy was in the hospital getting a check-up and he wanted his mommy and threw the hallucination, hoping she'd hear him. Except Doctor McNamara checked for me. Jimmy wasn't in the hospital or the clinic next door."

Neither Thomas nor Scott said anything, but she could see the two of them look at her, then look at each other, then look back to her again.

"I know it sounds crazy."

Thomas clicked on his keyboard again. "Not crazy, but if we have an unidentified Alt out there we need to find him. Where were you when you heard these sounds?"

"In Doctor McNamara's office. Not the one he has in the regular pathology department, the other one in the VIP level."

Thomas looked up at her with a frown. "Do you mean the clinic next door?"

"No, I mean the level under the regular pathology department. The one you need a special key to get to."

Both Thomas and Scott looked confused. "Hannah, I provide security for the entire hospital and for the clinic. There is no level under pathology."

"Yes, there is. I've been there, several times." A sick feeling sank her stomach. Doctor McNamara had said it was a secret, but she'd assumed Thomas would know. How could he not?

"Do you have this key?" Scott asked.

Since she'd already spilled the beans, she pulled out the key from her pocket.

"How do you use it?"

"I insert it into the side of the key pad in the main elevators. It only works when the elevators are empty."

The absolute stillness of both Scott and Thomas as they stared at the white card in her hand made her think maybe the screen had frozen. "I'm not lying. It's there. McNamara performed an autopsy with me right there."

She didn't tell them about bloodsurfing though the dead. This conversation was already complicated enough.

"Hannah. I'll need to see that key." Thomas's jaw hardened. His usual flirty self disappeared and was replaced by a rock-hard authority figure. "In fact, I want you to meet me at the hospital first thing tomorrow and show me exactly where this elevator is taking you."

"But, Doctor McNamara — "

" — will have to wait."

"I don't want to be fired." Oh, Lord, did she sound whiney? "McNamara worked hard to circumvent the Oversight Committee to get me this job. He's protected me from the Committee. I wasn't supposed to tell anyone, but I assumed you would know since you're a big VIP in Thunder City."

"Regardless, I want to see this mysterious level. I'll

bring you to the hospital first thing in the morning. No excuses."

She was so screwed, trapped between Carraro and McNamara.

"In the meantime, I'll put out an alert and assign someone to investigate this mysterious Alt, but with everything that's happening, it's going to be a low priority for a while."

She had expected as much. "I'll let you know if it happens again."

"Please do," Thomas said with a finality that brooked no more arguments. He looked at Scott. "You said there were two items you needed me to check."

"Uh, yeah. I'd like to know more about a Neutral who calls himself the Shield. I don't know what his real name is."

Thomas's frown deepened as he started typing. "I must be losing my touch. I used to know all of the Alts in Thunder City. This is the second Alt I'm not familiar with today."

"You've been more than a little busy," Scott said. "And more than a little tired."

"Aren't we all?" Thomas typed a little more. "What ability does this 'Shield' have?"

"Exactly what his moniker says. He can create a shield that can deflect pretty much anything, including bullets. It's a flexible shield he can wrap around himself and others. He can also extend it out to form a barrier."

Again, Thomas threw his son a concerned look.

Scott rolled his eyes. "I know, I know, it sounds like the ability my biological father had. I'm not that fragile, Thomas, you can say his name. I know who my real father is."

A small smile cracked Thomas's hardened features,

but the worried look remained. "I'm sorry, Scott, but there's no one in the database with the moniker 'The Shield' or just "Shield', nor is there anyone else with that ability."

Scott shook his head, his disbelief clear. "That's not possible."

"Why isn't it possible?" Thomas asked.

Scott hesitated, and Hannah remembered how the Shield had ordered them not to tell T-CASS he was with them as they fled the harbor.

"Scott — " She didn't say *tell him,* but her meaning was as clear as she could make it. Thomas was already stressed. Keeping more secrets from him was going to make matters worse if he ever found out.

"Scott, if there's something going on and we need to have a private conversation, just say so. I'm sure Hannah would understand."

Hannah held her breath, wondering if Scott would cut her out.

"He's been in the Arena." Scott ducked his head, like a little boy forced to tell the truth.

"Has the world gone mad?"

Hannah jumped. She'd never seen Thomas get so angry.

"You let an unregistered Alt into the most secure facility in Thunder City? What the hell were you thinking?"

"I didn't let him in, he was just there." Scott looked at his father, eyes begging for understanding. "I figured he was like Spook, a T-CASS member, but working only when called in for special assignments, and freelancing on the side. We've sparred a couple of times, and he's been helping with training. Not officially, but this afternoon I was able to pull all the beanbags Highlight laid out in front of me without even thinking about it."

Thomas rubbed his forehead. "There is no way anyone could bypass my system. We test it regularly. There's just no way — "

No one said anything until Thomas pulled himself together. "I have to lock down headquarters — hell, I'll have to lock down the entire Arena. No one gets in or out until we figure out who this Alt is."

"There's a basketball game tonight."

Thomas ignored Scott. He picked up his phone and punched a number. He turned away from the screen, issuing orders. Scott looked at Hannah. His distress at causing his father more aggravation at a time when the entire city was in an uproar was obvious. Hannah suspected she didn't look much better.

Thomas turned back to the screen. "Both of you, go to bed. Catherine's just been notified that Johnson has called for another hearing with the judge. We think he's going to press for an arrest warrant for both of you. We're heading to Harbor Regional first thing tomorrow. Then we're going to the Arena. I want these two mysteries cleared up before either one of you is arrested."

Thomas's side of the screen blacked out. Hannah couldn't think of anything to say, so she blew a kiss to Scott, which he caught and returned before he logged out too.

CHAPTER EIGHTEEN

Hannah stood between Thomas and Scott in front of the main hospital elevators after a quiet, tense ride from the Blackwoods' estate. She'd just finished her scrambled eggs and bagel when Thomas had appeared, car keys in hand, to ask if she was ready. She had abandoned her orange juice so as not to exacerbate his annoyance.

Now, Hannah held up her key card. "I don't know if this is going to work with both of you inside the elevator. McNamara said it would only work if the elevator was empty."

"The elevator is hooked to a system which tracks the weight it carries. The maximum weight is 6,000 pounds." Thomas didn't look at her. His voice, rough from what she suspected was too little sleep, spoke into his phone. "Isolate elevator number three as soon as it's empty. Bring it the main floor."

The phone chimed, and Thomas switched numbers. "Yes, dear."

He must be talking to Catherine.

"They're with me." He stopped and listened again. She could feel Scott slide up behind her, but he was careful not to touch her. "We're at the hospital. We're going to go exploring for this mysterious VIP level I told you about last night."

Hannah winced. Of course Thomas would tell his wife. Thomas continued to listen to whatever Catherine was saying.

"I'll let them know. Stall them for as long as you can. Joanna's on her way."

Thomas hung up and looked at both her and Scott. "Johnson's at the courthouse again, asking the judge to issue a warrant for your arrest. Short of a miracle, we might not be able to stop him this time."

Hannah's heart fled to her throat. "What can we do?"

Thomas slipped his phone under his jacket. It was the first time she'd ever seen him dressed so casually, almost rumpled. Even his hair had lost the perfect style of careful grooming. She could only imagine the pressure he was under. "Rely on the court of public opinion. I'll arrange for a press release to be issued. In the meantime, Joanna will mount a defense on your behalf."

"I can't be locked up." Hannah could already feel her urge to flee taking over her good sense.

"You won't have a choice if the warrant is issued. I warned you about this. Joanna will be with you every step of the way."

"Joanna's not exactly Ms. Tea and Sympathy," Scott said.

"Would you prefer a public defender?" Thomas snapped, then stopped. "I've tried everything I can to keep this all above-board. I warned you not to run from the Committee in the first place. The gray areas I have to work with are shrinking rapidly. Short of a jail break, there isn't much else I can do to protect the two of you."

The elevator arrived, the doors opening to disgorge

a group of people who looked as if they, too, had been through the wringer. Maybe they were relatives of those hurt at the harbor? Hannah stepped back to let them pass by.

Scott said nothing, but motioned Hannah to enter in front of them with Thomas following behind. The doors slid shut with finality.

"I'm sorry, Thomas." Her voice shook as the urge to flee intensified, but again, she dug her nails into her palms. She was sorry. For Thomas, for Scott, for everyone who had been so kind to her since her escape. The elevator walls appeared to creep closer. Her heart raced beyond her control. "I didn't mean to make things so difficult."

Thomas took a deep breath. "I know you didn't. I know you don't look for trouble, but by God you have a talent for finding it. I used to think Scott specialized in driving me crazy with his antics."

Hannah pulled out her key card, but her hand shook so badly that she had to run the card along the edge of the key pad three times before it disappeared.

Thomas snatched it when it reappeared. "I'm going to have this analyzed. You said McNamara gave it to you?"

Hannah nodded. She was beyond words at this point. Thomas had been nothing but kind and supportive ever since he'd evacuated her and Scott from Star Haven. It had to be the pressure of the harbor attack, plus the Committee investigation, that was making him so cross.

The doors opened and they stepped out into the hallway. The quiet only emphasized the unreality of the situation.

"What is this place?" Thomas looked around, as did

Scott.

"The autopsy rooms are this way." Hannah pointed toward the rooms leading to the emergency door. "There's also a room with a generator. McNamara's office is the other way."

Scott placed his hand on her back, a comforting rub along her tense muscles. It might be the last time he would have the opportunity to touch her.

"This place — it doesn't exist. It's not on the blueprints. I double checked them last night. How the hell did it get here?"

Scott cleared his throat. "Someone must have erased it from the blueprints?"

"Erased it from the blueprints *and* managed to install the elevator, surgical suites, equipment, electricity, plumbing, *without anyone noticing?*" Thomas pushed past them toward McNamara's office. The door wasn't locked and swung open.

Hannah followed him, but didn't try to enter the office because Thomas appeared to take up the entire space with his growing anger.

"This is where you heard the voice?" he asked. "And the dogs?"

"Yes." Her tears blurred her eyes. "I'm sorry. I trusted McNamara. He made it all sound normal. Everything sounded reasonable, so I just went along with what he wanted me to do."

Thomas slipped behind the desk, played with the mouse, then typed on the keyboard. He slipped out what she thought looked like an external drive and attached it. He started typing again. "What did he have you do Hannah? What haven't you told me yet?"

Her voice hitched. "I bloodsurfed through the cadavers."

"What?" Scott's outrage in her ear made her tears spill.

"At first, he just wanted to see if I could get into a body without blood. It worked, but I couldn't move, so he set up a cadaver hooked up to a cardiopulmonary bypass. It worked. I bloodsurfed through a dead body."

Thomas disengaged the external drive and shoved it into his breast pocket along with his phone.

"Did he tell you why he wanted you to do this?"

"He said it would be an experiment. To see what I was really capable of. He thinks — he treats me like I'm remarkable, that I can do things that I never even imagined."

A shout behind her shut her up. All three of them saw McNamara and the Shield enter the corridor through the emergency exit. No alarm sounded.

"Stay behind me," Thomas ordered.

Scott pushed her behind him, but she still followed him as he went with Thomas to meet McNamara and the Shield at the elevators.

McNamara got there first. "I'm disappointed in you, Hannah. I thought I told you to keep this area a secret."

Hannah stepped around Scott, then around Thomas, though he tried to keep her behind him. It all grew so tiresome, everyone trying to keep her behind them, trying to keep her safe. She faced McNamara.

"You told me it was the VIP floor. That it was a half-secret. Thomas Carraro is one of the biggest VIPs in Thunder City. He designed the security system for the entire hospital. How could he not know about this floor? How could I know he wouldn't know?" She looked back at Thomas, her old friend — anger — taking the place of her sorrow and fear. "Why does everyone blame me for making a perfectly reasonable assumption? Why are you blaming me when you've been manipulating me all this time?"

McNamara stared at her for a moment. "Good point." He held out his hand to Hannah. "I apologize, Hannah. I should have explained things to you from the beginning, but if you'll come with me, I will show you what you need to know."

"You'll show all of us," Thomas said. Scott stood side-by-side with his father.

McNamara pulled Hannah closer to him. "I'm afraid not." He turned to the Shield. "Shoot them."

"What?" Hannah tried to yank her hand away from McNamara, but he tightened his grip and dragged her closer until he clamped his arms around her body. She struggled but could only watch as the Shield raised two guns. "No! Stop! Leave them — "

Bang. Bang. Bang. Thomas fell, Scott fell, blood pooling on the floor.

McNamara's arms tightened even more. She had no breath left to scream. McNamara turned her away so she couldn't see what the Shield was doing to — oh, God, to the bodies.

Damn her gloves. Why did she have to wear them? If she hadn't obeyed the Committee's rules she could bloodsurf through McNamara right now. Kill him. And the Shield. Then save Scott and Thomas.

Instead, she could only kick as hard as she could, the whole way down the hall, as McNamara dragged to her to the emergency room door. She slammed her sneaker between his legs, almost forcing him to drop her.

"Leave the bodies," McNamara shouted back to the Shield. "Help me get her through the door!"

The Shield appeared in her peripheral vision. He

opened the emergency room door before grabbing her legs. With her legs locked together, she couldn't kick, but she could arch her back, desperate to gain some leverage to throw them off. She needed to remove her gloves. Just two seconds to remove her gloves. They couldn't stop her from fighting. She would fight to her last breath, damn them, and damn her for thinking McNamara cared. Despite her thrashing, they shoved her through the door.

"Get the syringe, top shelf to the left."

Oh, shit. The Shield dropped her legs, so she returned to kicking and slamming her head back, hoping to hit McNamara's nose. He dodged her attack. She knew she connected a few times, but his arms were like steel ropes.

The Shield pulled out a knife and ripped off one of her sleeves. The last things she saw was the needle jammed into her arm before her world turned black.

Scott forced one eye open against the clamps trying to keep them shut. The cold tile against his cheek prompted him to fight the urge to sleep until a familiar scent reached his nose. Blood. The Shield had shot him. He'd also shot Thomas. Where was Hannah?

Scott started to roll over, but a sharp pinprick tweaked his neck. Running his hand over the spot, his fingers brushed against something sticking out of his neck. Automatically, he yanked, and found a dart in his hand.

He tossed it away and crawled over to Thomas, who lay in a pool of blood nearby.

"Thomas?" Scott checked for a pulse. The rhythm was strong enough to push away fears of a near-death. Further searching located a bullet wound in his father's upper arm and another dart stuck in Thomas's shoulder. Scott removed his jacket to create a tourniquet. "C'mon Thomas. Wake up. I need you to wake — "

"Shhhhh." Thomas opened his eyes when Scott cinched the jacket over the wound. "Scott. What happened?"

"You've been shot. I'm going to get you out of here."

He could see Thomas looking him over for wounds, and added, "I'm fine. We were both hit with tranquilizer darts, but you have a bullet in your arm."

"How long?" Thomas's voice sounded fuzzy.

Scott checked his phone, which was still in his pocket. Both of his guns, his knife and his taser were also in place. "Fifteen minutes."

Thomas nodded and tried to sit up. "Where's Hannah?"

"McNamara has her." Scott nodded toward the emergency door. "I'm going to put you in the elevator and send you up to the lobby. Then I'm going after Hannah."

Thomas raised his hand to Scott's face, but the pain brought his arm down again. "Why didn't they kill us?"

"I don't — " *Don't you dare say you don't know. You do know, asshole. Give Thomas one damn good reason for me to not shoot both of you and save myself some aggravation._*

Nice to know The Shield's voice was still in his head. He tried again. "The Shield is a double agent. He was training me to recruit me into the Court of Blood and help him bring it down from the inside." At least that's what Scott hoped the Shield had intended to do. He still wasn't quite clear what the Shield's plan was. "The Shield shot you to draw blood. Make it look like he was shooting to kill. Then he hit both of us with tranqs so we'd lie quiet and McNamara would think we were dead."

Thomas closed his eyes against the pain. "I'm sorry I was so — "

"Don't. You had every right to be pissed. Hannah knows that, too. Just stay conscious, okay?" He could already see his father's face becoming more animated as the drug left his system. Scott could feel his own lethargy bleeding away. There was still a lot of blood loss for Thomas to have to fight. "I need you to get up to the lobby, call T-CASS and report Hannah as kidnapped. You'll also need to get the hospital to evacuate, but do it quietly in case McNamara is still here. We can't alert him to what's happening."

Thomas nodded. "Help me stand up."

Scott got Thomas sitting, then standing. Though they were both still wobbly, Scott managed to get his father into the elevator. "How are you going to get to Hannah? They might have already left with her."

"I haven't figured that part out yet."

Thomas leaned against the back of the elevator. "Why you? Why now?"

Scott shook his head. "I don't know and we can't worry about it. There might be cameras in this corridor. They could be watching us."

"I should have known. How could I have not — "

"Thomas." Scott grabbed his father's face between his hands. "You have one job. Report and evacuate. I'll take care of the rest."

Thomas leaned forward and kissed Scott on the forehead. "I'm so proud of you. Your mother is too. We couldn't have asked for a better son."

"And I couldn't have asked for a better father. Thank you for adopting me and reuniting me with Catherine. Now go!"

Scott hit the main lobby button, thankful he didn't need Hannah's pass key to send his father up.

His energy returning by the second, he jogged toward the emergency door. What lay on the other side? Before he could open the door to find out, the push bar squeaked. He pulled his Ruger from his shoulder holster and plastered himself against the wall behind the door. If it was McNamara coming through the door, the doctor was a dead man.

The Shield walked through just far enough for Scott to point the gun to the guy's head. The Shield froze in place.

"Where's Hannah?"

"She's safe."

"Where is she safe?"

The Shield put a single finger to his lips. Scott allowed him to step away from the door so it closed. "I'm out here to dispose of your bodies."

"You've had fifteen minutes to do that. What's happening behind this door?"

"We're evacuating. There's a small medical facility that the Court of Blood established down here for McNamara to use for experimentation. Thanks to you and your girlfriend, he has to destroy it and hide the evidence. We have thirty minutes before the bombs activate."

"Bombs?"

In a lightning move, the Shield slammed him against the nearest wall, his hand tight over Scott's mouth. "Any louder and they'll hear you in Star Haven."

Scott gritted his teeth. The Shield was right, but he shoved the Shield's hand away from his mouth. "How do we stop him from setting off the bombs?"

"We don't. You evacuate, go home, and stay the hell

away from the Court of Blood. I'll stay with the Court, McNamara, and your girlfriend."

"I'm not leaving Hannah behind. I'm not allowing McNamara to blow up this building. Thomas is alive. He's going to trigger an evacuation."

"Of course he is. Why do you think I aimed for his arm and not his heart? Try not to fuck up my plans any further and get the hell out of this hospital."

"He's also going to call in Hannah's kidnapping."

He expected the Shield was rolling his eyes behind the sunglasses. "This place will be destroyed before T-CASS can get down here. Even if your speedster could get down here without a key, he'd have to choose between saving Hannah, the hospital, or the other subjects."

"Other subjects?"

"I don't have time to explain to you what McNamara has been doing. If you leave now and help with the evacuation, everyone lives."

"What about Hannah?"

"Hannah will live. She's too important for the Court to leave behind. Everyone else is expendable. Stop wasting my time."

Scott closed his eyes, not caring about the Shield's time.

"I can't stay out here much longer." The Shield stepped away from Scott. "There are no cameras because no one was supposed to find out, but McNamara will expect me to place your bodies near the closest bomb so they're incinerated."

"Where's that? Is there more than one?" He needed more information. He wouldn't let the Shield pull one of his disappearing acts until he had what he needed.

"Whatever you're thinking — don't." The Shield

shoved Scott's shoulder, interrupting his train of thought. "You don't have the skills to disarm these bombs and even if you did, there's too many. There's one in the maintenance closet to destroy this level, the rest placed along the outside to trigger an implosion. There won't be enough of this building left for anyone to wonder why there's an extra big hole where this level used to be."

Which was exactly what Scott needed to know. "I don't have the skills, but I know people who do. I can make this work. You're just going to have to trust me. I won't leave Hannah behind. I can translocate her out of here and we'll run for it. We're pretty good at running."

The Shield was at the end of his patience. He threw his arms in the air in frustration. "You moron. You translocate her, then McNamara will know that I let you live. There are other lives at stake beyond Hannah's."

"Yours?"

"No." The Shield suddenly stopped, looked down, then away. Scott had never seen the man appear so uncertain about anything. "The subjects back there. Subjects like Hannah."

Scott's heart skipped a beat. "How many?"

"Too many." The quiet, vulnerable moment was gone and the Shield was back in fighting form. "Jimmy Chung is one of them."

"How is that even possible?"

The Shield ignored the question. "If you yank Hannah out of there, or go charging in full throttle and don't give McNamara the time he needs to get out, he will blow this place with them inside and he won't look back."

Nightmare on top of nightmare. How could he get those people — he refused to think of them as subjects — out of there and still rescue Hannah without McNamara knowing about it?

If you leave now, everyone lives.

"Wait. If he's evacuating people, he'll have to bring them up the elevator and through the lobby. If we can find what vehicle they're in — "

The Shield was already shaking his head. "There's another entrance. An underground tunnel that leads directly into the parking garage."

"Fine. I'll go in that way, find the others, find Hannah, and translocate them out. Can you knock out McNamara and make it look like T-CASS did it before he discovers I'm still alive?"

The Shield hesitated again. "This isn't going to work."

"It's better than leaving them behind."

The Shield took a long slow breath. Then he handed Scott one of his guns. "This is the one with the tranqs. There are three nurses. You can knock them out and translocate them too."

Scott took the gun. The Shield then handed him another key card. "Go to the second level of the garage. There's a jersey barrier blocking half of the compact car section. You'll see a door; it looks rusted, but it's fine. Run the card along the keypad next to the door. You'll have ten seconds to get inside before an alarm will alert McNamara."

"What about guards?"

The Shield snorted. "I'm it. The whole idea behind a clandestine lab underneath a hospital is to not attract attention. I was only assigned to the facility because the Anti-Alts really were threatening McNamara."

Scott glanced back at the door. "All right. If I fail, you get Hannah out. I don't care about the rest of it. Any of it. You get her out and you make sure she's safe. Understand?"

Instead of responding, the Shield yanked open the door and returned inside.

Great, Scott thought. *Just great.* He ran for the elevator and slapped the button for the main lobby. Thomas's blood smeared the wall. He wondered where his father was right now. Once on the main level, he headed toward the parking garage. Already he could see cars leaving, with police directing them in both directions. Ambulances also lined the street, with EMTs and nurses efficiently loading them. No sirens sounded.

Pathia. Emergency. Bombs. Please respond.

He kept walking until he hit the concrete of the first level. The scent of sugar cookies greeted him.

I'm here, Scott. Your father called for an evacuation of Harbor Regional.

Thomas was alive. That was all he really needed to know. Poor Pathia sounded so tired. He could only imagine what she'd been through since the quarry raid. *Good, but he doesn't know about the bombs. Where are Mach Ten, Blockhead, Ghost, and Captain Spec?*

One moment.

He hit the stairs leading up to level two, two stairs at a time.

Mach Ten and The Captain are at the courthouse. She knows about Thomas. An arrest warrant has been issued for you and Hannah. Blockhead is at the Arena running a drill with Highlight on the basketball court. Ghost is at the hospital already with Daniella Rose. Both of them are assisting with the evacuation.

Scott shoved open the door to the second level. *Tell The Captain, Mach Ten, and Ghost to meet me on the second level of the parking garage. All due speed. Tell Highlight to clear the basketball court and prepare for incoming hostages. Tell Blockhead I'm going to translocate him and to not give me grief about it when he gets here.*

Good luck.

He was going to need it. Blockhead had been a friend of his grandfather, and had no use for Norms. He'd never had much use for Scott, once it became clear that Scott would never develop Alt abilities. Scott needed him now, so instead he focused on the need to bring Blockhead here to save Hannah. Blockhead here. Protect Hannah. Blockhead here. Protect Hannah.

A subtle click in his brain, and the big Marine stood in front of Scott. Too close in front of Scott. He looked around, glared at Scott but said nothing. A second later Mach Ten came to a screeching halt, and his mother flew over the concrete barrier of this level. That left only —

Ghost surfaced through the floor, with a huge son-of-bitch holding onto him. Good lord, this guy made even Blockhead look small, the fierce face and rippling muscles offset only by a man bun. And he had a gun holster attached to his belt.

Before Scott could ask who, Ghost said, "This is Danny Rose. When I explained the situation, he insisted on joining the fun."

"I can't put my fist through concrete like this guy..." Danny nudged Blockhead with his elbow, although the latter didn't appear to appreciate it "...but I can get the job done."

Scott readjusted his instructions to accommodate the extra help. "The Court of Blood has set bombs all around this building. There's also one in a maintenance room on a level below the Pathology Department. This level does not exist on the blueprints. The only way to get to this level is by taking the main elevator in the pathology department and using this key card." He held up the card so they all could see it.

"Those bombs are on a timer. We have less than thirty minutes. Mach Ten and Ghost, you take the bombs on the outside of the building. No, I don't know where they are. Blockhead, you and Catherine will use the key card to get down to maintenance room.

"Once you are down there, Doctor McNamara will be evacuating his own people. Hannah is with him, as are other hostages. There is also a double-agent called the Shield. If you run into him, do not challenge him. He's on our side, but he's also armed to the teeth and will kill without hesitation."

Blockhead interrupted. "Is this guy going to help Hannah get out of there?"

"Yes, he will, but she doesn't know that, so she might fight him."

"Is he an Alt?" Catherine asked.

"Yes, he can create barriers to protect himself and others from pretty much anything you can throw at him."

He saw Ghost put his hand on Catherine's shoulder. She grabbed it, but Scott plowed ahead. "As much as I hate to say this, the bomb is your priority. If you can't disarm it — "

Blockhead nodded, knowing exactly what Scott was thinking. "The Captain will fly it out of there and into the atmosphere."

"Once the hospital is safe, go through the emergency exit next to the maintenance building. That's where

McNamara has been doing his dirty work. I'm going to be entering through this door here." He pointed to the rusted door with the key card. "If we're lucky we'll catch them in the middle and I can translocate the hostages out of there, just in case we can't disarm all of the bombs.

"Danny, you're our last line of defense. I don't know what McNamara's other subjects look like. If anyone comes through the door, stop them, but try not to hurt them unless they're shooting at you. Focus on the vans that are going to be arriving any second now to pick them up. That will be the Court of Blood. You can hurt them all you want."

Danny gave him a shit-eating grin. "Got it. Anything else?"

Scott looked at his crew. "Get out of here."

Ghost squeezed Danny's hand before he sank back into the ground. Mach Ten zipped past Scott so fast, the breeze ruffled his hair. The other three followed him over to the door.

"I don't know what to expect on the other side, but I'm closing it behind me. Hopefully, I won't need the key to get out."

The key worked, thank God. "All right. See you on the other side." Sparing a last look at his mother as he handed her the key card, Scott slipped through the door, then quietly shut it behind him.

CHAPTER NINETEEN

"Hannah."

She heard her name but didn't want to open her eyes. Bad things happened when your eyes were forced open, always. A hand touched her shoulder, pushed up her sleeve. Something cold and wet touched her, followed by a pinprick. Without warning her eyes flew open and she could see the fluorescent lights in the ceiling of...where?

Then she remembered. Scott shot by the Shield, who never missed. Thomas lying in blood right beside him. McNamara grabbing her, hauling her away despite her kicking and screaming. She tried to sit up, but the restraints held her down on a cold, metal table.

"Stop it. Stop moving. You're going to hurt yourself."

McNamara. He held her shoulders, his hands in gloves and a mask not unlike the kind worn by Division Six covering his face. She couldn't reach him even if she wanted to, which she did, badly. She spat because there was nothing else she could do.

He wiped the spit off his mask.

"Take me to Scott or kill me now, because I swear I'll kill you faster than Miranda Dane."

"I can't. The Shield is disposing of his body as we speak."

"You can. Who's in charge around here?"

"I am — but Hannah, we have to evacuate."

"I don't give a shit what you think you have to do. You will bring Scott's body to me now. You will hook him to an IV and a cardiopulmonary bypass and I'm going to bring him back from the dead."

McNamara stilled, his whole body going rigid and indecision scrawled across his face. "Can you do it? Can you bring someone back from the dead?"

"Scott, yes. You, never. And I will kill you, McNamara. Make no mistake about that."

McNamara swallowed hard. He was entranced with her power. He wanted to see what she was capable of. Good, she'd keep him guessing right up until she killed him.

"I have to admit, it's a temptation. I could get a mobile refrigeration unit and keep his body stored until we — "

The door to the room slammed open. Hannah took the opportunity to look around. She was in an exam room, judging by the medical equipment lying around. The Shield entered, marching over to the table she was strapped to, cutting off her search for an escape route. "Took care of the bodies. What do you want me to do with the other subjects?"

The Shield snapped McNamara out his consideration for her plan, double damn him. Hannah lay back down on the table because holding her head up was awkward. Scott was gone and there was no bringing him back. Her heart broke, then reformed and hardened to thick black ice. There would be time for tears later, when she was alone. Right now, she had to escape, but not before she destroyed McNamara and the Shield if it was the last thing she did before she died. She just had to buy herself time. She had to take back her control.

McNamara's voice changed from admiration of her, to the tones of a man in charge. "Gather the older subjects into room four with one of the nurses and get them ready for transport. The two other nurses will handle the subjects in the lab."

Subjects. Miranda had called her Subject A. She'd called Joe Austin Subject B. McNamara was no different than Miranda. He was experimenting on Alts. She was right back where she started, in the clutches of the Court of Blood.

The Shield left the room without even looking at her. McNamara returned to her side.

"I'm sorry, Hannah, but time is not on our side. I can't risk retrieving Scott's body for you. You will have the opportunity to try resurrecting someone, I promise, but we cannot risk not getting out of here before T-CASS arrives. The vans will be here in five minutes. I've already activated the countdown sequence."

"What sequence? What countdown?"

"I have to destroy this place to erase any chance of anyone discovering it was here. It's the way the Court of Blood operates. No one can acquire any evidence of our existence." He laid a hand on her head. "You're one of us. We created you and it's time to bring you back home."

Home? Created her? What the hell did he mean? "Wait. You're going to blow up the hospital? Why? There are hundreds of patients, plus all the personnel. Maybe a thousand of them. What did they ever do to you?"

"It's not what they did to me, Hannah. I can't allow the Court to be exposed like this. That's how the Court has survived all these centuries. If anyone realizes that this level has existed for so long undetected, they'll start searching for our other facilities...and they'll start searching for us. We cannot allow that. Our work is too important. You're too important."

"There's nothing I can do to stop you. Nothing you want that I have that I can bargain with to stop the bombs."

"I have you, Hannah. You're all I need." He swept her hair off her forehead. She fought not to flinch.

"Let me go."

"I can't do that —"

"I mean, let me get up and move. Keeping me chained here is only going to slow you down."

McNamara stared at her. "If you try to escape — "

"Oh, c'mon. Don't treat me like I'm some idiot. You just shot two people who loved me. You're about to kill over a thousand people. You claim that I'm important, that you want to bring me home, but nothing says you have to bring me home awake or in one piece. I'm not going to do anything to jeopardize myself."

He still wasn't sure about her. Hell, she wasn't sure about her, either. Everything she'd just said was true, but it also wasn't true at all.

"Look, you just said that the Court of Blood created me. I want to know where I came from. I only found out a week ago that Miranda wasn't my mother, and I just scattered the ashes of one of my step-fathers, so how about you give me a break? If the Court knows who my parents are, even if they're just egg and sperm donors, at least I'll know the truth."

It was all true, and still not true at all. She would find out from the Court about her parents, but that didn't mean McNamara had to live to see her triumph. Her murder scheme raged hot in her chest, but she fought like mad to keep it off her face. Kill McNamara and get the hospital evacuated.

He still looked down on her as if she were a bug. "I wasn't just any sperm donor. I was the *ideal* sperm donor."

Her ears closed to the words. If she didn't hear it, it wasn't true. And, yet...

"Us gingers have to stick together," he repeated.

Her stomach heaved. "Get me off this table before I puke."

McNamara must have believed her, because he released the restraints, but he didn't remove his gloves or mask. She heaved and McNamara grabbed a bucket. Her breakfast gone, he handed her a glass of water from a small sink. She rinsed out her mouth, then made her way to the sink to fill the cup again. She gulped down another two cups before wiping her mouth with her sleeve.

As she did so, she noticed that her phone had been tossed onto the counter. Using her body to block McNamara's view, she managed to grab the phone and shove it down the front of her pants. Not comfortable, but at least she had it. She rubbed her wrists to stop the shaking as she turned around, and quickly found them yanked back behind her and cuffed.

"What the hell?"

McNamara removed his mask at last. His red hair was the same shade as hers. Why hadn't she noticed before that it was the *exact* same shade? "I'm sorry," he said, "but I'm not taking chances. We have fifteen minutes to get out of here, twenty-five before the bombs explode."

She wanted to faint, but instead she remembered her mission. Save the hospital. Kill McNamara — commit patricide. She'd figure that one out later. "Fine. What do I do now?"

"You don't do anything. I have someone I think you'll enjoy meeting."

They walked down a narrow corridor. The decor wasn't much more inspiring than that of Miranda's quarry prison, but at least the walls were a more cheerful yellow and there was no grating over the light fixtures. McNamara stopped in front of a room. Hannah couldn't help but notice a large number 4 on the door. He scanned his key card. No voice activation or palm scanning like at the Arena. Interesting.

He motioned her inside first. The room was lit with indirect lighting, its walls splashed with pastel colors, and toys were scattered across the floor.

She looked around. A woman wearing light blue long-sleeved scrubs stood off to the side, with a dozen young children gathered around her. She was struggling to get them dressed from a pile of clothes folded next to her. She wore gloves, and a face mask obscured her features, but allowed tufts of curly black hair to tumble around her head.

McNamara walked over to the woman. "Keep doing what you're doing. We have some time. I just need to borrow this one for minute."

Hannah knew even before McNamara walked the small boy over to her what he was doing. "Hannah, I want you to meet Jimmy Chung. The *real* Jimmy Chung. Jimmy, can you say hi to my friend Hannah?"

A pair of wide blue eyes stared up at her. The small, adorable face under a mess of curly blond hair looked nothing like what Jimmy Chung was supposed to look like.

"Can you say 'hi' to Hannah, Jimmy?" McNamara

repeated.

The boy didn't say anything. Instead the word *Mommy* echoed through the room, just like she'd heard yesterday. Her throat closed, thick with a rage that went even beyond what she'd felt lying on the exam bed. "Why isn't he talking?"

"I don't know. He's been mute since the surgery, but his Alt ability is undeniable. We now have verification: Alt power is tied to the brain. We suspected it, but now we have proof."

Close. They were so close. She knew the truth about Alt power, but now that the Court of Blood had narrowed the search down to the brain, how long would it take for them to find the microscopic black thread? More importantly, what would they do with that information?

"Let me bloodsurf through him."

"No, we don't have time."

Hannah kicked McNamara. Damn that felt good. "Stop acting like an asshole. It'll take thirty seconds and I can fix him."

"There's nothing wrong with him." McNamara rubbed his ankle, getting himself down on one knee.

"Not from what I saw in...the other Jimmy. I told you the stitching was sloppy. What I didn't tell you was that the swollen nerve tissue you created is pressing against the bone. It's slowing down the nerve signals because of the uneven scarring over the wounds. That's why he was acting so odd. C'mon, let me do this. I'm about to lose everything I've ever wanted. Give me this. Let me take a closer look so that if you need to do this again, you can do it better, with less trauma. You're still a doctor. I'm a healer. Let me heal. Let me help. You don't even have to remove the handcuffs. Just one of my gloves."

Maybe there was still a hint of a medical ethics inside McNamara, because he checked his watch. "Thirty seconds. If you're not out in thirty seconds, I'll force you out."

Hannah had no idea how he would do that, so she rolled her eyes this time. "I have no more interest in dying in a bomb blast than you."

McNamara motioned for her to turn around. One of the gloves slipped off her hand.

"Hold him still so he doesn't move," Hannah said over her shoulder. McNamara still knelt on one knee, favoring the ankle she'd kicked. "Hey, Jimmy, want to see a magic trick?"

The boy nodded slowly, as if he wasn't sure if his head would stay on his shoulders.

"Okay, grab my hand."

Inside. She swam back to where she'd started from in the other Jimmy Chung: the place where the medulla oblongata ended and the spinal cord began. She soothed the bulge and allowed the signals to travel unimpeded. Then she returned to Jimmy's hand. If this was going to work, she'd have to move fast.

Back in her own body. She'd been so fast inside Jimmy, McNamara still hadn't reacted to the handcuffs and the phone on the floor. Before he could reach for her, she slapped one hand onto his cheek and surfed again.

Inside. How long did she have before McNamara pulled free? Already his arm had shifted. Did he wonder what would happen if he pulled away? She had no time to spare, so she pushed harder than she'd ever pushed before, surfing fast up the current to his brain. Not to kill him. Even if she wanted him dead, she couldn't bring herself to kill her own father.

The reticular activating system floated into view. She punched her way inside and scraped along the edges, creating a lesion. Almost immediately her center of gravity shifted. McNamara fell, his body no longer able to stay awake. Hannah swam up to the interthalamic adhesion. No black thread, so no Alt power. The normal firing of electrical activity slowed. She counted three beats, then swam back down his arm and fell back into herself.

Outside, McNamara had fallen forward onto her, firmly in a coma. Hannah shoved his body off her hers. Jimmy had run back to the nurse.

"Hey," the nurse shouted, shoving one of the kids off her lap, heading for Hannah to prevent her escape.

Hannah had no idea how suicidal McNamara's collaborators were, so she grabbed her phone and handcuffs and pelted the latter at the nurse's face. The nurse ducked. The delay was just long enough for Hannah to run out the door and slam it closed.

She headed back the way she came, but the Shield came into view. Damn it. She ran in the other direction, but another shadow appeared on the wall where another corridor intersected with this one.

Behind her, the door to room four banged open. Like McNamara, the nurse grabbed her from behind. She was well and truly trapped.

The door slammed closed behind Scott. The dingy stairwell only headed down, so he jumped the steps to save time. The final level ended at another metal door. Thank God he didn't need a pass key for this one or he'd have been screwed.

The corridor on the other side surprised Scott. Instead of the dull institutional look of the stairwell, the walls were painted a cheerful yellow with bright lights above to give him a clear view ahead. He kept the Shield's gun at the ready. The first door he could see was near an intersection. If anyone rounded that corner he'd have no place to hide, and he'd have to be the first one to shoot.

He jogged to the door and flattened himself against the wall to make himself less of a target. He slid past the door to a large window that stretched about ten feet across. He peeked inside and his jaw dropped.

Babies. Lined up in a nursery, tucked into cribs. Some cried, some slept, some flailed their tiny arms and feet around. Two nurses weaved through the room, moving the cribs onto carts and lining them up at the door. They were preparing to evacuate. Scott checked his time — ten minutes. He had ten minutes to translocate all of these infants to the Arena. He hadn't even had a chance to find Hannah yet, or the Shield.

He waited until both nurses had their arms full of babies and their backs to the window so he could dash past. If fate were kind, there would be no one around the corner —

A door slammed, followed by a female voice shouting, "Shoot her!"

"I'll fucking kill you! Both of you!"

Hannah, swearing up a storm. Subtlety dropped; Scott raced around the corner in time to see Hannah jam her hand up the sleeve of a nurse, making skin-on-skin contact. Hannah turned translucent and the nurse, screaming, dropped like a rock. Hannah reappeared, only to see the Shield standing over her.

"Walk away," she said. "McNamara's in a coma. He

can't help you. You touch me, you'll get the same treatment."

Scott's heart expanded at her tough talk. Hannah had not only taken out the nurse, but McNamara, too. He never should have doubted her ability to protect herself.

If the Shield was impressed with her threat, he didn't say so. "Stand up, so I can get you out of here alive."

Hannah froze, her bare hands raised, fingers curled to attack. Scott wanted to intervene, since Hannah probably couldn't get skin contact if the Shield had his barrier raised, but the Shield took that option away from him.

"I said, stand up." He grabbed her by the back of her shirt and hauled her to her feet. Then he shoved her toward Scott. "Move it."

Hannah saw him standing there. She broke away from the Shield and ran into his arms. He caught her, pulled her up so he could crush her to his chest, feel her arms wrapped around his neck.

"You're alive. I saw you lying there...Thomas...."

"Thomas is alive, too. He took a bullet to his arm, but he's alive."

Hannah kissed him, hard, soft, desperate, needing, and with all the power and passion he had ever wanted.

"We don't have time for this," the Shield growled, coming up from behind. "Bombs, remember?"

Hannah pulled away from him and he lowered her to the ground. "Why should we trust you? You shot Scott and Thomas."

"Do they look dead?"

Hannah had no answer to that, so Scott turned her back so he could cup her face in his hands. "His methods are brutal, but he's the one who kept us alive so we could alert the hospital and T-CASS. I need you to trust him."

Hannah blinked, getting her bearings. "There are children in the room back there. At least six. Toddlers. One of them is Jimmy Chung. McNamara performed a brain transplant. The others are also a part of his experiments."

Scott was surprised that he wasn't surprised. "I'll translocate them to the Arena, but there's something else you need to see."

He tugged her arm so she followed him back to the nursery, motioning her to keep her back flat against the wall.

"Oh, my God." Hannah whirled around to shout at the Shield. "You knew about this? You did nothing to stop it?"

"What do you think I've been doing for twenty-two years?"

"All right, enough." Scott pulled Hannah back from the edge before she antagonized the Shield into shooting both of them. "Like he said, we don't have time. I'll have to translocate both groups of children."

"How much time do we have left?" Hannah asked.

Scott checked. "Eight minutes."

"Can you do it? Can you get them and us out of here?"

Could he? He looked over Hannah's shoulder at the Shield. The Shield nodded, understanding Scott's silent question. "I can't do this if I'm worried about you. I need to know you're safe. My ability is still wild. I still might fail. For all of the strides I've made, I'm not going to take the chance with you. You are the only sure thing in my life."

Hannah swallowed. "What are you saying, Scott?"

He kissed her instead, but she knew what he was telling her. The kiss could have lasted a lifetime, but the clock continued to tick. He pulled away.

"Go." He turned away because he couldn't bear to look at her as the Shield forced Hannah to duck below the window and push her toward the exit.

Scott checked his watch. Six and a half minutes. Before he started though, he needed to make a phone call.

"Highlight," snapped the familiar voice.

"It's Scott. Is the Arena clear?"

"Clear and ready. You can do this."

Now she gave him her support? "I've got a nursery full of babies and a half dozen toddlers and a few Court of Blood agents. Watch yourself."

"Babies? Are you kidding?"

"I'm going to try to send the babies with their cribs, but no promises."

"Got it, Grey. Good luck."

So everyone kept telling him. He hung up. Pulling out the Shield's gun with the tranqs, he positioned himself outside the door. Three...two...one...

He slammed the door open. Both nurses turned around; one had a baby in hand. He shot the empty-handed one first, and the second held the baby close.

"You wouldn't shoot a woman with a baby, would you?"

"Put it down."

"No way. I'm getting out of here and she's coming with me."

Scott aimed for the woman's thigh and fired. Down she went. Scott could only hope the baby wasn't concussed. He looked around. The cribs had been arranged in crèches of four. It would be faster if he sent four at a time. The baby on the floor had started crying, which set off all of the others.

Scott focused on the four closest to him. He imagined his arms, longer than normal, wrapping around all of the cribs together. He pushed them all into an image of the basketball court at the Arena — the Arena he remembered from his childhood, looking down from Thomas's skybox.

The group of babies disappeared, cribs and all. He wanted to call Highlight to make sure they made it, but he couldn't waste the time. If his crew hadn't deactivated the bombs by now, he wouldn't make it. None of them would.

The next group disappeared faster. Maybe he was getting used to using his ability. The drills with Highlight had served a purpose — to get an Alt to feel what their ability could do without hurting anyone. If he hadn't been such a rebellious brat, he might have succeeded the first time and not fallen for the Shield's more brutal version of getting the job done.

The fourth group disappeared on the heels of the third. It was like his concentration had a good dosing of lube — his commands slipped through to actions with lightning speed. He scooped up the screaming baby next to the unconscious nurse and placed it carefully back in the crib amongst the fifth group. As soon as Scott had her tucked away, he sent them to the Arena. He'd have to come back for the nurses if he had time.

Two and half minutes. He had to find the toddlers. He located the door next to the third unconscious nurse. He left her and McNamara on the floor. If he had time he'd get them out too, he would, but first...

A few of the toddlers were gathered around McNamara, shaking him, trying to get him to wake up. "Hey, kids. C'mon, gather around me okay?"

Most of them waddled over, but he had to chase down two. One minute. More wasted time trying to keep them together. He'd have to leave behind McNamara and the nurses. He threw his arms around as many of the kids as he could and pushed all of them to the Arena.

The crying babies echoed through the cavernous chamber and sang in his ears. There was no explosion. No searing heat or flames to scorch him alive. Scott lifted his head and saw all of the toddlers — safe and sound and looking at him like he was crazy. He could live with that. They all could live... would live. McNamara had failed.

"Grey."

Scott staggered as he tried to stand, but his legs couldn't quite make it. He'd done it. Everyone had lived. At least he hoped so.

Highlight stood over him, in her yellow uniform, her fascinator clipped behind her ear. She knelt down next to him.

"You did it. You saved them all. I knew you could."

He couldn't respond; everything was spinning. All around him people were being pressed into service to soothe the infants. Even the basketball players who'd arrived for practice were bouncing babies in their arms. The spinning wouldn't stop, though. Was this how Hannah felt when she didn't drink enough water before bloodsurfing?

"Hannah. Is she here?"

Highlight shook her head. "I haven't seen her, but that doesn't mean she's not in the building. If she came in through the roof entrance or the main lobby, she might have gone straight down to headquarters."

Would the Shield have taken her here? Would he have used his access to get her inside? Would he have joined her?

Scott pulled out his phone. "I need to call her."

Her phone rang twice before a familiar voice answered.

"She's not here, Grey."

It was the Shield, not Hannah. "Where is she?"

"She's busy. It's a long story. I'll tell you when I get there."

"I'm at the Arena. I got all the kids out."

"I don't train incompetents. Stay there. I'm coming to you."

"But what about Hannah? Where is she?"

"I said I'll explain when I get there. Don't go anywhere until I talk to you." The Shield cut the line.

"He won't tell me where Hannah is."

Highlight's face softened. "C'mon. Let's get you away from here. I'll take you down to HQ. You expended a lot of energy doing what you did. We'll get you something to eat and drink."

She held out her hand, so Scott took it and tried to stand once more. Before he could topple over, Highlight secured a strong arm around his waist and guided him off the court. Before he left, he took one last look back. He did this. Hannah would be so happy.

<hr />

The Shield kept a firm hand on Hannah's shoulder as he pushed her toward the exit. She shoved open the door and walked into a war zone.

Three black vans in various states of destruction lay scattered across the near empty garage. Bodies of men and women, all dressed like commandoes, littered the ground, some of them still moaning in pain.

"What the hell —"

From behind one of the vans a giant appeared, dragging another body behind him. He tossed the body next to one of the piles and began to disarm it.

"Who the hell is that?" the Shield growled at her.

"I have no idea."

The giant straightened up and noticed them staring.

"Hi, Hannah!" The giant waved, then jogged over to them, each step like thunder on the concrete. "Let me guess, leather man must be the mysterious Shield."

"Uh, yeah. Who are you?" Hannah stepped closer to the Shield, who had his guns in both hands.

"Oh, right. I'm Danny Rose. Nik's paramour. You've never seen me shift, but it's me."

The giant pulled the elastic out of his hair and let it fall to his shoulders. It had the same brown waves with golden highlights as Daniella Rose.

"You did all this? Where's Nik?"

Danny put his hair back into a bun and the Shield lowered his guns. "Disabling the bombs. We need to evac in case they miss one. I'm headed to the lobby to see if I can lend a hand with last-minute stragglers. Where are you headed?"

"First level," the Shield said. "I'm getting her out of here."

"You've got eight minutes — get going." Danny clapped his massive hand on the Shield's shoulder. He looked at it, but didn't try to shove it off. Danny either didn't notice or didn't care. "I'd say take one of these vans, but I don't think they're in any kind of working order."

"I have a cycle on the ground floor. Easier to get through traffic. We'll take the stairs."

Danny motioned them to follow as he headed toward another stairwell. Once they hit ground level they parted, Danny heading inside, the Shield pulling Hannah in the direction of his cycle. He straddled the bike and motioned Hannah to get on behind him. Two minutes and counting.

The Shield didn't bother with a helmet. The engine revved and they peeled out of the parking space at high speed. Hannah held on for dear life. Not since she and Scott had stolen the muscle car from the Left Fists had she felt like she was about to kiss the pavement. The Shield kept his promise and weaved expertly through traffic, speeding through red lights. After the last red light, Hannah buried her face against his jacket so she couldn't see anymore.

The Shield rode until an explosion rocked the air. The cycle skidded into a half turn and stopped.

Hannah looked back toward the general direction of the hospital, but the explosion echoed from above. Up in the clouds, a light show rained over Thunder City.

Captain Spectacular must have flown one of the bombs into the atmosphere. Only she could have survived.

"Don't let go," the Shield ordered, and sped up the cycle again.

It took a few more minutes before it dawned on her that if the other bombs were going to go off, she would have heard them by now. She pulled her head off the Shield's leather-clad back and looked around. They were far away from downtown, in a sparsely populated area near a set of train tracks.

"Pull over," she shouted, but he couldn't hear her, so she banged on his shoulder. "Pull over," she repeated.

This time he did, finding a quiet area near a telephone

pole. Hannah dismounted as soon as the bike stopped. The Shield sat there waiting, patient. She paced back and forth a few times, feeling like she wanted to jump out of her skin. Emotions descended on her, and every feeling she'd shoved away from her heart for the past two days rushed through her, unstoppable.

"McNamara said he was my father. Is that true?" she asked.

"Yes."

"He told you and you believed him?"

"I looked at your file when the Court assigned me to McNamara's facility."

Hannah paused her pacing. "The Court has files on me? No, don't answer that, of course they do. Do you know who my mother is? My real, biological mother? Was she the one Miranda killed? The one who gave birth to me?"

The Shield shook his head. "No, the woman Dane assassinated was a surrogate who had second thoughts and tried to run. Your mother was too busy to carry a pregnancy. You're a test tube baby. McNamara and your mother mixed a bunch of their cells together in a petri dish because they thought the genetic mix would create a powerful Alt. They were right."

"So my mother is alive. Both my father and my mother are alive." The agitation crawled over her skin, so she started pacing again.

"We can't stay out here, Hannah. The Court is going to want to know why I failed to keep T-CASS away from McNamara."

She kept moving. If she stopped, she'd scream. She didn't even understand why she wanted to scream, except to release all of her pent-up fury. "Will they hurt you?"

"Torture me? No. They tried that. It didn't end well for them." He paused, looked away from her and lowered his voice. "There are other ways to hurt a man besides through torture."

He meant there was something valuable out there that the Court could destroy or hurt. Something or someone. She needed answers, because she had a decision to make when she barely understood the question.

"Who are you? Why are you working for them? How did you become a double agent?"

The Shield hefted his leg over the bike so he could lean back against it. "Come here."

Hannah walked closer to him, so close his pure aggressiveness almost repulsed her, but she held her ground and looked up at his face.

The Shield removed his sunglasses and looked down at her. His eyes looked normal, ox shaped, no scarring or obvious signs of disease. The pupils reacted to sunlight, the cornea was clear, the irises looked…gray. Cloud gray. The same shade as Scott's eyes. What were the chances of two men having the same rare eye color in such close proximity?-

"My God. You're Scott's father, aren't you?"

The Shield nodded, slipping the sunglasses back onto his head.

"Did McNamara know that when he ordered you to shoot Scott?"

The Shield nodded. "It wasn't supposed to matter. I wasn't supposed to care. Creating Cory was one of my first independent assignments for the Court. Cory wasn't supposed to mean anything except for a possible future subject for the Court. I wasn't supposed…to love him. I wasn't supposed to fall in love with his mother. I was young and I failed and I did fall in love and I've spent over two decades keeping the Court away from my family. This time, I couldn't."

"So you trained Scott instead."

"If I brought him to the Court, if I could keep him close to me, the less likely the Court would hurt him or Catherine. And maybe, just maybe, I would have someone to help me bring down the Court once and for all."

Her temple started to throb, so she rubbed it. "This is all giving me a headache."

He stayed quiet, giving her time to think, time to process. She knew what decision she had to make. She hoped Scott was successful in translocating the children, because there was only one way that she could see to bring this nightmare to an end.

"Tell me about the Court of Blood. What do I need to know to work against them?"

The Shield tilted his head to the side, studying her. For the first time since she met him, she had the impression he was taking her seriously.

"They're not a huge organization. There's no secret army of Alts looking to take over the world, or the government, or even Thunder City. At least, not now."

"What do they want?"

"To create Alts." He reached out to touch her hair, letting the strands slip through his fingers. "To find the source of Alt power. If they can create Alts, if they can decide what power an Alt will have before they're born, if they can bring about an Alt with more than one ability — that's their goal, their mission, the reason for their existence."

"For now," Hannah said, to confirm her suspicions.

The Shield nodded his confirmation.

"Are they only in Thunder City and Star Haven?"

The Shield shook his head. "There are other locations, but since Thunder City has a higher than normal population of Alts, their main headquarters is... nearby."

Hannah thought about that and a plan blossomed. The more she thought about it, the more determined she became to make it work.

"My mother. What's her role in all this?"

The Shield smiled, and almost managed to not look terrifying while doing it. "She's the Supreme Judge. She controls the Court. The CEO if you will. Everyone answers to her."

"She gives you your orders?"

The Shield nodded his head.

"You can't go back to the Court. McNamara failed, just like Miranda failed, but this time they'll blame you. Even if they can't prove you worked against them, they'll be suspicious. Thomas — he pulled records off McNamara's computer before you found us. All of T-CASS is going to be on the watch for the Court now. The more T-CASS moves against the Court, the more likely the Court will realize you helped me escape."

"So what do you suggest I do?"

He really didn't know, and Hannah didn't know what do with the responsibility he shoved into her lap. The Shield had always appeared to be a dozen steps ahead of everyone else. Why would he listen to her now?

Before Hannah could answer, her phone buzzed in her pocket. It was Scott.

"Answer it." She shoved the phone at The Shield. "Tell him I'm busy and you'll explain everything to him when you see him later."

"What are you up to?"

"Just do it!"

The Shield answered the phone. "She's not here, Grey."

Hannah couldn't hear what Scott said. It was better this way, not hearing his voice. She might lose her resolve if she heard his voice.

"I said I'll explain when I get there. Don't go anywhere until I talk to you."

The Shield cut the line and handed the phone back to her. Hannah pushed his hand away. "You keep it in case he calls again."

"What are you planning?"

Hannah sighed. "The Oversight Committee has a warrant for my arrest. I refuse to go to jail, not for a minute, not for a second, not for them. Not this way. I have to leave Thunder City for a while."

"Where do you want to go? I'll take you there."

Hannah shook her head. "You need to go home. To Scott...Cory. He needs to know who you are. It's his right to know you do care about him and how much you've sacrificed for him."

"If Catherine doesn't kill me first."

"Catherine will get over it." Her heart flipped, again and again and wouldn't stop. "How do you contact the Court of Blood?"

She had the feeling that the Shield knew where she was going with this, but he handed her his phone without protest. "There's only one number. Text the code 9000. When they answer, tell them who you are and where you are. They'll come get you."

She took the phone and shoved it in the pocket where her own phone used to reside. "If they ask about you?"

"Since there won't be a body, best to tell them I rode off into the sunset. They'll try to find me, but I'll lay low."

"At the Blackwood estate."

He laughed again. "I don't think that will go over very well with anyone."

"It's the safest compound in Thunder City and the last place anyone will look for you — living with your wife and her husband."

This time he sighed. "I should be talking you out of this."

"To what end? They'll never stop. The manipulations will continue on forever. There will always be another reason, another excuse to set up a lab and experiment on Alts. We have to bring this to an end. I can do that from the inside. I have to do this myself."

"You don't know what you're walking into." The Shield shoved her phone into his breast pocket. "The Supr — your mother isn't like Miranda Dane. Dane got things done by using a sledgehammer. The Supreme Judge is crafty, cunning, and capable of making you work against your best interests without you even realizing you're doing it."

"Like McNamara."

"Worse."

Hannah didn't doubt it. There was still one more thing she had to do before she chickened out. She reached up to touch the Shield's cheek, but waited for his permission. He leaned forward to let her touch him. There wasn't much for her to fix. For all of the scarring she saw, he was in great shape. Still, no matter how great your shape is, age will rob you no matter how hard you fight it. She couldn't rush this because she needed to touch every point of his body, and did.

When she returned to herself, she kept her hand on his cheek because she suspected it would be a long time before she would touch another human with such tenderness.

"What did you do?" he asked.

"I gave you the body of a twenty-two year old."

He raised his eyebrows.

"There's a war coming," she said. "Whether or not I succeed, T-CASS will go after the Court and the Court will retaliate. T-CASS will need you at the top of your game because you will fight for them, Shield. You will fight for your son, for your wife, and for me. Do you understand?"

He nodded. She lifted herself onto her tiptoes and kissed his right cheek. "That is for Catherine." She shifted and kissed his left cheek. "That is for Thomas." Keeping her lips closed, she kissed him on the lips. When she pulled away, she looked into his eyes. The same eyes as her lover. "That is for Scott. You tell him I love him. You tell him to wait for me. I *will* come back and when I do, there will be no more Court and we will be together forever. Promise me you will tell him this."

"I promise."

She believed him. He stepped away to mount his cycle. After he was gone, she texted the lone number on his phone. The phone rang a second later. A female voice answered before Hannah could even say *hello*.

"Shield, where are you?"

"This is Hannah Quinn, daughter of the Supreme Judge. Tell her I'm ready to come home."

ACKNOWLEDMENTS

If writing a novel is hard, writing the the sequel is twice as difficult. This book wouldn't exist if not for the support of my family, friends, and colleagues. To not name them here would be a disservice for all of the time, energy, and advice they poured into this project as if it were their own.

First, Madeline Martin, who made those pre-dawn writing sprints bearable, and for making sure all appendages were present and accounted for during the love scene. Next, Abigail Sharpe, for correcting those pesky grammar problems. Dawn Bonanno, for holding me accountable every week. Jan Jackson, for reading everything that I write and for safely driving me to all of those FCRW meetings. I only wish I could have attended more often.

I also have to thank my editor, Debra Doyle, for keeping up with my writing escapades and making sure my characters don't wander too far off track. Tina Condon for proofreading.

There are so many others, including Pat Esden for reading drafts and raising my spirits, Sylvia Spruck Wrigley, for blurbing and for exchanging airplane tales with me.

Once again, I must thank Cliff Weikal of Cliff's Books (https://www.cliffsbooks.net/) for stocking autographed copies of all of my books at his bookstore.

This book was a wild ride from beginning to end. Thank you to everyone for standing by me.

SPECIAL BONUS!

If you would like to be notified when Debra Jess's next novel is released, please sign up for my newsletter by going to:

http://debrajess.com

Your email address will never be shared and you can unsubscribe at any time.

Word of mouth and reviews are vital for any author to succeed. If you enjoyed this book, please consider leaving a review wherever you purchased it. The reviews do not have to be elaborate. A simple sentence or two sharing your thoughts about the book would be helpful to other readers. Thank you!

EXCERPT FROM:

A SECRET ROSE: A THUNDER CITY NOVELLA (BOOK 1)

Twenty years ago.

Eight-year-old Daniella Rose reached out and placed her hand on the large mirror over her dresser drawer. "I wish I may, I wish I might, have this wish I wish tonight."

Nothing happened. Dani hadn't vanished through the looking glass as Alice had done when she wished to visit Wonderland. No matter how hard she wished, she was still stuck in a dreary, dreadful world. Maybe tomorrow the words would work. The words must have worked for somebody or why would people say them?

Except she'd recited those same words every evening before dinner all winter. Dinner was the time of day when her parents aired their grievances about her — why did you get an A minus on that test, why didn't you braid your hair instead of letting it just hang there, why can't you sit still for more than two minutes — but it would be even worse now that Grandma Carmelita had moved in.

Grandma Carmelita had some very strange notions about girls. "Old fashioned," Dani had overheard one servant whisper to another.

Through the vents in the floor, she could hear her father arguing with Grandma Carmelita in the dining room. Something about hospitals, something about Robby. Robby was in the hospital again. Daniella would be going to the hospital tomorrow, too. Robby needed her liver or a piece of it, at least. Her father called it a transplant. Her Grandmother called it butchery.

"Doctors. Hospitals. You start putting the girl's body parts into the boy, and he will not be the same child. I tell you, this is madness. I have seen it for myself. Luca Fontane brought his child in for the same exact surgery. He came out a completely different child. Do you want your son to become like her? A vain, wicked creature? Always staring into mirrors, admiring herself? If only she were a boy."

Dani clenched her fists to keep from flying down the stairs and yelling at the old woman. It figured that her grandmother would think she was admiring herself. Heaven forbid she should compliment the granddaughter who'd done nothing but try to please her. She even wore the ugly, out-of-fashion dresses that her grandmother insisted she wear for dinner, for school, for church, for everywhere.

Dani squelched the tears before they flooded her eyes. Anger was better. Anger gave her power, even if it got her grounded more often than not. The fire in her belly raged hotter than it ever had before. Dani grabbed the flame and pulled it into her heart, keeping it there until it took hold. The fire burned until it hurt.

So, her Grandmother thought her vain and wicked? Fine. Vain and wicked the old woman would get.

Dani sat on the bed, her new plan more of a comfort than the bed itself. She could hear the crumple of paper under the mattresses where she'd shoved her most recent failure so she wouldn't have to see it. Stupid English teacher gave her an A minus. The Rose family didn't tolerate A minuses. Robby never got an A minus, but only because everyone felt sorry for him because he was so sick. He also got extra tutoring because he couldn't go to school. He got extra time to finish his assignments. It wasn't fair!

With a vicious tug, Dani yanked off one of the ugly patent-leather shoes her grandmother made her wear and tossed it at the useless mirror on her dresser. The shoe hit the mirror and knocked it off the wardrobe with a loud crash. Very good, the voice whispered in her ear. Vain and wicked girls throw things. Vain and wicked girls are powerful. But, what would a boy do?

Dani knew exactly what a boy would do. He would hit whoever was closest. Robby always hit her when no one was around to see. Dani tried to hit back once, but Robby ratted her out and she got her father's belt to her backside. How dare she hit her poor, sick brother?

The memory of leather on skin clenched her fist. Even to her eyes her hand looked small and useless. And, hitting the wall wouldn't hurt anyone but herself.

If only she could become a boy. Wouldn't that make her grandmother sorry? Vain, wicked, and a boy. Healthy, too. Her parents would hate her even more and it would be so delicious. Dani stripped off her dress.

"I wish I may, I wish I might, have this wish I wish tonight."

The gentle click in her brain took her by surprise. Fascinated, Dani watched as her skin stretched to accommodate her desire. It didn't hurt, but the odd sensation of spaghetti swirling in her stomach reminded her of the dinner she wasn't allowed to eat because of the A minus. It took less than a minute, but when when her skin stopped stretching, the swirling sensation also stopped, and Dani smiled.

Maybe there was something to the prayers her grandmother insisted she recite. God had made her a boy.

Joy washed through her. For a moment, she forgot about the vain, wicked child she'd sworn she'd become and raced to get redressed, this time in her jumper, which was big enough to cover her now-larger body. Finally, her parents would be satisfied with her. Maybe her grandmother would be happy to spend time with her.

As her hand touched the door knob, her eyes stopped on her fourth-grade class picture tacked up on her wall. Nikolaos Blackwood stood behind her. She'd cut everyone else out of the picture except herself and Nik. His hand rested on her shoulder, and

Dani remembered the joy of knowing he was right behind her, his eyes the color of Mystic Bay, his smile as bright as the sun reflecting water. Everyone liked Nik, the boy who could disappear into the walls and travel underground without even trying. Everyone called him "Ghost" because his voice sounded like a ghost when he talked from the walls. He was an Alt and all the girls loved him, including Dani.

Dani looked down at her body again. Would Nik like her if she were a boy? She knew some boys liked other boys the way that girls liked boys, but she didn't think Nik did. He was a year older because she had skipped a grade. He knew more about boys liking girls than she did.

The lump in her throat choked her. What did she want more? Her grandmother's approval? Her family's love? Or Nik?

She looked at the picture as more shouting rose from the vent. Reality sucked her hopes for a peaceful family down into the dusty vent. All her parents wanted from her were her body parts to give to Robby. Nik might love her if she tried hard enough, though. If she stayed a girl.

Dani turned away from the door and took off her jumper, hanging it back in the closet so she wouldn't get into trouble again. With the jumper no longer restricting her movements, Dani prayed again. "Please make me a girl."

The changed happened even faster this time. Dani put on her pajamas, the vain, wicked girl subdued for the moment. The argument downstairs still raged. Dani crawled into bed. She closed her eyes and imagined Nik. Would he think that not telling anyone about the boy side of her was lying? Nik never lied.

Nik doesn't have to lie, the vain, wicked girl whispered. His parents love him. He can disappear. He can travel fast. You're just Robby's little sister. Becoming a boy won't change that.

For Nik, she'd remain a girl.

OTHER STORIES IN THE THUNDER CITY SERIES

These are now available from Amazon, Barnes & Noble, Kobo, and iTunes !

Blood Surfer (A Thunder City Novel, Book 1)
A Secret Rose (A Thunder City Novella, Book 1)
Valley of the Blind (A Thunder City Short Story)
Slow Burn (A Thunder City Short Story)
Still Life (A Thunder City Short Story)

OTHER STORIES BY DEBRA JESS

Blood & Armor featured in Fragments of Darkness (Anthology).
Available in print only and only available through Amazon.

ABOUT THE AUTHOR

A Connecticut Yankee transplanted to Central Florida, Debra Jess writes science fiction, romance, urban fantasy, and superheroes. She began writing in 2006, combining her love of fairy tales and Star Wars to craft original stories of ordinary people in extraordinary adventures and fantastical creatures in out-of-this world escapades. Her first published novel, *Blood Surfer,* has won the National Excellence in Romance Fiction Award for Best Paranormal and Futuristic.

Debra is a graduate of Viable Paradise and is a member of Codex. She›s also a member of the Romance Writers of America and RWA›s Fantasy, Futuristic, & Paranormal chapter and the First Coast Romance Writers.

You can sign-up for Debra Jess's newsletter on her website at **http://debrajess.com.**

You can also find her on social media at:
Bookbub | Facebook | Twitter | Pinterest | Tumblr | Instagram